THE BEAUTY OF YOUR FACE

THE BEAUTY OF YOUR FACE

A Novel

Sahar Mustafah

W. W. NORTON & COMPANY
Independent Publishers Since 1923

Copyright © 2020 by Sahar Mustafah

All rights reserved
Printed in the United States of America
First Edition

Decoration by wonderfulkorea / Shutterstock

For information about permission to reproduce selections from this book, write to Permissions, W. W. Norton & Company, Inc., 500 Fifth Avenue, New York, NY 10110

For information about special discounts for bulk purchases, please contact W. W. Norton Special Sales at specialsales@wwnorton.com or 800-233-4830

Manufacturing by Lake Book Manufacturing
Book design by Dana Sloan
Production manager: Beth Steidle

Library of Congress Cataloging-in-Publication Data

Names: Mustafah, Sahar, author.
Title: The beauty of your face : a novel / Sahar Mustafah.
Description: First edition. | New York, NY : W. W. Norton & Company, [2020]
Identifiers: LCCN 2019027179 | ISBN 9781324003380 (hardcover) |
ISBN 9781324003397 (epub)
Classification: LCC PS3613.U846 B43 2020 | DDC 813/.6—dc23
LC record available at https://lccn.loc.gov/2019027179

W. W. Norton & Company, Inc., 500 Fifth Avenue, New York, N.Y. 10110
www.wwnorton.com

W. W. Norton & Company Ltd., 15 Carlisle Street, London W1D 3BS

1 2 3 4 5 6 7 8 9 0

For those struck down by hate,
your stories still keep you among us.

She's so young. Would you not let her blossom a bit more?

—*friend of Yusor Mohammad Abu-Salha*

Events matter little, only stories of events affect us.

—*Rabih Alameddine,* The Hakawati

THE BEAUTY OF YOUR FACE

Nurrideen School
for Girls

ANOTHER ANGRY phone call, and it was only Tuesday.

"It's very haram, Ms. Rahman! All that drinking and debauchery!"

Afaf Rahman inhaled deeply. She had cultivated a reputation for patience as principal of the Nurrideen School for Girls. This wasn't the first complaint lodged against a book. "*The Great Gatsby* is a state-approved text, Mrs. Ibrahim," she calmly explained to the parent on the other end.

"The state of Illinois is not raising my daughter to be a proper muslimah, Ms. Rahman." A swift retort. She could hear sneering through the line.

The fathers rarely called Afaf—a professional woman with two master's degrees—didn't bother speaking with a marra. The men coached their wives on what to say when they called her. She could tell by the weak persistence in their voices that some of the wives had not taken their husbands' positions against the liberal education of their daughters.

This mother, however, was raring to go.

Afaf's assistant Sabah appeared in the doorway of her office, holding a folder. Afaf waved her in. "Um Ibrahim, raising your daughter to be a proper muslimah is your job at home, and my job at this school." She rolled her eyes at Sabah. "I'm also responsible for providing each young woman enrolled at this school with a competitive education. I'm confident that no book could ever steer her—or any of my students—off the path of righteousness, Um Ibrahim."

My students—four hundred young, bright, and determined girls whom Afaf claimed as her own daughters. Her love and devotion to them were fierce.

Sabah pointed at a signature line on a document and handed her a pen. Her assistant wore a thickly knitted infinity scarf around her neck and a long sweater over her abaya. In the middle of February in Illinois, you could bet on a wind chill of ten degrees one day and wake up the next morning to a thirty-degree hike above normal.

"Have you read *The Great Gatsby*, Um Ibrahim?" Afaf asked the parent on the phone, quickly signing the form.

Sabah smiled, knowingly shaking her head, and replaced the document in a folder. She retreated to her desk outside Afaf's door.

"Well, no. Abu Ibrahim and I watched it on Netflix. Leonardo DiCaprio's in it."

Afaf massaged her left temple. "I see. Perhaps you and your husband should read it. I can arrange for copies to be sent home with your daughter Eman. Inshallah we can sit down once you've read it and discuss your concerns." A few seconds of silence. She scratched the top of her hijab with the antennae of her two-way radio, waiting.

In her ten years at Nurrideen School, Afaf wrestled with parents who never backed down—a few even withdrew their daughters' enrollment. The majority eventually relented and trusted her. Still, she chose her battles: contraception could be explored in health class, without encouraging premarital sex. And absolutely no discussion of abortion.

"No. That won't be necessary, Ms. Afaf. May Allah give you the strength and wisdom to guide our daughters in this frightening world."

The parent hung up and Afaf left her office, clutching her radio. She gave Sabah a thumbs-up.

Her assistant laughed. "By the way, the interfaith summit meeting is rescheduled to next week. They're sending us a revised agenda by the end of the day."

"Good. Who are the student ambassadors?"

Sabah scanned her desk. "Majeeda Abu Lateef, Jenin Muhsin, and Renah Abdel Bakir. Two seniors, one junior."

Afaf nodded. Jenin was her daughter Azmia's best friend and the two of them had started the first student chapter of Amnesty International at Nurrideen School. Azmia had been only a freshman that year, already championing human rights. Like so many of her peers, she'd paid close attention to the case of Malala Yousafzai, a fifteen-year-old student like her, shot in the head for wanting an education. Azmia had been rattled for days.

How can they do that? Aren't they Muslim, too? her daughter had wanted to know. Afaf had no good answer except, *They're not true muslimeen, habibti.*

Then Sandy Hook happened and Azmia helped mobilize a student rally that traveled all the way to Springfield, joining other groups demanding that Illinois legislators hold Congress responsible for the lives of those twenty young souls.

Azmia was a senior now, her eyes set on international law. Her friend Jenin had chosen premed with plans to volunteer with Doctors Without Borders. Sometimes Afaf stood outside a classroom, listening at the door as the teacher lectured, followed by an intermittent chorus of loud and unflappable responses. She was overcome by her students' sense of pride and purpose. There was an infinite number of choices for these young women.

At home, Afaf watched Azmia at the kitchen table, her head buried in a textbook, hair pulled into a bun, marveling at this magnificent creature who was nothing like Afaf had been at her age, wrecked and lost. Azmia was an extraordinary surprise at the saddest part of her life, growing up bold and assertive, her brothers fretting over her, though she constantly pushed them away, making room to spread her wings, to chart her own course.

When she was nine years old, the girls in her Brownies troop told Azmia she was lucky she didn't look Muslim. She'd come home fighting tears and begging Afaf's permission to begin wearing hijab.

Afaf had gathered her in her arms. *Why, my love? You're still so young.*

Azmia's eyebrows furrowed like two wings intersecting as they always did when she was about to cry—a rare occasion, as tough as she was.

I don't want anyone to make a mistake about who I am.

Hadn't every muslimah asserted this collective identity to the world? There could be no mistake about who they are, what they believe. Her daughter's brazenness still amazed Afaf; Azmia was so unlike how she herself had been at her age, a mousy girl with no sense of self, an invisible child. It's what your children did: erased your flaws, your tragedies.

Outside her office, Lou, the school security guard, sat at a small wooden table, spectacles propped on the bridge of his freckled nose, reading a newspaper. He didn't look up, the bill of his White Sox cap shadowing his eyes. He raised his two-way radio in greeting.

Afaf remembered his skeptical look when she hired Lou last year.

"I've been retired from the force for five years. I'd never worked with a Muslim population." He pronounced it *Moo-slim* and looked like he wouldn't have been disappointed if he didn't get the job.

And yet Afaf had wanted him. He had that self-assured way that white people oozed because they believed you counted on them to improve matters. After a series of bomb threats, a jittery school board swiftly approved the full-time hiring of Lou, an ex–Chicago cop.

She turned down the corridor past the cafeteria, where laughter and chatter rose and fell. Young girls—twelve through eighteen— ate turkey sandwiches and sipped from water bottles, their heads swaddled in the compulsory white hijab, their bodies hidden under shapeless forest-green uniforms.

The head of the cafeteria staff waved at Afaf with her metal tongs. Um Khaddar was a widow, ancient and ageless all at once, with nine grown children. She'd pleaded with Afaf for a job in the kitchen to fill her empty days. The students adored Um Khaddar; she was like a mother hen, plump and fretting over wasted food.

"Mashallah, ya sayidah Rahman!" Um Khaddar would proclaim. "These girls have every liberty nowadays. How I envy them!"

Afaf would nod and smile, hoping progress would continue and every one of her students would reach her full potential. They were no longer swayed by fancy marriage proposals and dowries of gold. Careers in law, medicine, and political activism glittered on the horizon of their young lives more brilliantly than diamond rings. Her own teenage years were a blur of indifferent white boys, a deep loneliness engulfing her.

Afaf waved back at Um Khaddar with her two-way radio, moving past the glass-plated window of the Student Services Office, past posters on good citizenship and high expectations. A framed photograph of President Obama smiled down on her. She would miss the noon prayers if she didn't hurry.

"Ms. Rahman! Ms. Rahman!"

Afaf halted, sighed, and spun around. A short and stocky girl with a round face beamed up at her. Najwa Othman, a senior. She was neck-and-neck with another student for valedictorian. Her mother and Afaf had been in elementary school together. She was shocked to see how well Afaf had turned out in the end.

"Salaam alaykum, Ms. Rahman! Have you had a chance to look over my proposal for the blood drive?" Najwa didn't draw breath, batting her thick black eyelashes in expectation.

"Not yet, Najwa. I will—"

She cut Afaf off. "The deadline is in three weeks, Ms. Rahman." Najwa bounced on the balls of her feet as she spoke, her excitement contagious, or annoying, depending on your mood.

"Three weeks is still plenty of time to—"

Najwa threw her hands up. "Inshallah I'd like to begin promoting as soon as possible, Ms. Rahman. I need your approval."

Despite herself, Afaf smiled. "Inshallah," she said. Exchanging a complete sentence with Najwa was as futile as predicting the weather.

Afaf hurried past the science lab. Last fall, Mrs. Sultany, the forensics teacher, won a state grant for an infrared spectrometer—Nurrideen School was the first in the area to acquire such a sophisticated instrument for chemical analysis and environmental testing. Her class had been featured in a community spotlight article while partnering with the Tempest Police Department on a case of a home burglary.

She turned east down another corridor, toward the farthest end from her office on the first floor. Snow-crusted windowpanes cast a blinding glare, and tiny dust particles circulated like small galaxies above her head. She stopped in front of a wood-paneled door with a lattice.

Afaf glanced behind her. No one was around. Dribbling balls and whistles echoed from the gymnasium on the other side of the building.

She slipped inside and pulled a light bulb chain, illuminating a space no larger than a janitor's closet. A worn cushioned chair was propped up against one wall, a small Quran on a lamp table beside it. This had once been a confessional, Afaf had learned on a tour of the building when she was first hired to teach ten years ago. Nurrideen School in Tempest, Illinois, had long ago been Our Lady of Peace, a two-story convent housing thirty Benedictine nuns.

It was built in 1929, facing east toward Lake Michigan, though they could not see its gray-blue waters. Behind the convent was a modest field—two acres, the size of a strip mall parking lot. The sisters of Our Lady of Peace did not squander an inch of it, planting potatoes, cucumbers, tomatoes, and cabbages.

During the Great Depression, it served as a way station for poor white families traveling north to Chicago from the central and southern regions of Illinois—some came as far as Joplin, Missouri. Escaping the threat of lynching, black men broke their journey at the convent, a few staying to help the sisters harvest the fields for a few cents a day. For white farmers ruined by the Dust Bowl, Chicago gleamed against their dull, economically stunted lives, traces of the eroded soil that had failed them still clinging to their clothes when they arrived. Travelers stopped at Our Lady of Peace, ate a meager meal of hard-boiled eggs and baked apples, and put up their horses until daybreak.

Young children were sometimes abandoned in the middle of the night. Afaf imagined the sisters tending to them, killing their head lice with apple cider vinegar and hookworms with warm milk and castor oil. Soon it became regular practice—white widows and unwed mothers depositing babies and toddlers for whom they could not afford to care—and the convent transformed into a place for orphans, the sisters of Our Lady of Peace plunging the fear of God into their young, displaced bodies like a vaccine.

Afaf loved the confessional. It was a place of escape, for solitary prayer and a break from the daily school operations. Before she removed her shoes to pray on a green velvet rug, Afaf sat on the chair and breathed deeply. She propped her radio next to the Quran and gazed at the door. A mural had been painted over it depicting the annunciation of Holy Mary. Afaf studied Mary's solemn face, upturned as she receives the angel Gabriel's message. The brown of her pupils had dulled and flaked over many decades, and the angel's pearly white wings had turned dingy. The image was the only Catholic relic—that and the confessional itself—left in the Islamic school.

The convent was closed down in the late 1940s when tuberculosis swept through, killing most of the nuns and whatever remaining children the welfare agencies could not reach in time. Over the decades, the state made it a halfway house for war-broken veterans. In the eighties, when President Reagan cut funding, the state turned it over to the village of Tempest.

It remained vacant until Ali Abu Nimir stood up at a board meeting one frigid evening in February 1995—two years after the Tempest Prayer Center first opened its doors only a few blocks away—and proposed a private Islamic school for children. He was a wealthy businessman—an immigrant from Palestine—who'd washed and waxed used cars before owning his first lot on the South Side of Chicago. After fulfilling hajj with his wife, he returned to Tempest with pockets tipped toward good deeds, ensuring his place in Paradise. Among them, donating to the Center and opening a school for the next generation of muslimeen who were more likely to recite the latest pop song than a verse from the Holy Quran.

Meanwhile, the white taxpayers of Tempest had been witnessing with trepidation a growing Muslim population. They'd nearly stone-walled the building of the Center in 1993; they weren't keen on the expansion of "un-Christian spaces," as one circulating pamphlet had charged. Ali Abu Nimir's proposal for a school was rejected—and rejected six more times after that. It appeared the small town of Tempest was more likely to bulldoze the old convent before "letting it go to Muz-lumz."

In the winter of 1998, its construction was finally approved with the help of a Pakistani American civil rights lawyer, and the following year Nurrideen School opened its doors, first to boys, then exclusively to young girls after a brother school opened in a neighboring township. Among the dignitaries cutting the ribbon was Ali Abu Nimir, who later resigned from the school board and returned to his Palestinian homeland, leaving behind his legacy—an engraved brick on the exterior walkway.

Afaf removed her shoes and stood up, planting her feet on the edge of the prayer rug. In two shifts, students and teachers filed into the gymnasium for scheduled communal prayer, temporarily halting games of volleyball and basketball. Most days, she preferred worshipping alone, avoiding the barrage of faculty requests and inquiries heaped on her as soon as she raised herself from the floor.

The confessional was peaceful, though not quiet. A piano tune floated from a vent in the ceiling, then a chorus of altos. Miss Camellia's show choir was preparing for the spring concert at Navy Pier. A faint rendition of Adele's "Skyfall" echoed above Afaf's head. During her brief escapes from her office, she'd sit on the cushioned chair, eyes closed, listening to the melodious voices flowing from the vent. But today she only had time for prayer. Aside from parent phone calls that morning, she'd been mulling over a new budget proposal and investigating an incident of plagiarism on a term paper.

Hands folded over her stomach, Afaf whispered: "Bismallah al rahman al raheem."

By her final prostration, Afaf heard a sound like a firecracker. She quickly finished and reached for her two-way radio.

Lou must have heard it, too.

She turned up the volume and adjusted the control. "Lou. Can you check that noise? Troublemakers again. Over."

People around the neighborhood tossed M-80s over the school fence on a regular basis. It was a message booming loud and clear: *You don't belong here.*

The vandalism had gotten worse, too. Last week they'd spray-painted a pig's head on the field house, and two days ago a beer bottle shattered the window of Mrs. Nawal Qadir's art classroom.

My husband's been at me to quit, the young pregnant teacher had informed Afaf yesterday, her hijab-trimmed face tight with apprehension. She rubbed her growing belly, waiting for Afaf's reassuring words.

We've taken every precaution, Nawal. And beyond that, it's in Allah's hands, she'd told the art teacher, sounding more exasperated than hopeful. It was a script she'd automatically recite. And when a local news van pulled up to report on the latest incident of vandalism, she'd recite another one:

We are a religion of peace, not terror. We are Americans, too.

Defying the board's recommendation, she refused to display more flags, particularly one outside the school's entrance for public view. One, to which an assembly of students and parents pledged allegiance during programs and graduation, was already prominently stationed in the small auditorium. *Is a flag the only proof of patriotism?* she'd argued to the board.

The radio crackled and Afaf set it back on the lamp table. She remained there on the floor, legs tucked under her, and closed her eyes.

Allah gift me with patience, she thought.

Eyes still closed, she gave du'aa for Azmia so she would do well on her AP psychology test this afternoon. They'd spent last night going over a dozen of Azmia's handwritten note cards on categories of abnormal behavior.

Afaf's cell phone buzzed. Before reading the text, she let her mind drift a moment longer in supplications for those she loved. She breathed deeply, whispered a final du'aa for her mother, who lived thousands of miles away yet still managed to disrupt Afaf's sense of confidence. She'd weathered years of Mama's undulating disapproval—or complete indifference.

Before she could text back, another explosion rattled the light bulb above Afaf's head. She scrambled to her feet. The round of firecrackers sounded closer, as though coming from inside the building. From the floor above her: Miss Camellia's music room.

Afaf looked up at the vent, her heart thumping.

The singing halted above her.

She snatched the two-way radio, her fingers trembling so badly she almost dropped it. "Lou! Come in, Lou! Gunshots! Over!"

High-pitched, wordless noise roiled from the ceiling. Young girls screaming. Terrifying and unfamiliar sounds, so unlike the swell and dip of laughter. Sounds that had lovingly crystallized in Afaf's heart over the years she'd been teaching at Nurrideen School.

Then came loud thuds. Like bags of cement dropping to the floor.

Afaf leaned against the door, obscuring Gabriel's wings as he hovered over Mary. Clutching the two-way radio, she listened, her face tilted up toward the vent.

1976

1

SHE DOESN'T answer her mother the first time she calls her name.

"Afaf!"

She keeps jumping on her bed.

"Afaf! Where are you?"

Majeed, her younger brother, is jumping opposite her on a twin bed. He freezes and cranes his head over the tune of "Aquarius." The two of them play it relentlessly on a secondhand record player.

A garage sale, to Afaf's father, is yet another novelty of American life. The first time he'd discovered one down their block, he told her mother, "These amarkan sell their own belongings for profit!" In the spring and summer, Afaf and Majeed accompany Baba on strolls up and down the alleyways of their neighborhood, searching for open garages, the white owners sitting on lawn chairs, drinking beers and tossing their cigarette butts onto the gravel, haggling with her father. Their wives wear terry-cloth shorts and halter tops, stark-white tan lines cutting through sunburned skin. Afaf can't tear her eyes away from their sagging breasts. On their last trip, Baba purchased a record player from a man with an unkempt beard and glasses like John Lennon's. And a desk lamp for a buck-fifty, though Afaf's family did not own a desk in their cramped apartment. They do their homework on a chipped coffee table in the front room that her mother wipes down multiple times a day.

Mama had turned her nose up at the record player—Massari

ala fadi, she scolds—a waste of money. The previous owner had thrown in an odd selection of albums: the Shangri-Las, Pat Boone, and Sam Cooke. Afaf and Majeed have so far memorized every verse of *Hair*, her favorite record. Baba listens to Leonard Cohen, improving his English through songs. "Suzanne" sounds like a bottomless well to Afaf.

On Sunday mornings, he strums his oud and sings ballads by his favorite Egyptian lute player, Farid al-Atrash. *Not as unhappy as Leonard*, Baba declares, as though both famous musicians are close friends of his.

"Afaf!"

The third time Mama calls her name it's a sure sign of something serious. Afaf hops onto the brown shag carpeting and bolts down the narrow hallway of the apartment, Majeed sliding behind her in his tube socks across the wooden floor Mama mops every day.

Her mother's on the phone, the yellow cord snaking around her fingers. A pot of fava bean stew boils on the stove and a stack of dishes has been brought down from the cupboard, but Mama hasn't set them yet. Something's disrupted her mother's dinner activity.

She's talking in frantic Arabic on the phone—Afaf guesses it's Khalti Nesreen on the other end, Mama's youngest sister, the only relative she has in the States, who lives two hours away in Kenosha, Wisconsin.

Mama turns to Afaf with wide hazel eyes, two amber stones with flecks of green or gold depending upon her mood. When she laughs, they are like tiny golden nuggets mined out of the earth. Fear and anger usually turn them green, the color they are now as Mama glares at Afaf. They're eyes only her brother Majeed has inherited. Eyes Afaf covets every day she's surrounded by a sea of white skin and darting blue and green eyes at Nightingale Elementary School. She has Baba's hair, thick and wavy.

"Yes, Mama?" Afaf stands as close to her mother as she bravely can. Mama scares her in a way she doesn't understand. Her mother is a beautiful woman who takes care of her and her siblings. She cooks every day, Afaf and Majeed coming home to pots of maklooba and pans of kufta, spices reaching them in the stairwell before they open the back door of the apartment. Before bedtime, she bathes Majeed—Afaf is allowed to wash herself now—and lays out clean clothes for the next day. But there are other days when they come home from school and find Mama in her bed, weeping. This lasts for a few days. On those nights, she hears Baba talking to Mama, his soft and consoling words muffled by her mother's sobs. Afaf moves carefully around Mama. She's like one of those floppy puppets at the carnival that you knock down with a ball. Afaf worries her mother might not get back up again from her bed.

"Did Nada tell you where she was going after school?" her mother demands, placing her palm over the receiver, though Afaf is certain her aunt hears Mama's desperate plea.

It hits Afaf: her older sister has not come home yet. She and Majeed have been distracted by their singing and jumping, hadn't paid attention to the creeping autumn dusk outside the apartment. Nada is required to be home before the streetlights turn on, before their father comes home from the factory.

"No, Mama. She didn't say anything to me." They both look at seven-year-old Majeed—a futile action. He shakes his head. Why would her seventeen-year-old sister tell her little brother—or Afaf—anything about her mysterious life outside their apartment?

Afaf is ten years old, patching together small pieces of her sister—

the hours Nada spends smoothing down strands of her thick brown hair, fastening them with tortoiseshell barrettes, or the sly smile that creeps across her face when she reads a letter on torn-out notebook paper, folded and creased many times. The quilt Afaf has assembled of her sister isn't a whole person—only glimpses of a double life.

"Ya rubbi!" Mama bawls into the phone. "Nesreen, where could she be?" Her shoulders shake with sobbing, but Mama still listens and nods as her aunt says things Afaf can't hear. Mama tucks frizzy strands of hair behind her free ear. Gray ones sprout from the crown of her head; she is due for a touch-up. Every month at the kitchen table, Khalti Nesreen drapes a plastic cape around Mama's thin shoulders while her mother cradles a tiny cup of thick coffee spiced with cardamom in her palm. They laugh at their childhood antics in Palestine and Khalti Nesreen shares tidbits of gossip about the other arrabi immigrants in her husband's circle, squeezing the plastic bottle of dye until the very last drop. Afaf understands a handful of Arabic words and sentences:

Massari. Money. Frequently uttered.

Bilad. The old country. Tinged with longing.

Ma assalama. Goodbye. At the end of long-distance phone calls, sometimes through choked tears.

Between the sisters, the crescendo in their voices signals an intimate merriment before their volume dips and sniffles replace laughter and Afaf hears Baba's name: *Mahmood.* She wonders how two syllables could carry such anger and bitterness each time Mama utters the name. Afaf understands little of her parents' marriage. At times, she finds them at the kitchen table, Baba in the middle of a story about a mishap at the plastics factory, and Mama laughs long and hard, her shoulders shaking as she spoons dinner onto his plate, grains of rice scattering off the edge. Other times, Afaf catches them at the kitchen sink, Baba reaching for Mama's waist, her hands soapy and wet, and she elbows him in the stomach, pushing Baba away, her lips pursed.

As Mama whines into the phone about Nada, Afaf wants to touch her arm, to soothe her, but it feels like she's reaching out to a hot pan of frying oil. Afaf thinks better of it. This is not like the perpetual tears streaming down Mama's temples, soaking the pillowcase. Mama is afraid, and this makes Afaf afraid. She looks down at Mama's dingy house slippers, once snow-white, now the color of dirty dishwater, before grabbing Majeed's hand and pulling him away.

They change into their pajamas and plop down on the blue velour sofa bed where Majeed sleeps in the front room. They stay out of Mama's way as she clanks dishes, slams kitchen drawers, muttering to herself. Her brother huddles next to Afaf and they watch *Three's Company*, a show that usually makes them roar with laughter. Tonight they can barely manage a giggle, for they understand the gravity of the situation: their favorite show always airs after dinner, when Baba has been home for at least an hour. Nada is beyond running late.

Afaf sometimes wonders what her older sister is doing outside of the apartment. Her clothes smell like cigarettes and her hair is disheveled, one barrette hanging lower than the other. She doesn't dare ask: Nada is secretive, snapping at Afaf to *mind your own business.*

At the end of the episode, when Mr. Roper stands hoodwinked again by Jack, Baba slinks through the front door and Mama rushes at him. He leans his leather oud case against the wall.

"Where have you been? Do you know Nada hasn't come home?" she shouts, twisting a dish towel into a rope.

"She's not home?" Baba looks at Afaf and Majeed as though they can offer him a sensible reason. Her brother begins to whimper. Afaf holds his hand.

Baba turns back to Mama. His work shirt is half tucked in, the back of it flapping over his belt. His name is stitched above a breast pocket along with the factory's name, Dyer Plastic. It's one of two Mama washes by hand at night and hangs over the bathroom tub. By morning it's dry enough for Baba to slip on again. "Where could she be?"

"This morning she told me she was going over to Laura's." Mama rolls the *r* in the other girl's name so it no longer sounds American. "To study for a science test, I think." She pulls at the dish towel like a tug-of-war between her hands.

"Tayib, tayib." Baba takes a tentative step toward her as though gauging her instinct to reject him, a gesture Afaf recognizes as a child who's also been held at arm's length by her mother. Mama's fingers untangle and braid hair, they straighten the collar of her dress on picture day, wipe her running nose when she's got a cold. But she can't remember the last time her mother's hands caressed her cheeks, or her slender arms pulled Afaf in for a hug. Baba gently clasps Mama's shoulders. "I'm sure she lost track of time, Muntaha. Did you call Laura's parents?"

Mama looks like she's been slapped in the face and jerks away. "No. But where have you been so late while I've been worrying myself to death?" Her cheeks flush pink.

Baba walks to the kitchen. "What's Laura's number?"

Mama's anger swells, squeezing out the sheer panic that has been filling the apartment. "Tell me why you're so late, Mahmood. Ah? More overtime, or were you with that sharmoota again?"

Sharmoota. Another Arabic word Afaf hears Mama spit out between sniffles at the kitchen table with her sister, uttered in connection to a woman Afaf doesn't know. Khalti Nesreen sucks her teeth, squirts more dye from the bottle: *ts, ts, ts . . .*

"Bas, ya, Muntaha!" Baba scolds, his voice trailing in the hallway. "I told you a hundred times, I've been rehearsing with the band."

Baba doesn't own a car. He takes two buses to the factory—sometimes one, when his bandmate Ziyad picks him up during the winter months. Afterward they rehearse in a small detached garage belonging to a third bandmate, Amjad.

Mama shuffles after him. Afaf jumps from the sofa bed, Majeed scrambling behind her, and they follow their parents. Majeed wipes his snivel on the sleeve of his Scooby Doo pajamas.

"Aywa! You're out playing with your cursed instrument, not a care in the world!" Mama punctuates each accusing word with a stab of her dish towel in the air. She remembers the fava bean stew and turns off the stovetop, slamming down a wooden spoon. Afaf and Majeed jump at the sound.

Baba pulls a slip of paper tacked on the side of the fridge with a magnet shaped like an apple. Afaf recognizes it as a sheet taken from her stationery pad, the one bordered with circus animals. She won it at the Valentine's Day party last year in the third grade for throwing five ping-pong balls in a row of buckets, like on *The Bozo Show.*

Still, it hadn't impressed Julie McNulty or Amber Reeves, the two most beautiful girls in her class. They would never invite Afaf to their birthday parties. That day, Afaf had proudly held her prize and Julie sidled up to her. *You didn't give Amber a chance to win it. Don't be stingy, A-faf. You don't really want it, do you?* She'd glanced at Amber, who stood silently watching Afaf, arms crossed, blue eyes glittering with tears that never fell. Without a word, Afaf handed over the prize to Julie. For the rest of the party, Afaf stood in the corner of the class-room, looking down at her empty hands. At the end of the games, she watched as Julie and Amber, their arms full of homemade heart-shaped cards, stood at the front of the line like they always did when the class filed out. On Amber's desk was the coveted prize; she'd carelessly left it behind. Afaf swiped it back—it was rightfully hers, after all, though she had relinquished it so quickly.

"Afaf." Her brother tugs the hem of her pajama top. They linger in the doorframe of their parents' bedroom, across from the kitchen table, out of their way.

"Shush, Maj!" She puts a finger to her lips and her brother's eyes widen. He nods, and they silently watch Baba squint at the list of names Mama compiled. She wrote the names in Arabic—strange characters to Afaf, the letters strung together like charms on a neck-lace, broken in some places. The numbers are printed in English.

"Hallo? Yes, this Mahmood Rahman speaking," Baba stammers into the phone. "Mahmood Rah—eh—Nada's father. Yes. Fine. And you?"

Mama stands close to Baba, her jaw set tight, her eyes shining. Her earlier dread returns, the anger toward Baba seeping out of her face. All that matters now is Nada coming home.

2

AFAF'S SISTER was born in 1959 in Mama's childhood house in Palestine. When they finally received sponsorship from his cousin, her father packed up his new family for America. He waited tables at a diner during the day and visited Chicago's Gold Coast nightclubs like the Pump Room, where Sinatra infamously had a private booth. Baba failed to persuade club owners to give him a chance.

He was no Leonard Cohen or Johnny Cash. His oud sung melancholic tunes, too exotic or "Oriental," as they called it. "Folks like to dance around here," they told Baba, shaking their heads at his pot-bellied oud.

His luck was no better in the South Side blues joints. Some of the managers were fascinated by Baba's instrument—the down-turned peg box, the way the notes on the downstroke bounced away when he transitioned to the upstroke.

But in the end:

"*You ain't singing in English, you ain't singing here,*" Baba recalls when Afaf climbs into his lap for stories of his musical life.

Baba's parents were forced out of their home in Haifa in 1950. They had one hour to pack up all of their belongings while the Jewish settlers kept close guard, pointing their rifles at them. His mother tucked the key to the stone entrance of their stolen home in a pouch sewn inside her peasant dress and they breathed in the sea for the last time.

"You could smell the salt of the sea from our window," Baba told Afaf. She wondered how it must have been for Baba to once have an entire sea and now merely a lake, though to Afaf, Lake Michigan appeared boundless during the summertime when Baba took them to the lakefront, outside the Adler Planetarium, to watch sailboats moving across the horizon.

Baba was a young boy when his father left them with a family in the West Bank, in search of work and a new home across the river in Jordan. They never heard from him again. His mother later died of a respiratory infection and he and his siblings were separated; two sisters were taken to El Khalil to live with a widowed aunt, and he and his older brother Jameel stayed behind with a foster family in Ramallah. While he attended school, Jameel apprenticed with a local blacksmith, hammering metal from early morning until the late afternoon prayer. The year Baba turned thirteen, his brother was kicked and trampled by a donkey on his way to the souk to barter goods for the blacksmith.

Baba was all alone in the world. The foster family was kind, but they could not quell Baba's passion for music, a useless vocation. He cut school and spent time with a villager who taught him to play the oud. Blind Wajee—Wajee al-Amee—procured a secondhand lute for Baba and trained his young fingers to strum and hold the strings.

"Was he born blind?" Afaf asks, her imagination stretching with faces and places of her father's first life. His second one began with Mama.

"La, la," Baba tells her. "Wajee was a member of a royal British orchestra in Jerusalem. He lost his sight in a terrible explosion during a riot." He kisses the top of Afaf's head. "But he never stopped playing, mashallah."

Not to be discouraged from all the rejections in Chicago, Baba enlisted a couple of fellow immigrants who worked at Dyer Plastic—Ziyad, a Palestinian from a small neighboring village who could play a heart-fluttering ney flute; and Amjad, an Egyptian percussionist who could seamlessly move between tabla and tambourine. They formed Baladna and played at arrabi weddings around the city. During the week, they lifted and drove pallets of resin at the plastics factory, carving out a new life for their young wives and their new American children.

Afaf loved to look at the black-and-white photographs from a shoebox her mother stored in a hallway closet, their winter coats grazing the lid. They are pictures she thinks she knows by heart, but then a new detail emerges like the way the feathery clouds obscure the sun, or how Baba's coat collar is turned up on one side. Her favorite is of Baba standing on the beach at the Dead Sea. He's wearing a pair of pressed slacks and a white button-down shirt. His hands are thrust deep into his pockets and he's squinting at the camera, a smile dancing across his lips.

"My best friend Bassim took that picture," he tells Afaf every time she holds it up for both of them to see. "Poor boy died of cancer of the blood. Maskeen."

Back in the old country, a young Baba honed his music while working at a muhmasa in Al Bireh, roasting watermelon and pumpkin seeds sold by the kilo.

Afaf pulls out another dog-eared photograph. In it her mother poses with a group of girls, their arms linked, sporting beehives and kohl-rimmed eyes. Mama is the tallest, standing in the middle.

"I loved your mother's dress," Baba tells Afaf, tapping the photograph. "You can't tell here, but it was a beautiful green mokhmal—

velvet with lace down her back. It was the first time I saw your mother."

But no photograph in the untidy pile in the shoebox could reveal the early turbulent periods of her parents' marriage. After Nada was born, Mama refused to have any more children until Baba had settled into a stable job and they could move out of his cousin's bungalow on Fifty-Third and Fairfield Avenue. They constantly fought and Mama had threatened to return overseas. It was an empty threat— they could barely make rent, let alone acquire a plane ticket.

When they could afford an apartment of their own, her mother conceived Afaf, seven years after Nada. Afaf often wonders what sort of child might have come after Nada. If her parents had continued having children immediately after Nada was born, who might exist between her older sister and Afaf? Would she still have been born? It seemed unlikely to Afaf when she watched Mama move around the apartment, a nervous energy causing her to spill glasses of milk and drop plates, their sound clattering down Afaf's spine as they hit the floor.

Mama is slow to smile at her and Majeed, though her eyes light up whenever Nada is home. It was the two of them for so long, Afaf and Majeed were like interlopers. Mama and Nada had been newcomers to this country though Nada has no trace of an accent, no recollection of olive groves and herds of sheep. For seven years, her only daughter had filled the void of the loneliness in a new country. Afaf finds in the shoebox a Polaroid of Nada, an olive-skinned, chubby toddler, bare-chested, and seated on a blanket spread over grass, with the children of Baba's cousin with whom they'd lived. And another shows Mama holding Nada as she stands next to Baba at someone's birthday party, his arm lazily draped around her shoulders, balloons floating behind them. There's something in her mother's face that looks like tentative joy—not a full smile, but her green eyes twinkle with mirth. When Afaf arrived, followed three years later by Majeed, they were merely more mouths to feed.

Baba twirls the phone cord and avoids looking at Mama. "Can I talk to Nada, please?" An interminable pause. "When? Two hours ago?"

Mama gasps, bringing the dish towel to her lips. Baba silences her with a wave of his hand. Majeed clasps Afaf's pajama top again, but he doesn't tug. He only holds on.

"No, no. That's why I call you." Her father's broken English makes Afaf even more afraid—how can they get answers if others can't understand Baba? Still, he is more fluent than Mama, who looks lost and flustered at the first error she commits in public places.

Afaf remembers, on a visit to the cousin's house, when Mama had taken the wrong bus all the way to the North Side. Though she was only four or five years old, Afaf still can glimpse the sun shining on Lake Michigan, the bus ambling along the lakefront. Her mother's face tightened and her eyes glistened. She instructed Nada to ask another passenger how to get home. Majeed, a baby, cried on her mother's lap while Mama bounced him. He kept reaching for an empty milk bottle in her hand.

It is Baba who registers them for school each fall, one of the only fathers in line, the white mothers smiling coquettishly at him, this dark and smiling handsome man. Afaf proudly holds his hand. And it is Baba who translates Mama's questions about vaccinations and fevers at the public health clinic on Ashland Avenue, the doctor's needle poised next to Afaf's bare arm. And it is Baba who gently squeezes Afaf's hand when the first awful sting occurs.

Mama is in charge of all of their important paperwork—birth certificates, medical cards, the lease. Though she can't always decipher them, she keeps them safely tucked in a plastic folder with a rubber band clasp.

"Should we call the police?" Mama asks once Baba has run through the short list of names. "Ya rubbi! Where is she?"

Baba is quiet for some time. He looks at Afaf and Majeed, his eyes clouded over like he's working out something in his head. The aroma of fava bean stew is sickly in the air. "What else can we do?" He lifts the phone from its mount and dials.

~

Twenty-four hours later, two white police officers, a man and a woman, arrive at the apartment, and a word is tossed around: *runaway.*

"In most of these cases, teenagers disappear for a few days if they're mad at their folks," one officer tells them. They wait for Afaf's parents to offer any details of an embroiling argument.

"She is happy," Mama declares, tears streaming down her face. Baba guides her to a kitchen chair.

Afaf isn't sure that's true. She pictures Nada and her white friends in their bedroom—the record player stays on an endless loop of "Made in the Shade." She's kicked Afaf out and threatened to beat her if Afaf persisted in knocking on the door. How many times had she caught Nada rolling her eyes at the other girls when Mama interrupted them asking if they were staying for dinner, a pot of maklooba emitting the pungent aroma of fried cauliflower and eggplant? Or how many times had she observed her sister's cheeks flush with embarrassment when Mama, in her nightgown and dingy house

slippers in the middle of a Saturday afternoon, answered the door
to a classmate who'd come to work with Nada on a school project?

And her parents never let her sister go to sleepovers, though
Nada begged Mama every time she received an invitation.

"Ayb! A young girl never sleeps outside of her father's home!
Shame!" Mama's green eyes blazed at Nada. These were the only
occasions when she became upset with her firstborn.

There was a standoff in the kitchen one time over a camping trip,
Nada and Mama the same height. They are opposites in every other
way: Mama's soft hair escapes from a loose braid down her back,
while barrettes barely contain Nada's thick waves. Mama's complex-
ion is like a pale custard; Nada's skin is an olive hue—the same as
Afaf's. But it doesn't matter to Mama. Nada is her world.

After giving up the fight, Nada slammed their bedroom door
shut, startling Afaf, who lay sprawled on the floor reading *The Pin-
balls*, a book she'd checked out from the library. It had been Nada
who'd taken her to get a library card, who'd shown her where to print
her name and guided her to the fiction shelves for books Afaf had
instantly loved before she even read them.

Her sister threw herself on her bed. "I can't stand it here! I hate
her! I hate both of them!"

Afaf didn't speak while her sister seethed, afraid Nada would
pounce on her.

"Don't you hate it here?" Nada demanded. "We're Americans
but they don't want us to act like it."

Afaf had silently considered this, never having quite felt like she
ever belonged the same way Julie McNulty and Amber Reeves fit into
the world like perfect puzzle pieces. And there was Mama, too, who
seemed to love Nada most. Afaf squeezes in and out of spaces, trying

not to make a noise around the apartment and at school. But Nada is bold and fearless. So different from her. So different from Mama.

Perhaps such a burden would make any child want to run away, Afaf thinks as the officers question her parents. Perhaps Nada had endured enough from the times she was required to ask strangers for directions on buses because her mother couldn't summon the words or courage.

"Please," Baba tells the officers. "Nada is a good girl. She never run away."

"Are her belongings or any personal items gone?" The female officer's thick body strains against her uniform, one designed for a man. Her ash-blond hair is pulled into a bun at the base of her cap. Static crackles through her walkie-talkie.

Afaf has already checked. Most of Nada's clothes are still in the wooden dresser Baba brought home from the Salvation Army—Afaf is allotted only one to Nada's two drawers. The bottom one is broken, and that's where she found her sister's diary. Nada wrote in it every night, shooing Afaf out of their room before she took it out and later stowed it away. On a hunch, Afaf carefully slides open the lopsided drawer. Wrapped in a red bandanna is Nada's diary. But she doesn't tell anyone she found it. She slipped it under her own mattress for the time being.

"Did your daughter have a boyfriend?" the male officer asks. He's a head taller than Baba, with pork chop sideburns. He's chewing gum, smacking it between sentences. "A fella we might talk to?"

"Boyfriend?" Baba looks confused. "Nada does not have boyfriend."

"Maybe not one you're aware of, sir." The female officer jots something down on her notepad. "Her friends might be of help on that point," she says to her partner.

The officer nods, smacking his gum. "'Gainst your religion, sir?"

"Well, it's . . ." Baba falters.

Afaf cringes. Her parents' humiliation and fear shrink the apartment. The police officers loom over them, exchanging disapproving smirks. Majeed huddles next to her in the doorway of their parents' bedroom.

"We'll go have a talk with her friends," the female officer says.

Afaf sees something deflate in Baba. He nods at the officers. There is nothing more to say. This frightens Afaf. Baba is the strong one, not given to hysterics like Mama. The look of despair on his face shifts something in Afaf's stomach.

When Mama sees the police officers close their pads, she starts to wail. "No, no! You must bring her back! Please! She my baby girl! My Nada!"

Baba peels her away and forcibly sits her down on the kitchen chair. He walks behind the officers, who are already heading out the back door.

Afaf follows them, halting at the top of the stairs. Mrs. Blakely, the landlady, is standing halfway inside her screen door, holding it open as she speaks to the police.

"I don't want any trouble," Afaf hears the old woman say.

"Nothing like that, ma'am," the male officer assures her.

3

THREE DAYS later, they still have no leads. They've questioned a young man who claims to be her ex-boyfriend, but he's been cleared.

"He's a harmless kid. Wouldn't hurt a fly," the male officer tells Baba.

Her father is silent for a moment, then translates for Mama, though she's already throwing her head back and forth, denying this information before Baba's finished talking. Their daughter is gradually turning into a stranger, like a kaleidoscope morphing into a new image, the same colors taking a different shape. Afaf's parents have lost someone they never knew.

"We'll be in touch with any news," the police assure them.

That night, Afaf pulls out Nada's diary and opens it for the first time. A soft rain patters against the window. October's close, the leaves on the maple trees that line the block have started to turn flaming red.

The cover of the diary is full of rainbow stickers and cut-out images of ABBA. The inside page reads: *PRIVATE! For Nada's Eyes ONLY!*

Afaf opens to the first entry, dated last year:

September 7, 1975

Dear Diary,

She's driving me bananas. A BAZILLION questions! Where are you going? Who were you with? She's so nosey. I can't stand it anymore.

Anyway, J. gave me a charm necklace today, like the choker Agnetha Fältskog wears from ABBA.

I ♥ it!!!

He's super nice to me. He tells me I'm pretty though girls at school are a hundred times prettier than me. I don't feel weird or different around him. He doesn't tease me like the other creeps he hangs around (his friends = phonies). I'm starting to like him-like him.

Gotta go! She's calling me AGAIN.

Yours Truly,
Nada

Afaf flips through the pages to another entry:

November 21, 1975

Dear Diary,

I hate my life. I hate J. He dumped me for Stephanie Brighton. He lied to me.

Everything about me is WRONG, right down to my dumb name. "Nothing's here! Nothing's here!" The boys tease me.

Everything I HATE:

1. my dumb hair

2. my gross skin

3. my HUMONGOUS nose

I wish I'd never been born.

I want to SCREEEEEAM in her face to LEAVE ME ALONE. She doesn't have a clue. All she does is—

Mama snatches the diary from Afaf's hands. She didn't hear her mother come into her room. Afaf's hands are still open, suspended for a few seconds as though she's waiting for something to fall into them. She folds them in her lap and swallows her fear.

"What's this?" Mama demands, flipping through the pages, though she cannot read her daughter's handwriting. "Does it belong to Nada?"

Afaf nods.

"Where did you get it, Afaf?"

She's silent, her heart thudding in her ears.

"Where?" Mama yanks her off the floor. Her eyes are a tumultuous green sea.

Afaf winces at the sharp flash of pain in her shoulder. "In the drawer," she whimpers. "I just found it."

"Mahmood! Ta'al! Ta'al!" Mama calls out.

Afaf instantly forgets the throbbing in her arm, worried Baba will be disappointed if he finds out she'd been hiding Nada's diary.

Baba appears in the doorway, his eyebrows furrowed. "Khair, khair! What's happened?"

Mama shows him the diary. "It's Nada's."

Baba slowly reaches for it as though it's some kind of ancient text, portending doom.

"What does it say?" Mama asks, sidling up beside Baba, gripping his arm.

He shakes his head. "Afaf, read to us." Baba extends the diary to her. He and Mama sit on Nada's bed.

When Nada was out with her friends, Mama always asked Afaf to read directions on a new appliance or a late notice from the electric company. Afaf would feel superior, possessing something she hadn't inherited, something for which her mother was not responsible. But reading her sister's diary out loud to her parents feels awful, as though Afaf's reading a dirty magazine, like the one Bobby Jamison had brought to school one day and hid in his desk. Somebody told, and her teacher rolled it up with a rubber band and sent Bobby to the principal's office with it.

Afaf peers over the diary at her parents. They look tired like they're battling the flu, their strength zapped from them. Afaf notices a deep line in Baba's forehead that wasn't there before. Mama's mouth is turned down in a way that seems permanent to Afaf.

"Yalla," Baba commands.

Afaf squeaks through each entry, her face flushing as though her sister's words are her own. Nada's alienation and self-loathing pour from the pages, each sentence stumbling from Afaf's lips like a script she's delivering, a part she isn't old enough to play. The last entry is dated earlier that summer: June 22, 1976. Nada's seventeenth birthday. But her sister left the rest of the page blank.

"Who's 'she'?" Mama turns to Baba. "Is she talking about me?" Her mother's eyes well up with tears and her lips tremble.

When she'd first found her sister's diary, Afaf soaked up Nada's anger toward their mother. But now, seeing the deep sense of betrayal flush Mama's cheeks, Afaf feels hollow inside. Nada's words are like tiny daggers, stabbing Mama's heart.

~

Ten more days pass and Nada hasn't come home. Afaf fills in the square on her calendar with a strawberry-scented marker she traded at school for a sheet of puffy stickers. She sniffs the tip before replacing the cap.

On a late Thursday afternoon—laundry day—Afaf and Majeed trail Mama on the sidewalk as she rolls a wire basket full of their dirty clothes five blocks to Kedzie Avenue. A jar full of change clanks on top of the load. At the Soap N' Suds Laundromat, her mother breaks down when she pulls out a pair of Nada's blue jeans, the bottoms frayed. Afaf quickly orders Majeed to help her sort the colors from the whites as she's seen her mother do each week, and they proceed with the laundry as Mama lays her head on the folding table. Afaf grabs the jar of quarters that Mama keeps below the kitchen sink and lets Majeed insert the coins into the machines. Mama sobs, low moans muffled by her folded arm. The other patrons leave her alone, their eyes trained on crossword puzzles, or they stare straight ahead at the automatic dryers where piles of clothes toss and twirl.

Much to Afaf's embarrassment, Baba called the principal at Nightingale Elementary School. Mrs. Belmont, her teacher, pays more attention to her now—more than just to give her extra reading time, though Afaf doesn't need it. She yearns to be a Cardinal—the top-tier reading group. Those students gather near the windows decorated with butterflies cut from construction paper, read silently from books like *Treasure Island* and *The Summer of the Swans*, books Afaf can easily read if she were given a chance. When no one is watching, she goes to a freestanding bookshelf against the back wall of the classroom and peruses a stack assigned to the Cardinals—they have red dot stickers on their spines—and runs her fingers across their hard spines. Afaf might have been happy to be a Blue Jay, too, but Mrs. Belmont keeps her with the Owls, the lowest reading tier. There are only three of them in this group: a white boy with thick spectacles and a speech impediment, and the only other arrabi child in her class, Wisam, whom Afaf also suspects could be a Cardinal if their teacher would only give them both a chance.

Mrs. Belmont stops her as everyone shuffles out the door at the end of the day and tells Afaf not to worry about "the situation at home." Afaf is unhappy with the interest her teacher has suddenly developed in her; the other kids look at her, mouths open in curiosity. She refuses to utter a word about Nada's disappearance.

The landlady stops her every day she comes home from school. Baba checks in with Mrs. Blakely every evening, sometimes bringing her fresh fruit or a gallon of milk when Mama sends him for groceries.

"Any word, dear?" The old woman's voice is raspy, like fingernails scratching sandpaper. Mrs. Blakely wears an auburn wig that looks like a helmet on her small head. Her bony hand grips the handle inside her screen door; she never opens it, never invites Afaf in. Afaf often wonders what the old woman's apartment is like. From the back stoop, Afaf can see a well-lit kitchen and the same narrow hallway as her family's.

Afaf answers Mrs. Blakely with a shake of her head, one foot dangling from the stairwell as she's ready to fly up to her apartment.

"Give my regards to your mother," Mrs. Blakely tells her. The old woman has softened toward Afaf and Majeed, no longer scolds them as they thunder up the stairs or slam the back door.

Khalti Nesreen comes to stay with them. She's a newlywed, not as pretty as Afaf's mother, though she's nice. Her black-dyed hair is teased and pulled into a high ponytail. She wears a bright-patterned polyester dress that hangs stiffly above her knees. She takes off her suede leather boots at the back door of the apartment and they remain there for a week while she cooks and cleans the place. She pads around the apartment in Mama's slippers, a size too big for her petite feet. She wears a pair of tube socks to fill them out. At night, Khalti Nesreen sleeps in Nada's bed and at first Afaf is angry that another person has invaded her sister's space. But in the middle of the night, when a car horn wakes her up or a metal trash can topples in the alley, Afaf looks over at her aunt's sleeping body, relieved the bed is not vacant.

Even with her younger sister there, Mama can't be consoled. She sleeps through late morning, sitting up in bed only to sip addas from a chipped bowl on a tray Khalti Nesreen sets on her lap. The green lentil soup looks like vomit and Afaf and Majeed refuse to eat it when they come home from school. Her aunt lets them pour bowls of Fruity Pebbles.

"Don't worry, my darlings," Khalti Nesreen coos. She digs in the cereal box, scooping a handful, munching as she watches them. "Nada will come home and your mother will be back to her old self again."

They nod, slurping the milk from their spoons, the colorful rice flakes turning soggy in their bowls.

Afaf wants to tell Khalti Nesreen that she doesn't want Mama's old self back, that she's terrified of that woman, that perhaps the return of Nada would finally transform Mama into someone who naturally smiles at her and Majeed. Nada's absence has confirmed Afaf's suspicion: her mother is a very unhappy woman.

But it couldn't have always been so, Afaf thinks. Hadn't she been different—happy—the first time Baba saw Mama at an engagement party? They were each a friend of the betrothed couple. According to the story she's heard a dozen times from Baba, he'd been invited to play his oud with the trio he had newly formed: a violinist named Hisham and a tabla player named Waleed. They were happy bachelors, performing cover songs at weddings and small gatherings. He'd tried to catch her mother's ear with his elegant strumming, but she'd been oblivious. Mama had no intention of marrying, let alone marrying a musician.

Before the end of the evening, he gave a short speech:

"May the couple lavish each other with love and remain always true to each other. And for the rest of us, may we bask in izz khaddar."

A lush-green happiness.

Every guest turned toward Mama in her green velvet dress, her cheeks flushed with embarrassed flattery. Baba proceeded to sing "Negoum Al Layl" by Farid al-Atrash, sealing his proposal.

"*Stars of the night, weeping over my love and hope . . .*" Baba croons when he tells Afaf the story, tickling Afaf's stomach.

Her mother's friends giggled and poked her arm, wishing they'd been the subject of such an ardent serenade. Despite her resolve, Mama smiled and nodded her approval at Baba from across the crowded room.

From what Afaf has stitched together from the rest of Baba's stories—Mama never shares any details with them—her parents were happy in the beginning. Baba rented a small flat in Ramallah. Afaf tries hard to picture this first home in a place as far away as ones she's read about in books, like Neverland. Below their flat was a bakery that sold the best bread in the city.

"Every morning I brought your mother khubuz so fresh I had to carry it with a towel!" Baba tells Afaf.

Mama agreed to a plan: Baba would pursue his music for two more years before they started a family. They didn't require much as a newlywed couple; they could live off Baba's gigs for a little while. But children were another matter.

"Between you and me," Khalti Nesreen tells Afaf in a low voice when she helps her aunt dust the front room, "I always thought your mother would never get married. She had every boy following her around the village, and she'd never bat an eye." With her fingers, she reaches out and combs Afaf's long bangs off her forehead. Afaf flicks them back—she wants to look like Davy Jones from the Monkees. "But your father won her over."

So why is she so sad? Afaf wants to ask her aunt.

While they wait for news of Nada, Baba comes home from work on time every night. He stops rehearsing with his band. He lifts Majeed and swings him overhead, landing him back on the sofa bed, where they watch TV, the sound on low. He kisses the top of Afaf's head and she pulls at the tips of his thick mustache, which tickles her cheek. He sits with Khalti Nesreen in the kitchen until it's time to sleep, sipping tea with mint leaves floating on the surface of their glass cups. They speak in low, respectful voices as though a person is dying nearby.

Some evenings, Baba sinks down between her and Majeed and plays his oud, softly singing in Arabic:

> *If only when I close and open my eyes*
> *I will find you coming back*
> *Coming back, O my loved ones*

Though Afaf doesn't understand every word, this ballad becomes familiar, like the meals Mama has cooked for them her whole life.

4

TWENTY-TWO DAYS pass. Khalti Nesreen has gone back to her husband, with the promise to return in a few days. Ammo Yahya came to the door to collect her. He didn't step inside, awkwardly apologizing to Baba.

Ziyad and Amjad stop by in the evening when Baba is home, carrying Pyrex dishes full of mahshi and kufta their wives have prepared. A few of the arabiyyat around the neighborhood also drop by to comfort Mama, bringing a thermos of Sanka as though she is incapable of even brewing coffee. From a wire basket at the sink they pull mugs that Afaf washes when she comes home from school, and between sips the women shake their heads and suck their teeth. *Ts, ts, ts . . . may Allah return her safely to you, Um Majeed.*

Afaf's friend Sameera visits with her mother and they play outside while Sameera's mother washes bowls and glasses, and Mama sits at the kitchen table, sobbing.

"Where could she have gone?" Sameera asks Afaf. Her friend's dark hair is cut in a short straight bob. Last summer, she crashed her bike into a rusty fence and a broken chain link sliced off the tip of her pinkie. Afaf never tires of studying it, begging her friend to let her touch the smooth scar tissue. It looks like someone bit it off. Ever since, Sameera is no longer allowed to ride a bike.

Afaf had overheard Sameera's mother telling Mama about it:

Shayfa, shayfa! See what happens when you give a girl too much freedom in this country? She loses a finger.

Luckily, it hasn't changed Mama's mind about Afaf riding her bike.

Afaf turns the knobs on her friend's Magna Doodle pad and shrugs her shoulders. "I don't know where she went." They take turns drawing on the sketch pad, black grains assembling like ants beneath the screen. Afaf pulls the lever and Sameera's fat rainbow and flowers disappear. She sketches a kitten with long whiskers. Afaf still desperately wishes for a pet, but Mama refuses to have any four-legged creatures in their home. They have a fish tank, but the novelty has quickly worn off. Afaf wants an animal to hold and cuddle; feeding indifferent fish is like any other chore she's expected to do around the apartment.

"I guess the police would have found her if she was hiding," Sameera speculates, laying her chin on Afaf's shoulder as she draws.

"Why would she be hiding, dummy?" Afaf doesn't intend to be cruel, but she wants to escape any talk of Nada, at least for a little while. She turns a knob on the pad, trying to join two arcs to form a heart, but it ends up looking like an uneven inverted triangle.

A young detective working the case buzzes the apartment one evening. Baba offers the detective a chair in the kitchen and Afaf and Majeed watch from the doorframe of their parents' bedroom. He is very young—ruddy cheeks and blue eyes. His thick blond hair parted on the side gives him the appearance of a schoolboy, not a homicide investigator.

"Detective Harold Jones." He shows her father his badge and tucks it back into the pocket of his corduroy jacket.

"Someone phoned about a suspicious man near the old Union

Stockyard." His eyes dart between her parents. "We investigated, and . . ." He turns toward Afaf and Majeed.

"Loolad," Baba says softly. "Go watch TV."

They bolt to the front room and sit on the sofa bed. Afaf listens hard, catching parts of the detective's sentences:

"We investigated and . . . a body . . . these photographs . . . can you identify if it's your . . ."

A chair pushes back. Mama's low moaning.

"Are you sure it's not her, Mr. Rahman . . . have any distinguishing marks?"

The moaning grows louder. Then shuffling slippers. The bathroom door slams shut. Mama's vomiting becomes the only sound in the apartment. Afaf runs to the kitchen.

The detective stands, gathering his photographs. Before he closes his folder, Afaf catches the image of an arm, badly bruised, and fingernails caked with dirt. "I'm sorry about all this," he tells Baba. "You should take comfort in the fact that she's still out there. We'll do our best to find her."

The dead girl in the pictures turns out to be Bianca Lopez, sixteen years old, gone missing a day before Nada.

Afaf knows that it is almost worse for her parents—it not being Nada's body, battered and broken—because it means more waiting, more not knowing.

∼

Halloween is cold and rainy. Khalti Nesreen agrees to take them trick-or-treating for one hour. She wraps herself in a white shiny trench coat, holding her collar closed with one hand, the other clutching an umbrella. She waits on the sidewalk each time Afaf and

Majeed run up to a house and ring the doorbell. They comb a three-block radius of bungalows, their plastic sacks bulging with Bottle Caps candy, homemade popcorn balls, and Bazooka gum.

Afaf is happy to move about the neighborhood in disguise. Her Wonder Woman mask shields her from questions about Nada.

In the last month, she can't ride her bike without being stopped:

No leads from the police?

Any word on your sister?

How are your folks doing, poor things?

She's become the sister of the girl who disappeared. She hates the pitiable head-shaking stares from the neighbors. Sometimes they stop her and Majeed on their bikes, waving them down with a rake on their front lawns.

Sameera doesn't come over as much anymore, as though Nada's disappearance is contagious to other Arab children in the neighborhood. Afaf blames her parents, and Mama blames Baba: *You let her go out with these amarkan, doing God knows what.* Afaf imagines Sameera's mother whispering with the other arrabi mothers: *Shayfa, shayfa! See what happens when you give your daughter too much freedom. This country will snatch her up.*

The white girls have grown fascinated with Afaf. Before, they used to ignore her or poke fun at her. Now they huddle around her at recess and beg her to tell them about Nada. It's the only time she doesn't mind talking about her sister—to get close to Julie McNulty and Amber Reeves. She exaggerates the details each time she reconstructs the story and ends with a *"Poof!* She's gone." In every version, Nada is still alive—only not anywhere the rest of them can see her.

"Do you miss her?" Julie McNulty asks her. Amber Reeves listens for Afaf's answer, her classmate's lower lip perpetually trembling.

Afaf does miss her sister, but not in the way her classmates expect her to. Nada's absence is like an earthquake rattling their house: nothing appears damaged, though every object seems slightly moved from its original place. Mama and Baba bicker even more—a noise as familiar as the chirping of birds on the telephone line outside the apartment window—but the silences in between are tomb-like. Sudden tears fall down Baba's unshaven cheeks when he hugs Afaf and Majeed good night. After school, she finds Mama standing at the kitchen, water running over a dish she's been holding for a long time.

On the sidewalk, they walk past a pair of children both dressed as Bambi and a tall boy from *Planet of the Apes*. Their fathers are in raincoats, smoking cigarettes and nodding hello at Khalti Nesreen. One mother drives slowly alongside her children, her windshield wipers squeaking back and forth.

At Mr. Cliverson's house, Afaf halts. Majeed is Bigfoot, the hem of his plastic costume pants dragging on the cement sidewalk. He runs ahead.

"Wait, Maj!" Afaf calls out.

He turns around and scampers back to her. "What's wrong?" His voice is muffled behind his mask.

Afaf pokes the edge of the damp lawn with the tip of her sneaker. "Let's skip this house."

Mr. Cliverson is a mean old man. He sits on his porch in the summertime scowling at the neighborhood kids who ride past his house. He calls them "little brats" whose parents "don't give a goddamn." He stoops to pick up littered soda cans and candy wrappers off his lawn.

Before they can turn and head to the next house, Mr. Cliverson opens his door and steps outside, a bowl of candy in the crook of his arm.

"Yalla, loolad!" Khalti Nesreen says. "Don't keep him waiting, maskeen."

Last summer, Mr. Cliverson sprayed Afaf with the hose when she passed his house. It wasn't meant in fun; when she glanced over her shoulder, he was waving his middle finger at her, a gesture that nearly threw her from her bike, one the older boys in the neighborhood sometimes flourished at them when she and Majeed rode past on their bikes. It was hard to imagine a grown-up behaving in such a way. Ever since, she's avoided passing his house.

Majeed looks at Afaf; the slits in his mask don't properly line up with his eyes and nostrils.

"Come on," she finally says. Today she is Wonder Woman; nothing can scare her. Still, she hopes the old man won't recognize them.

"Well, well. Don't you look like trouble," Mr. Cliverson says. He's wearing a pair of plaid flannels and a long-sleeved thermal shirt. Afaf has never been this close to him and he seems much smaller, his shoulders stooped, the skin of his neck hanging like a turkey's wattle.

She looks past the foyer and into the living room behind him. An old woman sits in a wheelchair. Her head dips to one side, her mouth slightly agape. Her fingers twitch on the armrests. Though Afaf harbors a fascination with the homes of white people, there's something unsettling about this one. She doesn't want any candy— she clenches her sack shut. She wants to get away from this house as quickly as possible.

Mr. Cliverson nods at Khalti Nesreen. "That's not your mother," he points out. He does recognize them after all.

"My mother's sick," Afaf says, a bit too hastily.

"I bet she is." He scoops a handful of cellophane-wrapped butterscotch candies and drops them into Majeed's sack. "How about you, missy?" His eyes are milky with cataracts.

Reluctantly, Afaf opens her sack and watches candy trickle down. "Thank you."

He cradles the bowl in front of him. "Any word on your sister?"

Afaf shakes her head, her stomach sinking. It's not the same tone the other adults use when they ask about Nada, the kind that sounds like they really care. The old woman coughs and Mr. Cliverson glances over his shoulder before steeling his eyes on her again. "I doubt she'll be back. That girl is gone."

Before Afaf can reply, Mr. Cliverson shuts the door and they're back on the sidewalk, trailing behind Khalti Nesreen.

Afaf's breath is hot beneath her mask. She no longer feels the cold whipping against the back of her neck. She fights back the tears, but they roll down her cheeks and drip onto her plastic costume, disguised by the drizzle of rain.

When they get home she goes straight to her room, defying their tradition of pouring all of their loot onto the kitchen table. She rips off her mask and tosses it aside.

Majeed faithfully follows her. "You wanna count it in here?"

She shrugs her shoulders, avoids looking at Nada's empty bed. Her brother turns his sack upside down and she watches his candy cascade onto the carpet. She turns on the record player, slides on ABBA, and listens to "So Long," Nada's favorite .

Majeed sorts the chocolate and nougat treats from the hard candy and bubble gum. In the kitchen, Khalti Nesreen prepares a pot of tea, and Mama emerges from her bedroom. Afaf dreads the day Khalti Nesreen leaves them for good, returning to her own life.

"Do you wanna trade?" Majeed asks her.

Afaf shrugs her shoulders again. She doesn't care if her brother takes all of it. Her favorite holiday has been ruined. Is this what it will be like from now on, Nada's absence casting a shadow over everything Afaf enjoys, days she looks forward to? She lies down on the carpet and props her legs on the mattress. She taps her fingers to the tune of "I've Been Waiting for You."

Majeed gnaws on a Tootsie Roll. "Is Nada really gone? Like Mr. Cliverson said?"

Still on her back, she reaches for a Bazooka gum from the pile and unwraps its joke:

How much dirt is in a hole 6 feet by 6 feet?
I dunno . . .
No dirt, stupid! I said it was a hole.

"Is Nada gone?" Majeed asks Afaf again.

"Yes," she tells him, balling up the wrapper and throwing it at the ceiling. "She's gone."

5

FIFTY-FOUR DAYS pass. The leaves have fallen off the maple trees that line the street. Afaf and Majeed can no longer go outside without a coat and hat. Soon Christmas lights will border the windows and rooftops of the neighbors' houses. Though her family doesn't celebrate Christmas, it is Afaf's favorite time of year. Baba takes her and Majeed for long walks around blocks of bungalows decorated with nativity scenes and snowmen with round bellies glowing with a warm yellow light.

Khalti Nesreen comes every other weekend. Mama returns to cooking and Afaf is grateful for that—her mother is a far superior cook than her aunt. She comes home from school each day and the aroma of broiled lamb and tomato stews spiced with baharat welcomes her. It almost feels like life is returning to normal.

Baba has begun to stay away again. He spends half his time rehearsing with his band, the other half with another woman. Afaf overhears her mother talking about her to Khalti Nesreen.

"How much more can I endure, ya Nesreen?" Mama wails to her younger sister. "Ya rubbi! What kind of life is this?"

They are plucking the stems of mlookhiya over sheets of newspaper spread across the kitchen table. Her aunt found a fresh bundle at a grocery in Milwaukee. A big bowl sits between them, a small mound of green leaves forming in it.

Afaf sits on the floor of her bedroom, her door ajar. All she can gather is that the other woman is arabiya—a singular affront to both her mother and aunt. Afaf wonders if it would be easier if it had been a white woman who'd stolen Baba.

After lunch one weekend, Afaf musters the courage to ask Khalti Nesreen, "Does Baba love another woman?"

She stands on a step stool beside her aunt at the sink, drying the dishes she carefully hands to Afaf. She broke a small dessert plate the last time Afaf begged to help. A portable television drones in her parents' bedroom. Baba bought it from a coworker and Mama accepted it without a word. He managed to fix the antenna until the screen finally cleared of static and images of people cut through.

Khalti Nesreen stops rinsing a glass and looks hard at Afaf. "What have you heard?"

Afaf shrugs, trying to be nonchalant.

Her aunt looks thoughtful for a moment. "You must not repeat a word of this to anyone."

Afaf solemnly nods as she rubs a bowl dry. She understands telling a child is like telling no one at all.

"It's actually a sad story when you get right down to it," Khalti Nesreen begins in a low voice, checking behind her for Mama's closed door. "Her husband was killed in a car crash—God rest his soul. She's a young woman, only twenty-four. It was naseeb, I guess. Our Lord has mysterious ways of bringing people together."

"Does Baba help her forget?" Afaf vigorously dries the bowl.

Her aunt hands her another one dripping with water. "Yes. I suppose he does love her. But that's not fair to your mother. Even if the other woman is sad."

"Mama's sad even when Baba's around."

"It's complicated, habibti. You'll understand grown-ups better when you get to be one."

It's not an appealing prospect for a ten-year-old girl. Months of observing her parents and their misery have brought her to a critical decision: Afaf will never get married. She would still have to grow up, but she would live on her own. On a farm like Fern in *Charlotte's Web*. Of course, she couldn't raise pigs—they're haram—but she would raise chickens and cows. Maybe she'd let Majeed come along, too.

~

The day before Thanksgiving is a half day of school. She and Majeed run home, jumping over puddles of rain, her brother careful not to damage the colorful turkey he's constructed from an outline of his hand. It's the same one she'd made at his age, one of many childish creations she'd present to Mama after what seemed like hours of carefully coloring inside the lines or delicately gluing cut pieces onto brown construction paper. For Majeed, it's yet another gift for Mama, like a potion that might break the spell of gloom—Afaf can see hope in her brother's face. Their mother's dresser is lined with macaroni art, a papier-mâché jack-o'-lantern, a color-by-number bouquet of flowers. Mama smiles at each offering, asks Majeed to explain how he'd made it, then she withdraws to her inner world. But, for a few moments, a curtain is drawn from her face and Majeed and Afaf can see someone vaguely familiar.

As soon as Afaf opens the back door, she senses something is wrong. The kitchen counter is full of half-peeled, half-sliced vegetables, and dinner plates have been smashed on the floor.

"Mama?" Majeed calls. He clutches his hand-turkey, eyes wide and afraid.

Inside her parents' bedroom, Baba's clothes are strewn everywhere. Mama's suitcase is laid open, a few of her dresses crumpled inside. It looks like someone was trying to escape but their plan was somehow foiled. Afaf's heart beats fast.

"Children?"

It's Mrs. Blakely, the landlady. Afaf grabs Majeed's hand and leads him back to the kitchen.

"Hello!" The old woman waves a hand, clutching the back of a chair. She's out of breath from climbing the stairs, and she's not wearing her wig. Her thin gray strands hang limply from her scalp. Afaf's stomach ripples with fear. "Your mother—she's not well."

"Where is she?" Afaf asks. Her palm feels slick against her brother's, but she won't let go. Majeed sniffles back tears.

"Your father's with her." Mrs. Blakely wipes her nose with a handkerchief she pulls from her sweater pocket.

"Where?"

"He'll talk to you as soon as he gets back." Mrs. Blakely grabs Majeed's hand. "Watch out for that broken glass. Oh, dear! What a mess!" She pats his cheek. "Come downstairs for some hot chocolate and marshmallows. Wouldn't you like that, sweetie?"

Her brother looks at Afaf, not certain if he should concede amid the chaos. Afaf nods at him and he wipes his nose with the sleeve of his coat. He sets the hand-turkey on the kitchen table and nods at Mrs. Blakely.

She holds up his project with liver-spotted hands. "How lovely! Did you make that for your mother? I'm sure she'll love it, dear."

Mrs. Blakely's apartment is tidy and sprayed in baby-blue paint everywhere you look. Afaf detects a strange odor—mothballs. There's a small piano in the front room, its lid covered with framed photographs. Most are black-and-white, scenes on a farm and in front of a white church. Mrs. Blakely had once been a pretty woman.

She sets them at the kitchen table with hot cocoa. They drop marshmallows in their steaming cups. Afaf watches a fluffy cloud swirl in the brown liquid.

In her bedroom, Mrs. Blakely speaks on the telephone in what she thinks is a low voice. Afaf puts a finger to her lips to stifle Majeed's anxious chatter and listens to the old woman as she describes the drama that was unleashed in her tenants' apartment. Mrs. Blakley had heard screaming—not those of an attack, but of sheer rage, she tells the listener on the phone. "Like a banshee out of hell!" Then dishes shattering. "I called Ma-mood at the factory and he came straight home, poor fellow. Took her straight to the emergency room."

Then an unfamiliar phrase emerges from Mrs. Blakely's one-sided conversation: *nervous breakdown.*

Two hours later, Baba knocks on the door. Afaf and Majeed run to answer, Mrs. Blakely in tow. He thanks the old woman.

"Yalla, loolad," he tells them.

"When's Mama coming home?" Majeed asks, clutching Baba's hand. "Are we gonna visit her?"

Upstairs, Baba gives each of them a brown paper grocery bag from a neatly folded stack Mama keeps tucked under the kitchen sink. Her mother rarely throws away anything. There's a drawer full of ketchup and mustard packets, extra twisty-ties for garbage bags, and rubber bands from weekly discount ads tossed outside their apartment door.

He tells them to fill the bags with clothes—a week's worth. Afaf helps Majeed and grabs the *Hair* album, not thinking whether or not Khalti Nesreen has a record player. That's all Baba has told them: they will be spending Thanksgiving with their aunt. It is the first time they have been to her house.

Ziyad, Baba's bandmate, drives them to Kenosha. They each exhale their cigarette smoke through a slit in their car window. There's a musbaha hanging from the rearview mirror. On the cassette player, Arabic ballads pour out against a background of static. Baba speaks in a low voice and Ziyad nods and sometimes says, "Khair inshallah. You must have patience, my brother." Ziyad winks at Afaf in the rearview mirror and she tries to smile back, but she feels too glum.

6

KHALTI NESREEN'S house is a white colonial with green shutters. Ziyad drives up a long driveway, past a mailbox post stenciled with roses. The closest house seems a mile away. There is a small pond in the backyard and an expansive lawn. An oak tree stands in the center, a wooden swing attached to it. On the west side of the house is a tidy berm with a wrought-iron bench. A red-painted birdhouse at the edge of the driveway instantly captivates Majeed.

He tugs on her coat sleeve. "Do birds live in it?"

Afaf shrugs her shoulders, curious, too. This new vista on nature is overwhelming. She's used to Chicago's straight lines, block after block of bungalows, and two-story houses buttressed by long staircases. Her aunt's neighborhood winds and dips, and contains more trees than she's ever seen in one place.

Baba escorts them to the door, carrying their paper bags stuffed with their clothes like groceries. He politely refuses Khalti Nesreen's invitation to come inside, nodding his head at his friend waiting in the car.

"I need to get back to Muntaha." Baba looks haggard and sad. A few white whiskers have crept into his mustache.

He drops down to his knees and gathers Afaf and Majeed in his arms.

"What happened to Mama?" she whispers in his ear.

Baba's eyes shine with tears that he blinks back. "She needs to rest for a while, habibti." He smiles and pats Afaf's cheek. He tickles Majeed's stomach. "Now go on, and don't give your aunt any trouble."

After she closes the door behind Baba, Khalti Nesreen pulls each of them close to her and kisses them on the forehead and nose. "Welcome, ya loolad!"

Majeed squirms out of her grip. "Khalti! Do birds live in that house?"

"What house, habibi?"

"The birdhouse!"

"I don't know, my love. You'll have to ask your uncle."

"When's Mama coming home?" Afaf asks.

"She's on a mishwar," her aunt says, smoothing Afaf's bangs out of her eyes. "A little trip. To relax and get better."

"But her suitcase is still at home," Afaf says.

"She won't need much on this trip, habibti. It's a short one. She'll be back before you know it. Now come help me with this tabbouleh." Khalti Nesreen leads the way to the kitchen.

Her aunt's words eerily echo from that day she assured Afaf and Majeed that Nada would also return.

Afaf drops her body down on a chair and sullenly squeezes the lemon halves into a bowl.

"Afaf," her aunt says, lifting her chin. Her fingers are fragrant with parsley. "Everything will be fine." She winks at Afaf and resumes chopping. Um Kalthum sings from a transistor radio with a cassette player. Mama always hummed the lyrics when she cleaned the house.

At dinner, Khalti Nesreen's husband regards them with detached courtesy, offering them orange juice from a glass jug instead of Coca-

Cola like Mama does at home. Ammo Yahya and Khalti Nesreen talk about the hospital and his patients.

"These amarkan are insufferable," he complains. "They ask a hundred questions about a simple procedure."

"You work very hard, my love," her aunt says. She spoons more tabbouleh onto his plate and checks the status of Afaf's and Majeed's plates. "Sahtain! Eat up!"

"Are there birds living in that house?" Majeed asks Ammo Yahya.

"Not anymore," he says. "They've flown south for the winter. They'll be back in the spring inshallah."

Khalti Nesreen chuckles. "I remember when we were kids, an old hajj in our village had over a dozen birdcages. He could hit a target from a kilometer away with his slingshot . . ."

Afaf chews on a halved slice of khubuz, its edges blackened on the stove. Her mind drifts to Mama and her stomach knots up. How can she possibly miss her mother and still be relieved to be away from her?

After dinner, her aunt leads Afaf and Majeed to a guest bedroom on one end of the second floor. There's a bay window with a built-in cushioned bench that overlooks the driveway. Majeed immediately goes to it to observe the birdhouse, kneeling with his forehead pressed against the glass.

"It's too dark to see," he says over his shoulder to Afaf.

She sits on a small, tidy bed in the center of the room. It's covered with a floral duvet of the same pattern as the curtains.

"I'll bring you an extra pillow, my darlings," Khalti Nesreen says.

Under the blanket, Afaf holds Majeed's hand, the only thing familiar to her in this place. She's never slept anywhere besides her apartment. Mama's words echo in the dark: *Ayb! A girl should never sleep outside her father's home.* Here in her aunt's house, Nada's absence looms in a strange way, like the ceiling fan hanging over Afaf, in a room neither of them had occupied together.

She stares at the ceiling fan. Where has Nada been sleeping all this time? She's still alive in Afaf's consciousness, living somewhere close to her family yet in a place none of them has been. She closes her eyes and runs down all the houses and apartment buildings on Fairfield, the ones on her way to Nightingale Elementary School. Then she scans the stores on the main street she knows—Grocery Land, Soap N' Suds—and ones she hasn't been inside before. Has Nada been in any of them? Could she be in one of them right now?

It's too alien a thought—Nada being dead. She hasn't known anyone close to her who's died. Her friend Sameera missed school for a week to travel to Detroit when her grandfather died. That's what old people did.

Outside, it is still—no car horns, no people laughing in an alley. The floor creaks as her aunt and uncle close their bedroom door at the other end of the hallway. Afaf hears a strange hoot—could it be an owl? It's a sound she believes Nada, too, might have never heard before.

~

Khalti Nesreen will host Thanksgiving. There is a small community of expatriates from Egypt and Iraq who live in Kenosha, among them a few physicians and their families whom Afaf's uncle has invited. Afaf can tell Khalti Nesreen is very nervous and doesn't want to disappoint her husband.

She bastes the turkey, curlers in her hair the size of soda cans and a frilly apron wrapped around her knit turtleneck dress. Her *Marie*

Claire magazine is propped open on the kitchen counter, a juicy, golden-roasted turkey taking up the centerfold. A bit of flour dusts the corner of an "Easy Turkey Day" recipe. Her aunt recites each direction out loud as she performs it, less clumsy in English than her mother. Afaf doesn't recall Mama ever consulting a magazine or a cookbook. There was no need: Afaf doubts the suppers they normally ate—maklooba and waraq dawali—could be found anywhere in a recipe book.

Khalti Nesreen permits Afaf to set the table, then returns and rearranges the silverware, approving everything else.

"Okay—I think we're all set," she says. "Let me do your hair, Afaf. Yalla! Before the guests arrive."

She pads up the carpeted staircase in fluffy pink slippers. Afaf remembers how her mother's dingy slippers had once swallowed Khalti Nesreen's feet.

The guests include a childless couple, newlyweds like Khalti Nesreen and Ammo Yahya. The woman has a hooked nose that makes her appear unkind. Her husband constantly blows his nose, much to his wife's annoyance, his handkerchief sliding in and out of his pocket like a magician practicing his act. He ogles Khalti Nesreen each time she stands up to serve or replenish a dish.

There's an older couple with two daughters close to Afaf's age. She attempts a polite smile at them, but they only snicker and whisper in each other's ears. Afaf tugs uncomfortably at the French braid Khalti Nesreen fashioned for her, adorned with a pink ribbon at its end.

The adults give Afaf and Majeed pitiable looks and wear phony smiles as though everything is okay. An ache churns in her stomach.

Majeed is oblivious, amazed by the impressive spread Khalti Nesreen has laid out.

Though the turkey looks rather pathetic—its skin is still pale,
not at all golden like the magazine photograph—there are platters of
Middle Eastern dishes to steer attention away from her aunt's failed
assimilation: mahshi koosa simmered in yogurt sauce; oozi rice with
spicy ground beef, carrots and peas; chicken musakhan with tangy
sumac. Yet it is the lamb roast that wins everyone's approval. The
charred fat still sizzles in the foil-lined pan. Khalti Nesreen beams
with pride.

The children sit at a small folding table with stiff metal chairs.
One of the girls keeps kicking Afaf's shin and apologizes insincerely.

More than ever Afaf wants to be home—she wants Mama
home—celebrating Thanksgiving in their tiny apartment despite
her parents' bickering. Mama always prepared chicken stuffing and
candied yams and her turkey was perfectly roasted. And a pan of her
mother's delicious waraq dawali was set out among the other dishes.
Baba sang and played his oud after they could eat no more. It was the
only time of year they all gathered around the table—Baba, Mama,
Nada, Majeed, and Afaf—to eat at precisely the same time. It was
the closest she'd ever felt like amarkan.

Afaf wonders if Mama is having turkey and gravy, wherever she
is. Does she even know it's Thanksgiving? Does she miss them?

And Afaf wonders again about Nada. She fights hard to keep
Nada's face sharp and clear in her mind, though it fades when Afaf's
away from home, where school portraits of Nada hang in the hallway
along with hers and Majeed's outside their bedroom. At her aunt's
house, Nada's face blurs in her mind, like it's out of focus. In their
apartment at last year's Thanksgiving, she and Nada broke the wish-

bone, her sister triumphing like she did every year. At Khalti Nesreen's table, no one goes for the wishbone from an inedible turkey.

Afaf carries her half-eaten dinner to the kitchen and spends a
long time in a bathroom on the second floor. She sniffs a potpourri
bowl on the porcelain sink, runs her fingers over scented soap
shaped like flowers.

Majeed knocks on the door. "What are you doing in there?"

Afaf finally emerges. "I hate it here, Maj." She presses the tip of
her shoe into the beige-carpeted hallway.

He shrugs. "It's not so bad. I miss Mama, too."

Afaf grabs his hand and they climb down the stairs, stepping
in sync.

In the main salon, Afaf sees Ammo Yahya pouring a honey-
colored liquid into sparkling glasses for the men. They light cigars
and lean back into leather chairs. The women help Khalti Nesreen
clear the table and prepare a pot of qahwa, the tiny demitasse cups
already arranged on a silver tray.

"Afaf? Why don't you take the kids into the sitting room?" Khalti
Nesreen says. "I've got Twister in there."

"I never play Twister," the older girl declares once they're out of
earshot of Khalti Nesreen. "I don't want a boy touching any part of
me." The sisters sit side by side on a wicker love seat, their chins jut-
ting out with moral righteousness. Their pristine white socks hold
up stiffly below their knees.

Afaf and Majeed look at each other. He shrugs. They sit opposite
the girls on two matching wicker chairs, staring them down. The
older one speaks in an Arabic dialect Afaf can't follow, then raises
her eyebrows at them.

"Do you understand what I'm saying?" she says in English.

Afaf doesn't respond.

"Dummies don't know how to speak arrabi!" the girl sneers.

Afaf grips the armrests of her chair as angry tears well up. "Shut your stupid, ugly face!" These hateful words startle her. They come from a place deep in her throat, and hurtle out of her mouth like a rocket ship. "Just shut up already!" she spits again.

This surprises the girl, too, because she tugs at the arm of her sister, who looks dumbstruck, and they leave the room, one closely following the other. Majeed grins at Afaf, impressed. He hops off the sofa and walks to the record player.

By the time "Good Morning Starshine" plays, Afaf joins Majeed as he sways his small hips, arms flailing above his head. She moves from side to side, soft-clapping. Khalti Nesreen pokes her head in. She looks like she's about to say something but only smiles before leaving them alone.

Good morning starshine
The earth says hello

They listen to the entire album until they no longer hear the words.

Nurrideen School
for Girls

IT HAD been easier than he imagined. He pulled into the loading dock behind the school, confident his white van wouldn't draw any suspicion. It resembled the ones that delivered food or serviced the building. He wore his old Excel company uniform jumpsuit under an oversized brown winter vest, concealing a .22 Ruger in his holster. The elongated metal toolbox he carried contained an Armalite M-15 rifle, unassembled, its parts perfectly fitted inside after he'd taken out the drawers that held his drill bits and bolts. Earlier that morning he'd tossed them all into the large dumpster behind his apartment building. He'd have no use for them after today. He plodded across the wet lot in work boots, crunching blue salt crystals dissolving what was left of a snowfall early that morning.

He'd woken to the snow, convinced he could hear the snowflakes settling on the windowpane. Eileen snored softly, her back to him, and he carefully rolled out of bed. His old dog Jeni painfully pulled herself up, arthritis slowing her joints. Her paws scratched the floor as she gathered her bearings and he waited patiently for Jeni before closing the bedroom door behind them. She followed her master down the narrow hallway, eager at the prospect of a much earlier outing than their normal routine.

The moon hung low through the kitchen window, illuminating the snow that continued to fall. It was very quiet, snowflakes padding the walkway outside of his apartment unit, and caking the roof and hood of cars lined up in the common parking lot. The plows were not out yet and he was grateful. The silence was comforting as the snow blanketed the world outside—a pure, clean white.

He didn't require sleep anymore; it was enough to have Eileen's touch. He'd try to absorb her perpetual warmth, though she sometimes flicked an arm at him, half woken and irritated. He let her sleep this morning, gathering his clothes in a bunch and dressing in the washroom. He'd decided against leaving a note—he couldn't summon any eloquent words to properly convey what he was about to do. His actions would speak for him.

He took Jeni for a walk, past the corner where children from the apartment building usually waited for the school bus, their backpacks bouncing up and down. On any other morning, he'd watch from the railing outside his second-floor unit, recognizing most of them, since he'd been inside their apartments, fixing a broken window latch or sealing a leak under a bathroom sink. He'd sip his coffee, panning the group of children, eyes fixing on brown twin boys who stood solemnly apart from their peers. At seven-thirty, the school bus would pull to the curb, a safety arm extending into the street. Earlier scattered and unruly, the children would fall into a single file and disappear onto the bus. The twins were always the last to board.

This early morning he seemed to be the only person awake. Jeni's gait slowed after they'd gone a block, her paws slapping against the snow. He felt terrible for his dog, a cross between German shepherd and Labrador, with black, white, and gray rings of fur around her neck. Jeni was almost fifteen years old. It seemed like a slow, tortuous decline, and now he regretted not having put Jeni out of her misery. He should have driven up north, found a patch of forest, and let her loose to cavort among the frozen-barked trees for a little while. Then he would have called her to him and gotten down on one knee to give her a final rub of her muzzle before pressing the barrel of his pistol between her eyes as she looked up at him. That's how he'd want to go—quickly and painlessly, avoiding the agony and pity of disease and age. If the day went as planned, it might go down like that.

He quietly reentered the apartment and spent a long time on one knee, rubbing his old dog's ears and muzzle. Jeni's faithful, tired eyes deeply moved him. A human being had never regarded him in such a devout way. He hoped Eileen would be merciful and put his dog down, save Jeni a bit of dignity.

∼

Inside the Muslim school, a few staff members milled in the short corridor from where he'd entered on the dock. He could see the security guard at a desk, his baseball cap obscuring part of his face. The guard was reading the *Sun-Times*, and looked up at the sound of his steps. He lifted his toolbox in a gesture of greeting and the guard waved back. No questions and no demands for an identification badge or a work order. Still, icy fear tingled down his spine as he rounded the corner past the cafeteria. He could turn around, pretend he'd forgotten a tool in his van, drive off the lot, back to Eileen and Jeni. But he walked on.

He'd had the rifle shipped to him last week and he'd opened it up, sweat beading his forehead. Eileen was at work and he sat on the edge of their bed assembling the rifle, the locking motions offering him a strange kind of comfort, like what he'd experienced as a boy when his father took him and his brother Joe hunting. It was the only time he could bear to be close to his father and not want to kill him.

His brother Joe had been brave, joining the army, leaving him alone with their parents. He'd started sleeping in Joe's room, burying his face in his brother's pillow, trying to muffle the low and deadly voice of his father through the vent, his mother's whimpers of pain. The next morning she'd be at the stove, cooking their oatmeal as usual, her sprained arm in a sling that she'd made from old cheese-cloth. Other mornings her lip was like a smashed cherry, her eye swollen like a plum.

Today he wouldn't be running away, and any thoughts of retreat-ing to his van were gone. He moved quickly down the hallway, eyes searching for a janitor's closet.

This school was like any other he'd ever been inside. There were bulletin boards with college posters and announcements for schol-arships. The floors gleamed under fluorescent ceiling panels. The old brown-brick exterior of the building contrasted with the mod-ern renovations he suspected had taken place over the decades. Except for the portraits of students showcased on the walls of the corridor—every single girl wearing a headscarf, grinning ear to ear—it was no different than other schools. He passed the gymna-sium and he could hear girls running across the court, dribbling a basketball, cheering each other on.

Next to a drinking fountain he spotted a door with a sign *EMPLOYEES ONLY*. He was about to enter when the gymnasium door suddenly pushed open. A panting girl came out. She wore track pants and a long-sleeved jersey with *Nurrideen School* printed across her flat chest, damp circles under her arms. He couldn't tell if her white scarf was wet, though her face glistened with sweat.

He halted, frozen, his eyes darting from the young girl to the door she'd bolted through. That old, familiar feeling of disposses-sion, of not belonging, coated his chest. Even this girl—thin black eyebrows raised as she took labored breaths from running—seemed to exude more confidence than he, a grown man, felt. She gave him a little wave before heading to a water fountain. He turned back to the door and quickly entered a closet full of cleaning supplies.

He'd hated school when he was a kid, though he'd made decent marks. He dreaded getting called on to solve an equation at the board or to read a poem from Wordsworth out loud while his classmates followed along in their textbooks. The only tolerable teacher had been Mr. Hillocks, a history teacher who'd been rumored to have been a spy for the Russians and in possession of Nazi silverware. Mr. Hillocks's classroom contained world maps and framed antique cartography. He would trace his finger along the distance between countries like Peru and New Guinea and where he was— maps made him seem closer to places he couldn't pronounce.

At first that had given him hope of a place bigger than Wisconsin, especially after Joe left. He imagined his brother living in a foreign country after his service, and he hoped a postcard would appear someday from Joe featuring an exotic city or a dazzling beach. But a postcard or a letter never came. Perhaps Joe had needed time to forget what he'd left behind in Vietnam. One day, government papers arrived proclaiming that Joe had been honorably discharged. His mother held the papers, looking them over and over, though she could not read English. She traced the official seal with her fingertips. He'd wanted to run away, too, to escape his mother's misery and his own intense loneliness.

Before he'd enlisted, Joe had never mentioned Vietnam. Even as they watched the images streaming from their television, his brother had never expressed an opinion about the war. They both sat on a woven rug in the parlor as Walter Cronkite reported events they could only see and hear: the *chop-chop* of helicopter propellers swooping over hamlets; the gray and black smoke billowing from once-lush forests. He could never imagine the stench of burned villages, bodies charred to unrecognizable clumps, or the diesel-like smell of Agent Orange sprayed over thousands of acres of vegetation. And how did it feel when your flesh burned, chemicals eating through your skin? Those horrifically visceral realities never penetrated through the television screen. Perhaps Joe had understood it more deeply, felt something that compelled a call to duty. Enlisting had at least given Joe a purpose their father could not rebuke.

But Joe left him, too, without even a note. The only thing he'd left under his bed was a walnut safe box with his .22 Ruger—a nine-shot revolver Joe had saved up two summers to buy. Discovering this, he pretended it was a farewell present from his brother.

His father carried on like he'd never had an older son. He'd realized then, fifteen years old and alone, how easy it was for someone to be discarded like an old blanket. People were disposable—even the ones you loved. One day, he'd leave, too.

A bell rang, yanking him back to the present. He could hear girls laughing and talking outside the door, a mixture of English and Arabic. He waited until a second bell rang, signaling the start of a new period. He slapped in a magazine of bullets, stowing additional ammo in his vest pockets. He closed the toolbox and placed it on a shelf near a stack of toilet paper, removed his vest. He touched the revolver in his holster and stepped outside of the closet, the rifle close to his side.

The school hallway was empty. He passed a wall mural with blue and green geometric tiles, then came to a stairwell where music drifted down to him and climbed the stairs.

He could have started in the cafeteria, but the faint sound of a chorus pulled him in another direction. His movements slowed as he followed the singing voices. Soon he would see their faces up close and he could soak up their terror, their pleas for their lives.

And he wanted them to see him, too. Not from a distance— some lunatic man wielding a gun like in all the other stories they'd heard on the news, never truly imagining it happening to them. He wanted to be close enough so they could catch an awful, desperate power in his eyes.

1985

1

MICHAEL WILSON whispers in her ear, "Don't worry, A-faf. I can do it in a way so you'll still be a virgin. I know how it is with your family."

Afaf is in his bedroom, his parents gone for the evening. Michael strips to his underwear, then sits behind her on his bed. He pulls off her shirt, unclasps her bra. Afaf lets the white boys touch her only over her clothes. She lets Michael Wilson go farther while she stares at a picture of him and his girlfriend Kelly McPherson—they're at the Six Flags amusement park, holding stuffed animals he's won for her—tacked up on a bulletin board. As Michael kisses her shoulders, lifts her thick strands of hair, Afaf wonders if Kelly's body feels the same to him. Perhaps the only difference is their hair: Kelly's blond tresses fall in shimmering waves down her back, not a single curl interrupting its flow, while Afaf's hair has turned frizzy from constant relaxers, her ends splitting into tiny brittle pitchforks.

Michael Wilson is a senior point guard on Hoover High School's basketball team, comes into the Dairy Queen where Afaf works after school and on weekends. His friends give loud and whooping orders for burgers and shakes. She didn't think Michael noticed her until last week. He came up to the counter a second time and asked if she'd like to hang out with him sometime.

We can watch a movie or something at my house.

Afaf knows he doesn't really mean that when he asks her out—none of the white boys do. They don't take her to public places and they don't want to watch movies at their houses on dusty VHS recorders in their family room. She knows what they say about her at Hoover High School: *A-faf will let you make out with her. She might even give you a blow job.*

And she knows Kelly McPherson is Michael's girlfriend, but Afaf doesn't care. She grabbed the napkin on which Michael had written his address and slipped to her across the ice-cream display case. She nodded at him and tucked it in the pocket of her uniform apron.

Afaf studies Michael's room as he sucks on her neck, sure to leave a few hickeys. She's learned to hide them behind waves of hair, though her parents don't regard her very closely. She'd once caught Majeed staring at one beneath her ear when she'd carelessly pulled her hair into a ponytail. They were watching television and he only looked at her like he does at Mama—a combination of pity and worry, and powerlessness. She tries not to think about what he's heard, in the boys' locker room, around school. Has he seen her name scrawled in marker on a washroom stall: *Call A-faf for a A-fuck?*

On one wall of Michael Wilson's room are mounted shelves with state championship trophies and all-star plaques. Afaf imagines how proud Michael's parents must be of their son. Had they known as soon as he was born that he would be a star athlete? Did they ever imagine he'd be messing around with an *Arabian girl*? What would they think of him now, almost naked, making out with a girl in his room? Would it matter less if it were Kelly McPherson?

Majeed has just as many baseball trophies. They're piled on a dresser in his bedroom, some on the floor near his bed. Baba and Mama make only the championship games, clapping proudly when

Majeed takes the plate, rotating his arms, digging his left toe in the turf. Mama clasps Baba's arm, sucking in her breath until Majeed's bat makes swift contact with the ball. At Hoover, he makes appointments with his guidance counselor, researches colleges and scholarships. He's going to have a career, an aspiration that seems so alien to Afaf, so optimistic. She isn't good at anything. She's always made decent grades with the least amount of effort, but nothing interests her beyond reading—luckily her elementary school teachers hadn't killed that joy in her. In two days she can devour a Sydney Sheldon novel—she's read all of them—and if she likes an assigned book at school, she'll look up the author at the public library and check out others written by them. She remembers when Nada took her to the library so she could get her own library card. How proud she'd been to neatly print her name where the woman pointed, how thrilled she was to finally check out books on her own.

Michael Wilson doesn't have any books in his room, only a calculus textbook tossed on the floor and a wrestling magazine folded over on his nightstand. He fumbles with her bra. Could Majeed be so bold with a girl? Has he even kissed one? Something suddenly turns in Afaf's stomach and she jerks away from Michael, snatching up her clothes and flying down the staircase.

"Hey! Where the hell are you going, A-faf?" Michael Wilson shouts down at her.

She hates the way her name sounds from his lips, like the others she's heard reducing her to an object: *A-faf. A-slut. A-virgin. A-lost girl.*

That's what Mama calls her on the phone with Khalti Nesreen. Bint dy'ah. Lost girl.

They don't know how far she goes with the white boys, that an invisible force pulls her back from crossing that dangerous ravine of sex. She pretends it's because she doesn't want to, but the truth—tucked deep in her stomach, in the place where she's always felt shame and guilt dwelling in her body—is that she's afraid to betray Mama and Baba in such a way. Her virginity is her last vestige of childhood, of innocence. She offers it up to her parents like a precious stone.

You're different, Michael had told Afaf when he'd first locked the door to his room. But she realizes it's not in a good way, because different is never good.

Maybe that's what her sister Nada was talking about in her diary all those years ago. Could it be why she left? It's what the young detective finally told her parents: Nada's case was classified as a runaway.

There's no evidence of foul play here. I'm sorry, Mr. and Mrs. Ra-man. It was 1980, four years since the first time Afaf had seen the detective. His blue eyes had dulled since that evening in their old apartment on Fairfield Avenue.

Mustaheel! Mama shouted, wiping away tears with the sleeve of her housedress. *Impossible! She never run away from me.*

Baba had gently grabbed Mama's shoulders, whispered something in her ear. She vehemently shook her head, but stayed quiet. The detective looked down at his notepad. Afaf and Majeed sat at the kitchen table, their mahshi growing cold on their plates. She liked to split open the stuffed zucchini, eat the rice first, then the skin. They'd been halfway through the meal when the detective arrived.

Ever since that night, Mama has been floating through the years like a ghost, moving around their family, hovering on the periphery of their lives. Baba disappears into himself, coming home late, stinking of alcohol.

Afaf runs out the back door, hops onto her ten-speed bike she'd left in Michael Wilson's fenced backyard.

"You bitch!" rings in her ears as she rides home through the alley.

2

IN HER bedroom, Afaf drowns out their shouting with her Walkman. It's the same fight between her parents: Mama wants to go back to the bilad. For good.

Angry words still break up the lyrics floating through Afaf's headphones:

"... can't afford it, Muntaha ..."

And do you feel scared, I do

"You drink it away ..."

But I won't stop and falter

"... think of your children ..."

And if we threw it all away

"... I have no life here, Mahmood ..."

Things can only get better

Afaf squeezes her eyes shut, turns up the volume.

There's a part of her that wants Mama to leave. The part of her that folds itself over and over again, tucking away the hurt every time her mother looks through her, never seeing Afaf, always seeing her firstborn. She comes home every day to Mama at the stove, cooking meals she won't eat herself. She looks like a withering tree, her thin arms like leafless branches, hands that appear incapable of holding more than a broom that she sweeps across the dull wooden floor of their apartment.

There's another part of Afaf that wants to shake the grief out of her mother along with all of the memories of Nada and the bilad until they're like specks of dust.

But her family has moved three times since Nada disappeared and her absence still occupies the most space in each small flat, squeezing out Afaf and Majeed.

~

In the school cafeteria the next day, something cool slithers across her scalp and slides down her face. Afaf catches globs of green Jell-O in her hand.

"Slut," Kelly McPherson whispers in her ear. She stands behind Afaf in the lunch line. Her friend Angela Malone cuts in front of her. They're all freckles and feral white teeth. Angela's shaking out a foam cafeteria bowl, freeing a few more green globs onto Afaf's sneakers.

Kelly's breath is hot on her neck. "Stay the fuck away from my boyfriend."

Though fear prickles her skin, Afaf slams her tray on the counter and pushes Kelly so hard she knocks down two other students behind her. A semicircle forms around them, razzing and hooting. Afaf can't hear what Kelly's shouting at her from the floor. A crushed pint of milk pools near Kelly's butt.

Angela grabs a fistful of Afaf's hair and yanks her backward. She whirls around and catches Angela's chin with her fist. Then someone pins Afaf's arms to her sides and carries her out of the cafeteria. A peanut-butter-and-jelly sandwich hits her face to a chorus of laughter.

In his office, Coach Phillips, one of the deans, hands Afaf paper towels to wipe off the Jell-O from her hair. The sheets stick to the sugary residue. She sinks into the chair opposite of him at his desk.

His shelf is full of trophies and ribbons. Framed photographs of Hoover High School's wrestling team are on the walls, perfectly aligned from 1972 to 1984. In every one of them, Coach Phillips strikes an identical pose: arms behind his back, shoulders rounded, stomach tucked in. In the very first photograph his hair is thick and long and sweeps across his forehead. As the years progress, his hair grows thinner and shorter, and in the most recent one—last year— it's all gone, shaved to the scalp. And he's fatter now. But nothing changes about his stance—an unsmiling, dead stare at the camera.

He thumbs through a file and dials a number on his office phone. "Mrs. Ra-man? This is Dean Phillips from Hoover High School." He pauses, tapping his pencil on the edge of the desk. "Do you speak English?" He nods at Afaf. "Good, good. I have your daughter A-faf in my office. She struck another student, ma'am. Hit a girl. Yes. . . ." He neglects to tell Mama that it was Angela Malone who grabbed her hair first. She did feel a certain satisfaction in the way her knuckles crunched into Angela's cheekbone. But getting blamed for the entire incident?

The bell rings and the hallway outside the dean's office fills with the pandemonium of another passing period. Lockers slam shut and footsteps thunder to the next class. Afaf tries not to squirm in her chair.

Coach Phillips says into the phone, "You'll need to pick her up. Three-day suspension, ma'am." A pause. "Yes. She'll be waiting for you. Thank you, ma'am." He hangs up and jots something down in her file, closes it. He leans back in his swivel chair, hands folded across his potbelly. "Are you planning on not graduating, Miss Ra-man?"

Afaf folds the soiled sheet of paper towel over and over, ignoring his question, pretending to be cool. But it's the second time this semester she's been in his office. Last month, she cursed at a boy in her physics class. Mr. Biggs had posed a problem about velocity and a classmate had snickered something about the speed of a camel.

But cursing out a classmate is one thing; laying your hands on them is another. Perspiration trickles down Afaf's back. The adrenaline from punching Angela has faded, and the dean's lack of compassion leaves her feeling hollow and alone.

"Three strikes and you're out, young lady."

Afaf stares icily at Coach Phillips. No matter what, she'll never show them she's scared. Never reveal how truly weak she is. Every year the social worker calls her down to her office, and Afaf listens to the same lecture: *You have choices, A-faf. We can only control what we can in our lives.*

The social worker had wanted to know: *Are your parents strict, A-faf? Are you having trouble at home?*

Afaf had suppressed a laugh. *Strict?* White people think she's locked up the minute she gets home, that she is oppressed and not free. Mama and Baba barely acknowledge her, let alone care what she does outside of school. Maybe if they did, she wouldn't be sitting in the dean's office again.

"You need your diploma, young lady. Wouldn't want your father selling you to a harem, would you?" Coach Phillips chuckles, scratches the bridge of his nose with a meaty finger.

She fights hard to control the flush of red across her cheeks. She wants to grab one of his trophies and smash his face. It's a joke she's heard him make before to the prettier Arab girls at Hoover. They smile back politely. He has an assortment of insults reserved for the arrabi boys, too: *No oil deals during the school day, fellas.* His tone is always playful, not fully masking his distaste for the nonwhite element at Hoover High School. He's among a dangerous kind of adult: a smile suppressing their true feelings about you. Like Mrs. Cass, her English teacher. She ignores the only two black students in Afaf's class unless they ask questions, then she gives them a phony smile. Or Mr. Abbott, the study hall supervisor. He lets the white kids slide on tardies, but diligently writes up everyone else.

Coach Phillips hands Afaf a pass. "Wait for your mother outside. And you better keep outta my office." He swivels to a filing cabinet on his left. Afaf leaves his office without having uttered a single word.

3

SHE WAITS for Mama in the main office, throwing defiant looks back at students passing in the hallway and slowing to peer through the plate-glass window as though she's a zoo animal. Sameera and a few arabiyyat walk by and they lock eyes. Their friendship fizzled in elementary school and now Sameera and the other girls keep away from Afaf like she's got the plague. Sameera seems to forget when they were ten years old and used to play "Miss Mary Mack" over and over until they burst into giggles. Afaf's always been on the wrong side of the window, unable to conform to a mold Sameera and the other arabiyyat easily fit. They flirt and giggle with the arrabi boys, never crossing that line of chastity. Their fathers own food diners and gas stations, buy them whatever their hearts desire. Their curls shine from expensive perms and their eyes are lined with thick kohl. They wear twenty-four-karat gold amulets inscribed with *Allah* in Arabic. They are beautiful and spoiled—no different than most of the white girls at school except for their olive skin. Sameera quickly looks away as Afaf sinks deeper in her chair.

An hour later, Mama comes into the office, clutching her purse like she's in the wrong place, ready to turn on her heels until she spots Afaf. She's wearing her long gray winter coat with the oversized buttons, though it's the start of April. Her long hair is loose and stringy, her graying roots giving her a wild look. Her pink polka-dot pajama pants peek out of rain boots. Afaf cringes, wishing she could have walked home herself.

Two freshman boys waiting next to Afaf snicker. She glares at them, daring an insult.

"Mrs. Ra-man?" The secretary gives Mama a tight smile. "Please sign here." Mama grabs the pen while the white woman eyes the spot where a button is missing on her mother's coat.

The secretary jerks her chin at Afaf. "She can return to school on the fifth. Is there someone to pick up her homework? We can hold it here at the end of the day."

"Yes. Her brother." Mama's voice is low, like the volume turned down on a radio, her words barely audible.

"What's his name?" The secretary's pen is poised above a yellow legal pad.

Mama is suddenly distracted by the reality of the situation. She looks at Afaf like she doesn't recognize her daughter—perhaps she never has, Afaf thinks.

Afaf stands up. "Majeed. He's in ninth," she tells the secretary.

The woman's phony smile is gone when she looks at Afaf, no effort to feign kindness. "I hope he doesn't give you any trouble like this one." She points her pen at Afaf as she addresses Mama again.

"He's the perfect child," Afaf bites back. "Every parent's dream." It isn't too far from the truth. Before the secretary can respond, Afaf is already out the door. Mama has never been called to school for Majeed fighting another classmate. The only time he's come close was at a state championship game last spring. Majeed hit a home run in the bottom of the eighth inning. The pitcher on the other team had called out, *Look at the camel jockey go!* as Majeed rounded the bases. They'd almost come to blows and the game had nearly been forfeited.

Mama trails behind her in the hallway. Afaf is grateful sixth period has begun. There are only a few stragglers around, slurping from the water fountain, dragging their bodies to class.

In the parking lot, Mama speaks to Afaf for the first time. "You hit a girl," she says in Arabic. Her parents switch to this dangerous tongue when she's in trouble.

Afaf slides onto the passenger seat of Baba's blue '79 Buick Riviera. The suede cushions are worn down, once a shiny silver-blue, now dull gray. She can't recall a single new thing they've ever purchased—except for mattresses—even when they moved to new apartment buildings. Nearly every piece of furniture they own belonged to someone else first, holds some other family's story— always a happier one, Afaf imagines. This had been their first car. Baba had bought it from his bandmate Amjad and, though it was used, it was new to them.

The school bell rings, signaling the last period of the day. From outside, it sounds like an alarm, and Mama startles for a moment. Her green eyes dart around the parking lot and her fingers tremble as she unlocks her car door. Her skittishness has grown worse since Nada disappeared. When the doorbell rings at the apartment, or a car horn blares from the street, Mama jumps and wrings her hands. She won't answer the door if she's home alone.

Afaf climbs into the passenger seat. Mama throws her purse onto the backseat and turns the ignition. The engine rattles for a few seconds before catching and roaring to life. The first time Baba drove it home, Afaf and Majeed squirmed in delight. He'd managed to persuade Mama to go for a ride and they all climbed in, giddy with excitement, awed by the spacious interior. Afaf had breathed in the scent of coconuts from a deodorizer that hung from the rearview mirror. Now nothing can mask the stench of her father's cigarettes.

Baba taught Mama to drive a few months after he bought the Buick.

In this country, you give up your freedom if you do not drive, Baba had told her. He gave Afaf and her brother a stern nod, making sure they'd heard his wise words. Afaf remembers sitting in the backseat with Majeed, perfectly quiet as her father gave Mama instructions. Mama would brake hard and their small bodies would jerk forward. The first time Afaf and her brother laughed, Baba turned around, narrowing his eyes at them. *You do not laugh at someone who is trying. Only at the fools who do not give themselves a chance.*

That shut them up for the rest of Mama's driver's education. Baba was a patient man. Every mistake Mama made, he responded with encouragement. *That was a challenging turn. You will get it next time.* Or, *Muntaha! Azeem! Excellent parking—and your third time, no less!*

In the car, glass clinks on the floor of the backseat when Mama turns out of the school parking lot. Empty liquor bottles roll against each other behind Afaf's seat.

At first it was a strange smell on Baba's breath when he squatted down to kiss Afaf after work—like cologne he patted on his cheeks on Eid, but sweeter. After Mama's breakdown, when Afaf and Majeed stayed with Khalti Nesreen for two weeks, Baba came home later and later, Afaf and Majeed already asleep, knocking into an end table, stumbling down the hallway. Majeed still slept on the sofa bed, though they'd carried Nada's old bed to every new apartment because her mother would never let a single thing go. But as soon as Mama began her angry crying at Baba's drunkenness, Majeed scampered from the front room and hopped into Nada's bed. Some nights, Baba plopped down next to Majeed on the sofa bed and sobbed, holding her brother until he passed out.

Over time, the smell grew more permanent on Baba, like a new layer of skin. When she was twelve years old, they were on their way to Khalti Nesreen's one weekend and Afaf had kicked something under the passenger seat. She pulled out a nearly empty bottle of Jack Daniel's lodged there. An amber liquid swished around the bottom. She had quietly unscrewed the top and sniffed it. A pungently sweet odor. She let Majeed get a whiff, too. He crinkled his nose. While Baba and Mama drove without speaking to each other, Majeed snatched the bottle from Afaf and took a swig. He coughed violently.

Mama craned her body over the seat. *Khair! Khair!*

Baba parked on the shoulder of the road and got out. He pulled Majeed out and rubbed her brother's back as he wretched on the asphalt. Mama was at his side, too, shaking Majeed's arm.

Lah, lah, lah, was all Baba had said when Afaf handed over the opened bottle. The remainder of the liquid had spilled on the floor mat, and Afaf had watched the silver fibers absorb it, turning dark gray, like the stains from melting snow cones or rain-muddied boots.

It's not enough you're ruining your own health, you've got to ruin our children, too, with your shurub! Mama had shouted. She wiped Majeed's mouth with the palm of her hand and inspected his eyes as though Majeed had been poisoned. Her brother hugged Mama, while she glared at Baba. Baba turned the car around and they drove home. The day was ruined.

4

MAMA GRIPS the blue leather-covered steering wheel, a few seams broken, her knuckles turning white. Her fingernails are bitten down to the quick. A few broken cuticles have turned scabby. She doesn't utter another word. Doesn't ask Afaf what could have possibly provoked her to hit another student. Doesn't demand to know why Afaf is miserable at school. Afaf's chest burns. Wickedness flashes across her heart: Afaf wants to tell her mother why those girls came after her. She wants to list their names—all the white boys she's let feel her up—like the grocery list her mother hands to Baba every week. Maybe then Mama will have more to say to her.

Sophomore year it had started with Tim Mackey in his car. Truth is, Afaf didn't even like Tim—she doesn't like any of the white boys, not even a little. None of them make her feel any better, only that she exists, that someone notices her. After years in elementary school, she's never been able to figure out who she is, how she wants others to see her. Girls like Kelly and Angela and Sameera seem to have figured it out. Tim drove Afaf to Marquette Park and kept his eyes closed the whole time he kissed her neck and face and touched her breasts over her shirt. She'd listened hard to Simple Minds on the radio, drowning out his soft grunts: *"Don't you forget about me..."*

Afterward they drank strawberry-flavored wine coolers that Tim's older brother had bought for him. By the third one she guzzled, she felt a nice buzz, numbing her for a short while, allowing her to forget where she was. She pressed her forehead against the cool glass of the passenger-side window, ignoring Tim's hand on her thigh, drowning out his promise to keep it a secret.

At first she'd felt a power over these boys.

Like junior year with Jonathan Duke. He'd sat behind her in U.S. history and tapped her shoulder with his pencil. *Your hair's so dark. Like a bat.* She'd meet him in the library, in the microfiche section that no one ever used. He kissed her with chapped lips and touched her with rough fingers.

A few months ago she'd started working at Dairy Queen, and her first manager, a twenty-three-year-old college dropout, rubbed her shoulders as she wiped off each tub of ice cream in the freezer display case at the end of her shift. *Would your father shoot you if he saw me doing this?*

They think she's exotic—not beautiful. Her nose seemed to double in size by the time she reached puberty; her skin was dark like a peanut husk. To the white boys, she's something to conquer and explore, not keep. And she doesn't hold on to them, either. Before they're finished with her, she's already moved on to the next one.

Mama drives in stony silence past blocks of bungalows, spring flowers blooming in rectangular planter boxes. Yellow and purple tulips pose in the afternoon sun, elegant, indifferent. Afaf fights back her angry tears, bites down hard on her bottom lip. She pulls a book from her backpack. Lately she's been obsessed with George Eliot, her favorite so far is *Silas Marner*. The story captivates her: a golden-haired child wanders into an outcast's life. What if her parents had abandoned Afaf, left her on someone's doorstep? Would life have been better? She wonders if one alteration in a person's life can undo everything that's happened, like pouring red dye into a bucket of clear water. What if she'd never been born? Would Nada have disappeared? Might Baba have still been unfaithful? Or maybe you'd have to go further back, when Baba first saw Mama in her green mokhmal dress, strumming his oud to the symphonic clapping of the other guests. And instead of saying yes, Mama turns down his proposal and never sets foot in this country with a young daughter, thwarting loneliness and loss. And Mama wouldn't be Mama, but Muntaha Saleem, the oldest daughter who'd never wanted to get married. *Only no one outwits naseeb*, as Khalti Nesreen used to say to explain so many tragic stories. *It's already been written, habibti.*

They enter the apartment through the back door. Baba's snoring on the sofa bed. For the last two years, he's been working the night shift at the factory. The mattress creaks as he turns over. There's a batch of pressed grape leaves on the table. Mama was in the middle of rolling waraq dawali when she'd gotten the call from Coach Phillips. She goes to the refrigerator for a bowl of the rice and meat stuffing she'd prepared before fetching Afaf. She's still wearing her coat.

The phone rings. It's Khalti Nesreen, wondering where her mother's been for the last hour, why no one answered the phone. Baba hadn't stirred once since her absence.

Mama commences her railing. "Ya rubbi, Nesreen! She hit someone! Is this how normal girls behave?"

Afaf escapes into her room, slamming the door behind her. Her clothes blanket the floor and she kicks through them, plops facedown onto her bed. Mama's voice seeps through the door in rising snippets. She tries to read her book again, but she can't concentrate.

Mama's words echo in her ears: *Is this how normal girls behave?* Afaf, too, wonders how normal girls behave. Are they like Kelly and Angela? Beautiful white girls beyond reproach? Or more like Nada, who pretended to be the perfect daughter until she disappeared one day? Did she let the boys feel her up, too?

Afaf tosses the book aside. In the corner of her room the old record player sits on a tarnished console, a crate of albums beside it. She pulls out *ABBA* and slides it onto the spinner. It still works, but the arm jumps sometimes in the middle of a song. She doesn't mind—every scratch and cut of static strangely consoles her in a way her Walkman eludes her. She turns up the volume and lies down on her side, hands tucked under her cheek. Her thoughts begin to scatter and drift under fluttering eyelids. Mama's voice on the phone fades and her body gradually loosens—she's so tired. Before the end of "Dancing Queen," she's fast asleep.

Her dreams of Nada come in wriggly, uncanny visions, so real Afaf's convinced they actually happened when she wakes up. Sometimes Nada walks into the Dairy Queen, orders the most elaborate item on the menu, then leaves before paying, and Afaf gets in trouble from her manager. In other dreams, she shows up at Majeed's baseball games, sitting alone in a row on the opposite bleachers. Afaf's never close enough to Nada to touch or smell her. In today's daydream, Afaf's walking behind Nada at Hoover High School, wearing her favorite Cheap Trick T-shirt—the one for the 1980 *All Shook Up* Tour. Nada's wearing the same clothes she had on the day she disappeared: a pair of flare jeans, a pale yellow T-shirt. The hallway is strangely noiseless, though students pass them, their mouths opening and closing in silent speech. They arrive at the cafeteria, and Nada opens a brown paper bag. A pungent tomato-and-vinegar aroma wafts from it—Mama's waraq dawali. Coach Phillips comes over to their table and asks Nada for her school ID and Afaf tells him she's only visiting—she won't be staying long. He grabs Nada by the arm and tells her she doesn't belong. Then Mama barges into the cafeteria wearing her winter coat. She's holding a plate of stuffed grape leaves, stacked like cabin logs. She calls Afaf's name.

"Afaf, yalla!"

She jolts awake, disoriented. Her arm is slimy with drool. She looks around her bedroom.

"Throw out the garbage!" Mama calls from the kitchen.

It's still light outside. Afaf peels herself off the floor and stumbles to the washroom. Strands of her hair stick together from the Jell-O. She shakes out her ponytail and wipes down the crown of her head with a wet towel. She splashes cold water on her face. It feels good.

Majeed's not home yet from baseball practice. Baba's awake, watching TV. When he hears the running faucet, he calls Afaf's name.

He's sitting with a tray table, sipping from the same coffee mug with a world map sprawled across its circumference, the one he always drinks from. There's a plate of yesterday's leftover okra stew he's barely touched.

"I hear you have trouble at school today." His English remains somewhat stilted, though he's picked up more expressions over the years.

He'll tell her and Majeed, "Another day, another dollar," if they've successfully completed their chores, how something "cost an arm and a leg" when an appliance breaks in the apartment. His favorite is, "I'll take a rain check," to disengage from an escalating argument with Mama when he knows they are listening.

Afaf is silent, her eyes darting everywhere but on his face. She settles on his oud, propped up in the corner of the room where he always leaves it. Baba still plays all of the old tunes, but the melodies sound strained and joyless.

When she finally looks at her father, she regrets it. His face is bloated from exhaustion, his eyes watery and yellow.

"You are a good girl, Afaf. Okay?" *A good girl.* What Baba told the officers who'd shown up the first night Nada disappeared. How little they'd known about her sister then. How Nada had secretly hated them.

Afaf nods, chews the inside of her cheek.

He looks like he wants to say more, words forming on his lips.

"Do you miss playing with the band?" she suddenly asks him.

"I miss the boys," Baba says, a smile creeping across his face. The Baladna band broke up shortly after Mama's breakdown. At first he'd started skipping rehearsals and Afaf overheard his excuses to Ziyad and Amjad about needing to stay home, *to keep an eye on Muntaha.* Had Baba been afraid of something even worse happening to Mama? Was he worried Afaf and Majeed would find themselves alone with her when it happened? She knows how much it hurt Baba, losing the band.

Afaf glances at his oud, nods, and turns to go.

"Wait, Afaf." Baba stands up and pulls her in for a hug. She can't remember the last time she's been in her father's arms and she feels herself unfold in his embrace, his body absorbing her weight. She wants to hear him say, *Everything will be okay, habibti.*

Before her tears come, she slips away. In the kitchen, Mama rolls the last grape leaf. She jerks her head at the back door. A black Hefty bag sits there in a lopsided heap.

"I'm going to the library. To return a book," Afaf tells her, zipping up her jacket. She really just plans to ride her bike around the neighborhood, but she needs an excuse to escape the apartment for a few hours.

Mama eyes her suspiciously, though she won't stop Afaf. Her parents have never grounded her or Majeed, a practice they hadn't adopted from amarkani parents. You got yelled at and spanked, then it was over. The last time Mama laid her hands on her, Afaf was eleven years old, and she and Majeed had been running through the apartment and her brother knocked over the small aquarium her father had started. Afaf and Majeed had gone with him to the pet store, begging for a puppy or kitten, as a clerk explained the fresh-water options for a beginner tank. They came home with a betta fish, a few fan-tailed guppies, and fiery red barbs. After a week, the betta floated belly-up and she and Majeed lost interest in the tank. Baba assembled the aquarium on a console table in the front room, removing souvenirs Khalti Nesreen brought back from the old country—a replica of the old city of Jerusalem and a handmade trinkets box with an inlay of smooth ivory.

Baba had been so proud of the aquarium, cleaning the filter and shaking food flakes through an opening in the lid. Every month, he introduced a new fish, calling Afaf and Majeed over to watch as Baba held the bag with the new fish inside the tank, acclimating it to the temperature before releasing it to its new home.

You see how happy they are? Everyone has room to swim, everyone is safe.

One afternoon, she and Majeed had rounded the coffee table and her brother tripped, hands in front of him, falling against the aquarium, and it shattered on the floor. They hid under Afaf's bed until their mother pulled them out and whacked their behinds. She dared them to move a muscle before Baba came home to his aquarium, now in shards in a garbage bag along with java ferns and hair grass and dead fish.

Lah, lah, lah, was all her father said to Afaf and Majeed that day. They sat on her bed, kicking their feet against the frame, nervous, fearful. He sank down on Nada's bed, dropped his hands in his lap. *What a pity, all those fish. What a pity.* Months later, Majeed found the blue castle ornament that had rolled under the sofa bed and kept it on his dresser for a long time after.

Baba's words were enough to make her feel horrible for weeks. She tried to recall exactly each fish, to honor its brief life. And they'd disappointed Baba; that was worse than any smack from Mama.

Afaf is too old to spank now. She snatches the garbage bag and slips out the door.

5

THE BACK tire of her ten-speed bike needs air, but it should carry her ten blocks to California Avenue. She wishes she had a car like Sameera and the other arabiyyat at Hoover; she's had her driver's permit since last summer. She rides past bungalows and two-story houses, *For Rent* signs in the windows. Nearly every block has an Arab or Mexican family. The O'Malleys across the street are now the Hernandez family, the Richardses have become the Saladins. A spattering of Polish families remain, keeping to themselves as they trim their bushes. They never wave hello.

Five blocks away from the apartment her rear tire deflates.

"Shit," Afaf mutters. She walks her bike across the street to a gas station.

She squats down next to the free air pump, ignoring catcalls from a passing car. The nozzle hisses; she can't seem to properly latch it.

"Can I help you with that?"

She looks up. Rami Asfoor peers down at her, a smile on his lips. He's a senior, the leader of a pack of arrabi boys who play intramural basketball after school but never join Hoover's team.

"I got it," Afaf tells him, her back stiffening. He's never spoken to her before at school.

"Here." He stoops down and takes the air hose from her hand. "When you pinch it that way, you're losing air." He inserts the nozzle on the valve stem and the wheel suddenly inflates. "You see?"

"Thanks." Afaf stands up and kicks back the stand with her heel.

Rami clamps a hand around the top of her bike tire and jostles it up and down, checking the tire pressure. Satisfied, he lets go. "Can I talk to you for a minute?"

Afaf clutches the handlebars, circles her bike around him. "About what?" Like the arabiyyat, Rami and his friends ignore her at school. She's seen Sameera laughing with him in the cafeteria while Afaf sits at a table with other loners.

"I know your brother Maj." He smiles, his brown eyes dull like pudding, but his tone is friendly. "C'mon. We'll go for a drive. Don't worry. I'm cool."

It's been a long time since someone hasn't accused of her something or called her terrible names. She softens. "What about my bike?"

"Leave it here. You can pick it up later." He climbs back into his car, dips his head through the passenger-side window. "Yalla! Hop in."

Afaf locks up her bike against the chain-link fence that runs the perimeter of the gas station. The sun has begun to drop in the sky; she doesn't think she'll make it home before the streetlights turn on, but she doesn't care. She's been suspended for three days—how much more trouble can she get into?

A combination of aftershave and stale cigarette smoke hangs inside Rami's car. A tiny replica of the Quran dangles from the rear-view mirror. She saw the same one in Amjad's car, the one Baba bought from his friend. Mama had immediately taken it down. And though neither of her parents were religious, it had felt like the loss of a talisman—something that might keep them all safe. Afaf sometimes wonders, if they prayed—the way amarkan went to church every Sunday—whether things would have turned out differently.

If they believed even a little bit, maybe they could get through the worst that could ever happen to a family. Maybe God listened. Hadn't Khalti Nesreen's prayers been answered after all those miscarriages? It had taken years, but her cousin Amal finally arrived.

Rami's wearing an expensive watch that jiggles on his wrist, ill-fitting and clunky. Afaf predicts that, like so many of the other arrabi boys, he'll take over his father's liquor store or gas station one day. She's seen Rami around school, playfully swiping the back of a friend's head before running down the hallway. The Arabs eat lunch at segregated tables: boys at one, girls at another. She doesn't recall Majeed hanging around them. He mostly sticks to his teammates, coming home right after practice. Afaf wonders what Rami wants from her, what he's heard.

They drive to Marquette Park on Kedzie Avenue. Afaf remembers her history teacher, Mr. Slade, telling her class about the infamous protest twenty years ago in the park where demonstrators marched, holding signs demanding *Keep White Neighborhoods White*. Martin Luther King, Jr., was hit with a rock that forced him to one knee on the ground. Some of the people Afaf sees through the windows of parked cars lining the lagoon are brown and black, but most are still white.

Rami pulls to the curb on an empty stretch. His eyes flick a few times to his mirror, as though he's making sure the coast is clear. Afaf's stomach tightens and she starts to regret getting into his car. He turns off the radio and drums the steering wheel with his thumbs.

"So you know my brother Majeed?" Afaf says, cutting the awkward silence.

"Yeah, I know Maj. All the guys do. It's a shame he's got a sister who's such a sharmoota."

Before she can flinch at his insult, Rami slaps her. His hand mostly catches her ear and part of her cheek. She instinctively drops her head, shields her face with her arms.

He pulls her hair, forcing her to look up. "Quit slutting around and respect yourself! Respect your people! Ifhimti?" He lets go. "Now get the fuck out of my car."

Afaf fumbles with door handle, then spills onto the curb. Rami spits out his window before his tires peel away.

She pulls herself up and looks around, dazed.

"You okay?" someone shouts from a nearby car that's pulled up beside her.

"I'm fine," she yells back, not looking at them, her legs shaking so bad she shoves her hands in her pockets just to keep her body steady. The car drives away.

She remembers her bike.

"Shit!" she curses out loud. She sniffles back tears and turns toward the gas station, nearly six blocks away. The sun has set and an evening wind howls in her ears as she walks as fast as she can without running. She tells herself to stay calm, to keep walking.

She touches her face. Rami's slap still stuns her, but what he called her stings even more:

Sharmoota.

What Mama had called that other woman years ago. The faceless, nameless person with whom Baba had spent hours away from her and Majeed, for whom he'd betrayed her mother.

The affair still continued for a few years though other things had stopped after Nada disappeared, like a train coming to a sudden halt, its brakes screeching in fury. The Baladna band, Mama's rare laughter. The loss still lingers like an arthritic ache, flaring when it rains, forgotten in the sunshine.

The chain-link fence is bare. Her bike is gone. She runs inside the gas station. There's a line at the cash register. A tall man in a navy-blue jumpsuit and work boots is buying lottery tickets. Behind him an old woman with curlers and a hairnet holds a gallon of milk with both hands.

"Someone stole my bike!" Afaf blurts out.

The cashier continues punching numbers. "What are you talking about?" His face is pocked with acne. He's wearing an Iron Maiden T-shirt.

"I chained it to the fence."

He hands the tall man in the jumpsuit his lottery ticket. "Who told you to leave it there?"

Afaf's speechless. The old woman gives her a sad smile, shaking her head. Afaf rushes out of the station, her head swimming.

Mama's right. She is a lost girl.

6

MAJEED KNOCKS on her door. "You okay?" He pokes his head in.
His hair's wet from a shower. "Where have you been?"

Afaf turns over on her bed, faces the wall. "Leave me alone." It'd
taken her a half hour to get home. She had gone straight to her room,
Mama still in the kitchen where she'd been when Afaf left hours
before.

"So what happened at school?" Her brother speaks with a patient
tone, as though he's the older one.

"None of your business," she snaps.

Majeed sighs, leans in the doorframe. "Why do you have to act
like this, Afaf?"

She whips around to face him. "Should I be perfect like you?"

"I'm not perfect." His voice drops. "You don't have to make
things worse for Mama. She—"

"You always take her side. Did it ever occur to you that maybe
she's the reason Baba is so miserable? Why he fucking cheated on
her?" Her voice drops, too, dangerously low, her words toxic—she
wants to poison her brother's hallowed image of Mama.

It's the first time the affair has been uttered between her and
Majeed. Like everything else in their lives, they've always tucked
away things over which they have no control, no say.

"That's not fair, Afaf, and you know it."

"What do I know? Huh?" All the rage and hurt suddenly bursts in her chest. Her stolen bike, the lash of Rami's hand, Coach Phillips's warning, Jell-O in her hair, Michael Wilson and all the other boys.

She buries her face in her pillow and sobs until her eyes are raw. Majeed stands over her, then goes to the record player and slips *Hair* on from a worn case that's slowly peeling at the edges. He slides next to her on her bed and wraps his arm around her shoulders. He doesn't say a word, doesn't make a sound except for his soft breathing near her ear. She doesn't push him away.

"Easy to Be Hard" comes through the speakers, and she listens with her brother, like they did when they were kids.

~

The telephone rings. The arm of the record player is skipping.

Afaf rubs her tear-crusted eyes. "What time is it?" Her mouth feels full of cotton. The ringing from the kitchen is interminable.

Majeed bolts for the telephone, and Afaf can hear him in the kitchen as he answers. "Hello? Yes. This is his son."

Afaf stumbles out of bed. "Who is it?" Her voice sounds hoarse to her, unfamiliar.

Seconds later, Mama's hand is on Majeed's shoulder. "Khair!" Her eyes are green with terror.

He holds up a finger, signaling them to be quiet. "Yes, yes. We'll be right there. Thank you, ma'am." He replaces the receiver and rubs the back of his head. "Baba had an accident."

Baba's crushed body under a load of pallets on the factory floor flashes across Afaf's mind. She feels dizzy. "Oh, my God!"

"Ya rubbi! What's happened to you, Mahmood?" Mama wails.

Majeed picks up the phone again, dials a number. It's two o'clock in the morning. "Hello, Ammo Ziyad. It's Majeed. No, no. We're fine. It's Baba."

At the hospital, they learn Baba never made it to work at the factory. He slammed his car into a streetlight a few blocks from the apartment. His right eye is swollen shut, his nose broken. His wrist and two of his fingers are broken. His left ankle is sprained. It's a horrible inventory.

Mama stands over his unconscious body, smoothing his forehead. "Laysh hayk, Mahmood? How did this happen to you?"

Afaf chokes back tears, covering his right hand with her own.

Beside her, Majeed whispers in her ear, "He could have died, Afaf." His voice is shaky.

"He's going to be fine," she says loudly. Tubes snake from his right wrist to a mobile IV stand. A heart monitor blinks above his head. The odor of ammonia and metal is strong. It's the first time Afaf's ever been in a hospital. When Mama had taken her "little mishwar" in the past, Afaf and Majeed weren't allowed to visit. She'd known then it wasn't a regular hospital.

A white nurse enters with a chart and looks them over. She's wearing an ugly brown sweater over her pale green scrubs, pulls a pen from an oversized pocket. "It could have been much worse," she tells them. "Much worse." She checks Baba's IV. "I'm Patricia. First shift. Doctor will be in shortly to talk to you. Let me know if you need anything." She speaks loudly and slowly to them, as though they can't understand her. It's a habit Afaf has observed in white people.

Baba's eyelids flutter, his lips twitch, but he does not wake. A surgeon in pale blue scrubs comes to talk to them. He's young, his hair parted to the side like a schoolboy's. "I'm Dr. Morrison. Attending surgeon." He shakes each of their hands.

"How this happen?" Mama asks, clutching a fistful of soiled tissue paper.

"He was intoxicated"—he glances at his chart—"Mrs. Ra-man."

Mama stares wild-eyed, not comprehending.

"He was drunk. Blood alcohol level was point-ten when he was admitted."

Afaf's mind spins in panicked confusion. Hadn't he just been holding her in the apartment? *You're a good girl.*

A few minutes later, a police officer directs them into the corridor. Ziyad approaches from the waiting room; only family are allowed in the patient's room. He had driven them to the hospital in dress slacks and sandals. His graying hair is uncombed.

The officer slowly recaps what happened. Her father called his boss from a pay phone at a bar on Ashland Avenue. The bar owner had alerted the police that a man—"A-rab, or Puerto Rican, maybe"—had been drinking all night.

The officer says, "He's lucky he didn't kill anyone. The car is totaled."

Ziyad silently shakes his head, puts a hand on Mama's shoulder. "La howla wala koowa illa bi lah."

There are people all over the corridor, nurses rushing past with clear bags of saline, patients in wheelchairs, visitors hugging and clinging to each other as they receive good and bad news. This floor is full of victims: a hit-and-run, people with stabbing and gunshot wounds, kids with broken arms and legs. Across from Baba's room Afaf can see a pair of hairless legs poking out of their hospital garb. An old woman reads from a Bible at the foot of the bed.

Mama's sobbing and Majeed wraps an arm around her shoulders. He's grown taller than her mother—taller than Afaf, too.

After the police officer's done with them, they leave Mama alone with Baba. Once he's discharged he'll be taken into custody for driving under the influence.

Ziyad gives them change for the vending machines, returns to the waiting room. Afaf and Majeed head to the hospital cafeteria.

"I can't believe this is happening," Majeed says, drinking his Dr Pepper.

Afaf waits for her hot chocolate to finish spewing into a cup. "The nurse said it could have been worse, Maj."

"He's going to jail, Afaf!" His voice is shrill and Afaf sees the little boy who'd always clung to her sleeve when they were kids.

She doesn't say anything more. A DUI. Scenes from her driver's ed class swarm her mind: terrible reenactments of drivers fumbling with their keys while her classmates snickered; the faces and names of victims scrolling at the end of a segment and a message from Mothers Against Drunk Driving. She can't recall Illinois' penalty for a first offense. She taps her fingers on the rim of her cup, hoping Majeed doesn't notice she's trembling.

The two of them linger in the cafeteria, watching orderlies and nurses on their breaks having toast and cereal. There's a family of five adults huddled around their Styrofoam cups, shoulders hunched, eyes wet with tears, sniffling between sips of coffee. Her chest inflates with something she can't name.

7

WHEN HE'S finally discharged a week later, two Chicago police officers wheel Baba to an armored police van, along with a few other men who have recovered enough from their injuries to be transferred. Mama's pride keeps her from calling Khalti Nesreen and asking for her husband's help to post bond for Baba. Instead, she instructs Majeed to dial Ziyad's number again and he and Baba's other bandmate Amjad take Mama to the precinct on Twenty-Sixth and California Avenue. She pulls out a small wad of twenty-dollar bills, cash she keeps tucked in her dresser.

"This won't be enough! Ya rubbi!" she whimpers. She's been saving it for years, putting a little away from Baba's checks.

"Don't worry, Mama," Majeed assures her. "Ammo Ziyad and Amjad will know what to do."

It turns out that a first offense in Illinois is considered a misdemeanor. Since Baba has no prior record, a judge fines him five hundred dollars, sentences him to eighteen months of community service, and probation. His license is suspended for ninety days.

Baba's bandmates pay the fine and bring him home. They carry him two flights of stairs to the apartment. Like her father, both men have aged, but their faces are different than Baba's. Lines of happiness etch their foreheads and crow's feet proudly stamp the corners of their eyes. Baba's face is a battlefield, wrinkles deep like trenches. Ziyad's two sons are married—Nada would have been their same age—his first grandchild on the way. Amjad's middle daughter is recently engaged.

They settle him in her parents' bedroom, a place he'd only enter to retrieve his clean clothes or leave some cash for Mama on their dresser. She props a bunch of pillows behind him and makes sure he's not too warm beneath an extra blanket. Afaf catches a long gaze between them—unfamiliar and strange. Mama doesn't complain how far five hundred dollars can go, how humiliated she is to be in debt to other men. Quietly, she prepares afreekah with chicken—just the way Baba likes it. She sits with him until he's sopped up the last morsels of barley soup with a piece of khubuz.

Something reignites between them, and Afaf and her brother stand back and watch, confused and hopeful. Khalti Nesreen whispers to them, "Like newlyweds again." It is Majeed who calls their aunt, and she stays for the weekend with her baby daughter, helping Mama wash clothes and prepare meals for the week. Once in a while she steals a few puffs from Mama's cigarette, exhaling through her nostrils. Mama has started smoking since the crash, long and thin Virginia Slims that she sends Majeed to buy from Pixie's Drugstore around the corner from the apartment. She insists on single packs, though they're cheaper by the carton.

Afaf takes her baby cousin Amal for a walk around the block, pushing the stroller as though she is hers. The baby coos at the dogs that stop to sniff her, their owners smiling and nodding at Afaf. Her aunt has endured years of infertility and two miscarriages. *Naseeb, my darling*, her aunt had whispered in her ear when Afaf had bent down to kiss Khalti Nesreen as she lay recuperating in her bed in Kenosha after she'd lost the second one. She patted the back of Afaf's hand, smiling sadly at her with wet eyes. When baby Amal arrived, her aunt and uncle's joy was palpable. Children, Afaf understands, are supposed to be a blessing.

At the apartment, Baba is a quiet patient. When he can finally use his fingers, he plays his oud and the tunes float from their bedroom like a spirit summoned from some long-forgotten place. In the past, Mama had complained that when he played, she couldn't hear the TV as she cooked. Now she keeps quiet as Baba plucks his instrument, and Afaf catches her mother humming a song to his familiar melody as she dries the dishes or chops vegetables.

When Afaf comes home from school, she hears them laughing in their bedroom. This stings her a little, being left out of this slice of happiness. She's tempted to say hello, but changes her mind. She doesn't want to disrupt their sweet sounds, and quietly grabs a soda can from the fridge and gets ready for her shift at Dairy Queen.

∼

Baba's doctor clears him for mandated community service. His arm is still in a sling when he takes the bus to Twenty-Sixth and California Avenue to join a cohort of other men on probation. They'll be clearing highway debris on I-55. Though his ankle has healed, Baba's lower back still aches from the impact of the crash. Afaf catches her father wincing each time he stands, but he never complains. His nose is slightly crooked in a way that makes Baba look more severe, betraying the warmth restored to his eyes, a glow Afaf hasn't seen in years.

It's May and the days are warmer. Afaf is weeks away from graduation. She avoids Rami and his friends, cutting down a staircase, changing direction in the hallway. Sameera and the other arabiyyat whisper as she passes them. Kelly McPherson and Amber Reeves hiss at her in the cafeteria, but she won't confront them. Since Baba's crash, she's determined that there will be no more incidents at Hoover High School, no more trouble. She can't explain it, but something's changed in her since that phone call in the middle of the night. She rarely leaves the apartment, only to work at Dairy Queen when she's not in school. It's as though being close to home will somehow prevent another calamity—perhaps much worse than Baba's crash.

Even Mama has softened a bit. It's like new skin once you've peeled away the scab. She'll touch Afaf's shoulder as she rounds the kitchen table, clearing it of platters once full of her delicious meals. Her smile comes more easily, like a breeze rustling through an open door. It's a smile Afaf has seen in pictures in the old shoebox, rarely in person.

Tonight, Mama's malfoof steams from a silver platter. She stands at the sink, scrubbing down a large pot. All the pots and pans have to be scoured before she sits down to eat with them. They've been eating together more frequently, engaging in strangely polite, yet guarded conversation.

"A priest came to see me," Baba says, holding up his fork.

Afaf scoops a half dozen of the rolled cabbage leaves onto her father's plate. "What priest, Baba?" she asks. Majeed looks at Baba, his hazel eyes curious, alert.

"At the hospital. They send priests. You know—to pray with people who are very sick. Or dying." Baba clears his throat as if those last words scratch his membrane.

Mama turns off the faucet and faces them. "What are you talking about, Mahmood?"

"He say to me"—Baba switches to English—" 'I know you are

not Christian, my son, but you believe in God, yes? Your God save you, my son. He give you second chance to live. To live right.' "

Afaf steals a glance at Majeed and he raises his eyebrows at her. She shrugs her shoulders. Baba has never spoken about God or religion. He and Mama don't pray, never fast for Ramadan as she knows Khalti Nesreen and Ammo Yahya do. She knows it is Eid only by the long-distance phone calls Mama makes to her parents in the bilad.

Baba reaches for her mother's hand. "Samheeni, Muntaha. Please forgive me."

Mama looks stunned. Then an old, irrational expression spreads across her face like blood seeping from a cut. Baba has punctured something and they all watch her mother's face collapse.

"So you've found religion?" Her words are slick with disgust, her eyes turn emerald, dangerous. "After all of these years you think God will ever forgive you? I certainly will not." Mama storms out of the kitchen, slamming her bedroom door shut.

Baba turns toward them. Afaf, too, is stunned. What has come over their father? "She has every right to be bitter, loolad. It will take time, but I'll make it up to her." Baba grabs their hands across the kitchen table. "I am sorry," he tells them in English. "I make things right for everyone."

For a moment she feels her mother's sense of disorder. It's cataclysmic, this apology from Baba, this acknowledgment of how broken their lives have been. But her father isn't the only one to blame—Afaf has always known this. They're all culpable. Since Nada's been gone, she's turned into herself, nursing the pain as it slowly leached her, believing her grief was the worst. Hadn't they all done the same thing, their deep, collective loss cementing them from moving forward? Baba is the first to drive a jackhammer into it, unsettling the ground, jostling them back to life. But can they be so easily repaired? There seem to be too many sharp fragments to reconfigure them into something resembling normal. So much time has been lost.

Her father returns to the sofa bed that evening and Afaf gives him his pain medication and tucks him in, gently placing the covers over his aging body, careful not to disturb his healing bones.

8

BABA LEAVES the house early every evening before his shift begins. After his DUI, his boss at Dyer Plastic fired him. He started a new job at a gas station owned by a wealthy Palestinian immigrant who knows his friend Amjad. It's menial and less money, but Baba is happy to take it and, as with every other hardship, he doesn't complain.

He prays at home every evening, facing the eastern corner of the family room after a washing ritual in the bathroom. Afaf stands in the hallway, watching her father, his back to her. He lays out a red velvet rug with a palatial mosque woven in the middle, minarets in golden thread. She wonders where he got the rug. His body folds over in prostration, then he lowers himself to the floor, legs tucked underneath him. When Baba pulls himself up, she hears a slight *hmph* and she, too, bears the pain of his lower back. She quietly escapes into her room before he's finished.

Summer is almost over. Baba is busy with a new group of men—the organizers of the Islamic Center of Greater Chicago. They want to build a mosque to replace the old civic center on Sixty-Third and Kedzie Avenue, a dilapidated gathering place where mostly men congregate to pray on Fridays and during Eid. The women host Ramadan potlucks and run child care during the day. They've found a plot of land outside the city, off Interstate 55, in a small town called Tempest, and have begun petitioning for it.

Baba's religious awakening rattles Afaf. It's a new side of her father that she can't quite understand. She's happy he quit his drinking and devotes himself to recovery. But it's like he's stumbled upon a spring of water and he wants them all to drink from it. She's uncertain if it's safe and hangs back. She can tell it makes Majeed nervous, too. Her brother remains guarded toward their father, as though he's walking on a bridge that might collapse at any moment.

"Do you know how many churches there are in the state of Illinois?" Baba rails one night. "A thousand. And how many Buddhist temples and synagogues? Ten, twenty." He pumps his hands in the air like he's counting for a child, stressing the immensity of this fact.

"And how many masjids are there? Ha?"

Afaf has heard about the mosque Khalti Nesreen's husband drives forty-five minutes to attend in Milwaukee every Friday. It was founded by a group of men exiled from Yemen in 1979.

"Wahid." Baba points his long finger in their faces. "One. We, too, have the right to gather together and pray. It's our human right."

Afaf's family hasn't observed Islam beyond small celebrations of Eid with Khalti Nesreen. Mama reluctantly puts on a dress and they drive the hour and a half to Kenosha. It's a religion she knows very little about, one limited to notions of what's *haram* and *ayb*: gambling, drinking alcohol, premarital sex. She remembers a painting hanging in Sameera's house of an old man carrying an ancient city on his back, a gold-domed mosque towering over stone houses with orange-tiled roofs. Afaf would stare at it for a long time, imagining the old man was the God of Arabs, who'd carried and protected her parents' ancestors, eternally carrying His burden. He was an unadorned figure, barefoot and wearing a turban. As she grew older, the old man faded from consciousness and another kind of God emerged—a faraway, ominous being with whom you reckoned when you died, like the one who commands Moses in the movie that played every Easter Sunday night. She'd never prayed to either God, not even when her sister disappeared.

Majeed smiles at their father's magnanimous decree.

"What are you laughing at?" Baba snaps.

"Nothing. It's just that . . ." Majeed looks at Afaf, but she keeps quiet. She, too, is unsure how to react. "It seems like a dream, Baba."

"Yes, yes," Baba concedes. "It is a dream, habibi. One that will come true if we all have faith. Say *inshallah.*"

"Inshallah," Afaf says. It's such a simple word that seems full of promise, yet without the pressure of failure. A word conceding to a power that might ultimately decide all of their fates, lifting the burden from themselves.

Majeed is silent. Baba says it again: *Inshallah.*

The TV volume in her parents' bedroom lowers. Mama is listening. The spell between her and Baba has broken since her father started talking to them about the prophet Muhammad, an illiterate shepherd, and how Allah had revealed His word through texts Muhammad could miraculously read and spread to the community. Afaf can't understand it: Baba seems to want to improve himself, and Mama berates him for it.

"The Lord has given us a purpose in this life. To pray, to fast, to take care of the poor, to fulfill hajj. And above all, to believe in His beneficence, that He is the only God, and that Muhammad is His true Prophet."

Afaf thinks of the evangelical preachers on TV, the only programming at one a.m. when Baba's at work and she's battling a fit of insomnia.

"The Prophet says, 'Worship God as though you see Him, but if you do not see Him, know that He sees you.'" Baba sounds so sincere, his face light and airy, the wrinkles across his forehead dissolving a bit. "It is never too late."

Mama suddenly looms in the doorway, a shadow inside her darkened bedroom. Her hair is in a loose braid, gray strands threading it. She holds a cigarette like an actress in an old black-and-white film—the wicked woman who's about to foil a good-hearted plan. "Then why has the Lord turned away from the suffering of muslimeen? Ha? Why has he forsaken the Palestinians? You think your precious masjid will make a difference?"

But Afaf sees in Mama's face the real question: Why has God taken Nada away from her?

Afaf, too, wonders why.

Baba smiles at Mama. "This earth is temporary, ya Muntaha. Allah has a plan and we must be patient and heed Him. Our suffering is temporary. 'Shall I tell you of better things than those earthly joys? For the God-conscious there are, with their Sustainer, gardens through which running waters flow . . .'"

It's the first time Afaf hears her father quote the Quran. He knows the words to every Um Kalthum song, memorized Nat King Cole's "Mona Lisa." But he recites this verse as though the words are his own, summoning them from a deep well of serenity. It is a new song to learn—faith has become his instrument.

Mama sneers, sucking on her cigarette. "All of it is haki fadi." To Mama, such words are like Velcro, holding fast until you strip them away with your actions. She tosses her cigarette in the sink and it hisses. "You can keep your foolish words." She retreats to the bedroom and the TV booms, drowning them out.

"Your mother has suffered greatly, but she will see how easy it is to cast off her suffering as soon as she opens her heart to the Lord." He pauses. Something sad flickers in his eyes. He resumes his sermon. "And you, too, loolad. I'll keep failing you as a father if I don't lead you on the lighted path."

Afaf shifts in her chair, uncomfortable. How did they fit into all of this? She thinks about the boys whose hands have roamed her body, and the resentment toward her parents that has rooted deep in her heart. Her bitterness toward an absent sister seizes like a tidal wave in her chest.

"I want you to come with me tonight to the masjid," Baba declares. "I took the night off work for a special meeting. Young people will be there, too. Every hand, big and small, must lay down a brick. It's your future we're building today."

It sounds like Baba's reciting from a salesman's script, but each word is doused in sincerity. Still, Afaf can't fathom any day beyond tomorrow. She'll be starting a new job at Pine Forest Mall, in a kiosk that duplicates keys. She'd quit two others since her graduation. Graduation was an event that extracted nothing more than a few awkward hugs from Baba and Majeed, and a strained dinner afterward at Leo's Steakhouse, where other small parties of families were celebrating their children's diplomas, bouquets of balloons floating above their tables. Mama had pretended to be sick. She'd given Afaf an envelope with thirty dollars.

"What do you say?" Baba says, his bright eyes imploring her and Majeed.

Afaf nudges her brother with her eyes.

"Okay," her brother says, glancing at Mama's closed door.

9

AN HOUR LATER, Baba pulls up to a furniture storefront building, a sign blinking though it's closed for the evening. On a security door there's a smaller sign indecipherable from the street: *The Islamic Center of Greater Chicago: Welcome.* Rain drips from the eaves of the roof. A woman pushes a grocery cart past, her translucent hair cap glistening.

"Here we are," Baba announces, beaming at them.

Afaf remembers this place. She and Majeed have been here before, perhaps a decade ago. Before Nada disappeared. Mama had dressed them up for gatherings when her parents still socialized. Snapshots flicker in her mind as Afaf gazes up at the building: Baba playing his oud while the arrabi men sang old folk songs and danced dabka. She can still hear the lamentation in their voices, an aching for a stolen homeland—their bilad—a country she's only seen in old photographs and heard about in stories Mama and Khalti Nesreen recollect over qahwa.

Baba climbs out and walks quickly around the front of the car, winking at Afaf. His backache seems to have temporarily disappeared.

Afaf looks over the passenger seat at Majeed. He reluctantly slides out and stands beside Baba. They wait for her, their chins tucked into their chests against the cold rain.

Afaf taps the door handle of Baba's replacement car, a black Toyota Camry. The men inside the Center had collected enough money for a small down payment and one of them had cosigned on condition that Baba make the monthly payment without fail. They would repossess the car if he drank again. This new group of muslimeen— gas station owners, dentists, mechanics, and the retired—had embraced her father, given him a chance. And here they are, Afaf and Majeed, his children, about to enter their community.

Afaf hasn't belonged to any place. Sameera and the other ara- biyyat flash across her mind. The taste of rejection is sharp on her tongue.

Still, she climbs out of the car, and Baba squeezes her shoulder.

The older muslimat immediately flock around Afaf. They hug and kiss both of her cheeks, smoothing her hair, squeezing her shoulders.

"How lovely you are, mashallah!"

"I think I see a bit of Abu Majeed in that face!"

Afaf nods and smiles, her cheeks hot in response to their effu- sive attention pouring on her all at once. They usher her to the side where the women congregate. It's not so different from the arrabi kids at school: men on one side, women on the other. The children find a space in between. Majeed and Baba are welcomed by a heavy- set man—the imam—with a long, graying beard, and Afaf hears her brother plunged into the same gushing affection.

A few of the women wear headscarves, loose-fitting around their faces, strands of dark hair that have strayed from the fabric. She thinks of Mama and Khalti Nesreen, how they wouldn't be caught dead in a headscarf. There's a black woman with a daughter Afaf's age. They both wear turbans, green and orange, their faces shiny. A few prayer rugs like the one Baba brought home hang as tapestries on one wall.

A large woman shaped like a bell waddles over to Afaf, chubby arms outstretched in her abaya. "Ya habibti! Come, come! We're so happy you're here!" She presses Afaf to her heavy bosom and Afaf smells lilac and sweat. "Why haven't you come sooner?"

She is called Um Zuraib, though she doesn't have any children. Afaf finds out later she's been widowed since her early twenties, never remarried. It's rumored her husband was among the Palestinian liberation fighters who'd fought and perished in the Battle of Karameh. "Come meet the other banat."

The girls smile at Afaf and introduce themselves. The only one she recognizes is Kowkab Suleiman. She's the only young person Afaf has seen wearing a headscarf at school. Not loose and fashionable, but snug around her face, her neck disappearing beneath the folds of her scarf.

If that had not been sufficient reason for others to torment her at Hoover, Kowkab's name clinched it. Freshman year, Afaf's English class was assigned to tell the origin of their names. Kowkab had stood quietly in front of rows of lanky, pimply white boys and stuck-up girls and announced, "Planet."

"Your name means 'planet,'" the teacher repeated.

"Like 'your anus'?" one of the white boys had called out. The class descended into laughter. Afaf watched Kowkab slip a finger inside her headscarf as though tucking away an invisible strand of hair. She looked down at her desk.

"That's enough," the teacher warned.

The awful nickname had stuck. "Here comes Your Anus!" the

boys taunted. Kowkab found notes on her desk with crudely drawn illustrations and immediately crumpled them up without reading them and stuffed them into her backpack. She'd settle into her desk, crack open her textbook, and stare straight ahead, her headscarf like horse blinders. The more blatant insults thinned out by the end of the year, but Afaf suspected Kowkab found a glob of spit or chewed gum stuck to the back of her headscarf on some days.

"Hi," Afaf says, sensing Kowkab won't make the first move.

"Hi." Kowkab smiles shyly at Afaf. She gestures to a table with trays of hummus and baba ganoush, freshly baked khubuz sliced in quarters. "I think we had a class together sophomore year," Kowkab says. "Seems like forever."

"It was freshman year. English," Afaf tells her, following her.

"Oh, yeah. Mr. Ryland." Kowkab's eyes do not betray any humiliating memory.

This girl had been the easier target. Afaf grew invincible to her classmates' barbs a long time ago, her skin gradually hardening from the name-calling and insults: *Where'd you park your camel? You got oil in your backpack?* She refused to cower. Had Kowkab heard about her? Does this girl know how many hands have groped Afaf? She feels her cheeks flush with the fresh sting of Rami's slap across her face.

Kowkab's smile doesn't contain any judgment—more a guarded politeness, like she's trying not to offend Afaf.

They don't say any more and turn to observe the other girls for a while. They're a hodgepodge of ages: grade-school-age and teenagers, young and married pregnant mothers, and a few wearing engagement rings. The older women hover like doting hens.

Afaf doesn't notice anyone else from Hoover High School. It

occurs to her that, aside from Kowkab, she is anonymous here. It suddenly feels like a chance to start over—the same as for Baba, maybe. People deserve second chances, right? Isn't that what Silas learns with the arrival of his golden-haired Eppie? Isn't that what drew Afaf to her favorite books? Through near-spirit-breaking ordeals, the protagonists still overcome. It's what hope is, after all. Baba found it after the car crash and now he wants to blanket her and Majeed in its folds. For Baba, hope is religion, though it's a more complicated shape to Afaf, as she knows so little about Islam.

The imam makes an announcement that she doesn't understand and suddenly everyone shifts from their places. Men roll out two massive Persian rugs, their fraying edges touching on the middle of the tiled floor. They are burgundy and forest-green, giant flowers adorning the center, smaller ones tracing their perimeter.

The women and girls move to a corner of the room where home-made prayer clothes hang on wooden knobs. Some of the shape-less tops and bottoms are mismatched, simply stitched fabrics. The women quickly slip them on and suddenly their previous forms disappear. They look like Russian nesting dolls, their faces poking through the fabric, their hands peeking from under small tents. They quickly assemble in lines behind the men. Everyone faces the eastern wall, which has no windows. Kowkab hands her a pair of prayer clothes. Afaf hesitates.

"Yalla," she encourages. "It's time for salat. Do you have wudu?"

Afaf nods, though she doesn't understand.

It's easy to follow Kowkab's orders, her tone kind yet insistent. Afaf slips the bottom over her jeans, hitching the elastic band over her hips. She pokes her face through a hole in the material and it hangs over her head and torso like a tent, billowing around her shoulders.

Kowkab gestures for Afaf to stand beside her. She searches for Baba and Majeed and finds them in the second row of men and boys. Her brother turns around a few times, stealing glances, until he finds Afaf and grins. How funny she must look!

"Just follow my moves," Kowkab whispers as the imam begins the prayer.

"*Allahu Akbar . . .*"

She watches Kowkab in her peripheral vision, folding her hands across her stomach as Kowkab does. It's the same way Baba begins when Afaf watches him from the hallway.

"*Subhanakal-lahumma . . .*"

Everyone bends at their knees. "*Allahu Akbar . . .*"

The blood rushes to Afaf's head for a second and she feels strangely vulnerable as she bows to some unforeseen presence that she imagines can, at its own whim, punish her in hellfire or gather her in its folds.

"*Subhanna rubbal azzeem wa bi hamdeh.*"

Everyone pulls their bodies upright. "*Allahu Akbar . . .*"

Then they're suddenly on the floor, their legs folded beneath them. Afaf watches Kowkab touch her forehead to the rug and she hesitates, lifting her gaze to watch the others. The folded bodies look peaceful. Afaf touches the rug, her forehead at first bristling at the scratchy, woven thread. She remembers to breathe.

"*Allahu Akbar . . .*"

They repeat this pattern three more times and conclude in the sitting position.

"Peace be upon you," Kowkab says to a woman on the other side of her, then turns to Afaf. "Peace be upon you."

Kowkab is like a proud teacher. "Good job, Afaf!" She pats Afaf's shoulder. "You'll learn the words in no time. If you keep doing it."

Afaf feels like a stranger who's finally come home, one who's forgotten the language, the mannerisms of her people. She's nervous, tentative.

Um Zuraib's words ring in her ears: *Why haven't you come sooner?*

10

ON THE ride home, Baba talks to them with a new kind of excitement, his one-sided speech jumbled with scripture and triumph. His voice rises above the pounding rain against the windshield.

"Your mother will finally see," Baba declares. "The adults must first reveal the path and children will follow."

Majeed rolls his eyes at Afaf when she looks back at him in the backseat. She doesn't feel very changed, either, though the kindness of Kowkab and the women still glows inside her. Do you have to believe in God to join the masjid? She won't dare say it out loud, but it wasn't at all what she'd expected. Kowkab and the others had made her feel at home. And the strange ritual of praying—it had turned out to be peaceful and soothing. Afaf couldn't quite explain it. It wasn't exactly a spiritual thing. It was more like she belonged among them, those strangers.

At home, Mama emerges from her bedroom when they arrive, her eyes glinting with expectation. Arms folded, she looks from Afaf to Majeed. Her lips curl in a sneer.

"A bunch of fools, mish ah?" she says, patting Majeed's cheek, tousling his hair.

Afaf watches Baba pull himself up straighter to face Mama, slightly wincing at the pain in his back. "It takes time, Muntaha. We have to encourage them."

Afaf imagines Kowkab's parents gathering them for prayer, leading them through every prostration, reciting each verse until the words become automatic expressions, her family moving in the same direction toward a common joy. Mama is like a giant boulder, splitting the river—Afaf and Majeed surging forward on one side, Baba on the other.

Mama lights a cigarette and leans her back against the sink, no longer listening as Baba tries to convince her. She's looking right through them, emotion vacating her eyes.

"It takes time, ya loolad." Baba's words trail behind Afaf as she heads to her room. Majeed has already locked himself in the bathroom. "You'll see."

Afaf wishes, for Baba's sake, and her own, that he's right.

The key kiosk sits on one end of the Pine Forest Mall and Afaf is grateful she is somewhat tucked away from the crowds of customers who sweep past her. A half dozen people show up during their lunch break each day. For the rest of her shift, she reads novels, learning to drown out the backdrop of echoes from the boring instrumental music incessantly floating from large mounted speakers, and the clacking of footsteps along the diamond-shaped slate tiles.

It's a pretty easy job for Afaf. She quickly learns how to adjust the blank key in a vise along with the original the customer hands her. It is a largely motorized process, but she takes her time, forcing a polite smile for the impatiently waiting middle-aged landlord, or a retired couple who need a set of keys for their adult grandchildren to walk their dog.

"We're going to Europe!" the chatty woman tells Afaf. The husband regards her with suspicion, nudges his wife into silence.

One late October afternoon, Afaf lifts her head from her book and catches Rami Asfoor approaching from the western entrance. He's with two other arrabi boys. Afaf's cheeks flush, the sting of Rami's slap returning, more intense now. She wishes she could shrink and disappear. But she's stuck in this lame kiosk, soldered to a stool.

"Hey, maybe you can make me a copy of your house key," Rami taunts. "You know—so I can make sure you're safe and sound in your bedroom, not whoring around in the streets."

"Doesn't your brother give a shit?" one of the other boys chimes in. "That pussy only cares about baseball, huh? Wallahi, that's fucked up, dude."

They laugh as her hands shake. She clenches the small counter that separates her from these horrid boys. "Listen, you ass—"

"Afaf! You work here?" A soft voice from behind her.

She turns around and faces Kowkab. She's wearing a pink flower-patterned scarf and a beige peacoat over stone-washed jeans. She looks completely out of place at this mall. She smiles her crooked smile, her eyes bright. A surge of relief runs through Afaf's chest.

"Hi, Kowkab. Yeah. I just started," Afaf squeaks, her fingers still trembling.

"Mashallah!" Kowkab beams, as though duplicating keys is the most noble job Afaf could be doing.

Rami and his friends suddenly look confused. Kowkab stares evenly at them, unblinking. Finally, they retreat, throwing a few icy glances at Afaf.

Afaf turns away from Kowkab, fighting back tears and pretending to look for something on a shelf behind her. A hand on her shoulder pulls her around.

"Forget about them. Only Allah judges," she hears Kowkab telling her as she cries.

"I've done a lot of dumb things," Afaf whispers.

"Yeah, but they don't define you," Kowkab says. "Mistakes make us better muslimeen."

Afaf tears a sheet off from a heavy roll of industrial paper towel she uses to clean the machine and dabs at her wet face and dripping nose.

"Did you have fun the other night?" Kowkab asks her.

Mall patrons pass by and Afaf catches their quizzical expressions, the nudges they exchange behind Kowkab's back. "Sure. I mean, it was a little weird, you know?"

"When's your shift over?" Kowkab appears oblivious to the world around her, her smile never faltering when she speaks to Afaf.

"Six."

"Do you wanna come over to my house and hang out?"

Afaf can't think of the last time she received an invitation from someone who didn't want something in return. And one from a girl. Her last true friend had been Sameera. After that she'd hung out with the outcasts at the video arcade on Kedzie Avenue, or on a weatherworn bench at Marquette Park—a place she's vowed she'd never return to after Rami had driven her there that night. At Hoover High School, she was among a social class of losers on the lowest rung.

She gazes at Kowkab and remembers how Kowkab had led her to the line of worshippers at the masjid, how the other women had hugged and talked to her as though knowing her their entire lives.

Afaf accepts, gazing at the pretty pink flowers blooming across her new friend's dipped head as Kowkab jots down her address.

———

Kowkab's house is a small bungalow with a tidy browned lawn. Small urns of orange and yellow chrysanthemums line the short flight of cement steps to the front door. It's the kind of house Mama's envied for years, the kind with a finished basement and two and a half bathrooms, and a nice yard where you could grill in the summertime. When Afaf steps inside the living room, she's greeted by an enormous cross-stitched rendition of the Dome of the Rock hanging from the center wall. There are school portraits of Kowkab and her sisters; she and the oldest one are wearing graduation caps over their headscarves, bearing the same crooked grins. Baba went to Woolworth's for a cheap wooden frame and nailed a picture of Afaf holding her diploma above the sofa bed. Mama had watched him from the hallway, smoking a cigarette, as Baba hammered away.

"Ahlan, ahlan, habibti, Afaf!" Kowkab's mother embraces her, kisses each of her cheeks.

Kowkab's sisters Nadia and Muna are watching TV. They look up at Afaf, polite smiles pasted on their faces. For a moment Afaf wonders if this is a mistake. She's sure Nadia, a year older than her and Kowkab, knows all about her bad reputation. Why would she approve of a girl like Afaf to hang around her younger sister? Nadia says hi and returns to watching TV.

Inside their home they are bareheaded, and Afaf marvels at their ink-black hair. Kowkab's wavy strands are loose around her shoulders; her mother and sisters have pulled theirs back in low ponytails. She looks like a different girl and she chuckles at Afaf's bewildered expression.

"Do you think we live and sleep in hijab?" Kowkab says.

"Let's eat!" Kowkab's mother ushers her into the kitchen, where a table is laid out for six. Kowkab's father is already seated at one end of the table and tucks his newspaper on his lap. "Welcome to our home, ya Afaf," he tells her. "You light up our table."

Afaf smiles, embarrassed. Kowkab's parents welcome her without reservation. Kowkab motions to Afaf to sit beside her, her sisters opposite them and her mother on the other end, closest to Kowkab.

"Bismallah," her father recites, and they all lower their heads. "And with the blessings of Allah I begin."

Between bites of musakhan Afaf's eyes dart around the table as Kowkab and her sisters engage in actual conversation with their parents. With work and practice schedules, Afaf and Majeed rarely sit down at the same hour for dinner. Afaf usually carries a dish full of rice and cauliflower, or mahshi with yogurt sauce, into her room and eats alone, headphones on, a book propped open on her pillow. After practice, Majeed turns on the portable television in the kitchen and watches the middle innings of a game while he eats. Mama used to wait for Baba and they'd sit across from each other, mostly quiet, eating together. Ever since Baba began praying, Mama leaves him a plate covered in foil in the microwave. Baba sits alone; the nightly news, turned up high, streams out of their bedroom, breaking the silence of the kitchen.

Kowkab's father asks them about their day, how Nadia's internship at the social services agency is going. Kowkab's mother updates them on the latest events at the Islamic Center. Even Muna, the youngest, has something to contribute about her volunteer work at the day-care center.

"And, elhamdulillah," Kowkab's mother adds. "The state has finally approved the children's free milk program."

"Elhamdulillah," the others respond in unison.

Kowkab's father asks Afaf about her job at the mall, and it seems like such a trivial thing compared to what's been shared over crisped chicken topped with tangy sumac and onions. She's glad when the subject changes to the recent hijacking.

"It makes life difficult for God-fearing people in this country," Kowkab's father says.

Afaf remembers the other day when she stopped at a 7-Eleven across from the bus stop after work. A newscast from a portable television set behind the cash register blared the latest on the terrorist investigation. She'd overheard a white man joke, *TWA—Trouble With A-rabs*.

"Inshallah peace," Kowkab's mother sighs.

"There won't be peace until the U.S. fixes its foreign policy," Nadia declares. "Until the Palestinians are fully recognized."

"I understand, yabba, but violence only breeds violence," Kowkab's father counters. "We're a civilized society. Once talks break down, we're all lost."

Afaf listens and eats, observing each small, intimate gesture exchanged at the table—Kowkab's mother tucking a strand of her sister's hair behind her ear, Kowkab's father refilling his youngest daughter's plate with rice before she asks for more. Dejection thickens in her throat, making it difficult to swallow her food.

So this is how a family is, she thinks as Kowkab's mother offers her a plate of glossy green olives and pickled beets. But would they be the same if they'd lost a daughter, a sister? Would their closeness suddenly shatter like a glass that slips through their fingers?

By the end of the meal, a familiar anger ignites in Afaf's belly. She holds it in, this fireball of rage and jealousy, wanting to spew it at this loving, well-intentioned family, though she hungers to be a part of this togetherness as long as possible. Kowkab's mother tasks Kowkab and Afaf with clearing the table and Afaf's fingers tremble as she gathers the silverware, forks clattering on plates. Kowkab looks up at her and smiles.

In Kowkab's room, stuffed animals crowd the top of a wooden dresser, and posters of the Bangles, George Michael, and Cyndi Lauper hang on the wall. Nadia's room is across from her parents' master bedroom. Kowkab and Muna have matching sky-blue comforters on their twin-sized beds.

Kowkab sits on the carpeted floor, quiet for the first time since dinner, as if she can hear the anger roaring in Afaf. She joins Kowkab on the floor, pulling her knees to her chest, huddled against the hurt she's terrified will leak out. They don't speak. Kowkab pulls at the fibers in the carpet.

"Time for salat, ya banat!" Kowkab's mother calls from the hallway.

Kowkab reaches over to the bottom drawer of the dresser and pulls out prayer clothes. She holds out one set for Afaf. "We can do wudu together."

"Why do you want to be my friend?" Afaf blurts out, her cheeks hot, a lump of tears gathering in her throat. "I'm not like you. I'm a rotten person."

"You're not rotten. You're just lost," Kowkab says. She reaches a hand out to Afaf, and Afaf looks up into a face of sheer sincerity. The word *lost* turns into something else. It's not wrapped in the same hopelessness as when Mama calls her that. "You just need to take your time and Allah will guide you. He wants us to be happy."

Afaf wants to know if prayer and fasting and charity could magically change her mother and make them a family, though really Afaf has always known they've never been a close-knit family, even before Nada's disappearance. Had religion been the missing force, the thing that could weld them to each other so that when something terrible befell Afaf's family they would be unbreakable?

"You'll see." Kowkab stands, extends her hand to Afaf. "Now let's get ready for salat."

Afaf takes her new friend's hand and pulls herself up from the floor, repelling the gravity of her self-loathing, at least for a little while.

Mama's scrubbing a pot, one arm disappearing to her elbow. "Where have you been?"

Afaf wants to tell her mother about Kowkab and her family but doesn't. "At the library." Kowkab's mother had insisted on driving her home. Before they pulled away, she looked over the driver's seat at Afaf. *Say hello to your mother, habibti.*

No more questions from Mama, only the sound of steel wool scraping the bottom of a pot. "There's maklooba in the fridge. Why do I even bother cooking anymore?"

Majeed's probably at the indoor batting cages, and Baba's at the Center, where plans to build a proper mosque are still under way. Kowkab's father had mentioned the fund-raising was close to its goal.

Afaf shuts herself in her room, kicking off her sneakers, tossing her bag aside. Lying on her bed, she stares at the ceiling, Kowkab's words hanging above her: *It's never too late. Every day we can be better. There's no limit. No end. You only have to believe, Afaf.* She said these things to Afaf after they prayed with her family.

It seems too easy, like the keys she duplicates at the mall. You've got the original one, then you make a copy that's identical in every curve and cut. Can she really be someone else, in this same body? Is change possible?

She reaches for her bag, pulls out a book she started today—
The Unbearable Lightness of Being—and tries to focus on the typed
print, her eyes trekking from word to word but her brain incapable
of absorbing meaning. She turns the page, only to realize she doesn't
know what transpired paragraphs before.

She mutters, lays the book on her chest. It's not like she didn't
enjoy herself that night at the Center, the rain beating against the
windows while bodies fell into prayer. More than that, it had been
a strange feeling at first, but a natural one, like instantly mastering a
new skill she'd never imagined she could. And at Kowkab's house,
nestled between her new friend and her sisters in their family room,
their bodies facing east, the same sensation washed over her: it was
like coming home for the first time.

She thinks about Kowkab, how she wears her headscarf like a
badge of honor—defiance, even. Afaf is impressed; she's tried hard
her whole life to be like amarkan, only to be rejected and used.

Afaf drops her book to the floor and rolls onto her stomach, the
pillow cool against her face. What more does she have to lose?

Um Zuraib embraces her with the same exuberance as before,
delighted that Afaf has returned. Baba is pleased, too. He pats her
back and heads toward the men's congregation. Majeed made up
an excuse about extra practice this week. "I knew you would come
back. Everyone always does. Inshallah you'll be blessed for the rest
of your life."

Kowkab's mother kisses her on each cheek. "You've come on
a great evening," she gushes. "We're baking ma'moul in honor of
Ibtisam's newborn son, mashallah." The other women nod and wave
at Afaf.

"I'm so glad you came," Kowkab tells her, lightly touching her arm. Her sisters nod at Afaf, their smiles more sincere than yesterday. "Here, put this on." She hands Afaf an apron and they sit at a long retractable table covered in a plastic sheet. There's a large bowl of mashed, pitted dates, a container of Crisco, and a long silver pan already lined with the first batch of cookies. Cinnamon and cardamom waft toward her, a warm and calming aroma.

"Like this," Um Zuraib instructs Afaf, pinching a small portion of dough from a large, kneaded ball. The older woman flattens it in her palm and spoons a dollop of the mashed dates onto the dough, then seals it. She grabs a juice squeezer that now functions as a mold and presses the filled dough inside it. When she plops it out, the dough looks like a small, flattened spaceship with ridges. "Now you try."

Afaf is afraid she might ruin the batch, but Um Zuraib takes her hand and repeats the process, guiding Afaf's fingers. The buttery dough feels good in her palm.

When the final batch is in the oven—they've baked five dozen ma'moul—it's time for salat al-maghrib, the evening prayer.

"Are you ready?" Kowkab asks Afaf, holding out a set of mismatched prayer clothes.

Something stirs inside Afaf—it's small and feeble, like a narrow shaft of light straining under a heavy, sealed door. "I'm ready," she says.

Nurrideen School
for Girls

HE DIDN'T hear the bullets leaving the chamber. Like lyrics suddenly dropped from a sound track, then the treble fading out. All that was left was bass: bodies thudding to the floor. He reloaded without pause, the action of his fingers as automatic as the rapid discharge of his weapon.

The first girl to look at him didn't have a chance to scream. His shooting wasn't haphazard, sloppy. He examined each target before pulling the trigger, keeping his hand steady. He took his time. The teacher, a tall and thin woman in a lilac headscarf, pushed a few girls through a nearby door. Only moments before, she'd been at a piano, one hand conducting the students. He aimed at her and held the trigger until her right arm nearly separated from her torso.

The students, heads shrouded in white, were like swans bobbing on water. It almost moved him. He thought about their parents for the first time and what it would be like to lose your child. Did it matter how? Was it less tragic if it were a car crash or a drowning? Did the grief of a mother or father lessen in the how rather than the why?

He didn't think about the futures of these girls, telling himself that he didn't care as he surveyed their bodies on the floor, a few gasping for breath until they were silent.

He walked out of the music room, closing the door behind him. The faint wail of sirens was drowned out by the screams of girls in the hallway, a deafening, numbing noise only his gunshots could penetrate.

He wanted them to see him, too, but they would not turn around, so he shot them in their backs as they clogged the stairwell, and watched them fold over each other on the steps. He made his way over their bodies and down to the first floor where the janitor's closet was located.

It might have been different for him—maybe if he'd never left Wisconsin—and perhaps someone else would be here and now in his place, the rifle at his side, boots clopping across the linoleum floors of the school. If this wasn't his destiny, would someone else claim it? Could events be altered, time distorted to undo them?

Decades ago, Chicago had opened up like a giant clam that threatened to swallow him. He felt utterly alone in the city. The elevated trains kept him awake until early morning. He'd park at the Adler Planetarium and sit on the hood of his car, watching the sailboats pass on Lake Michigan. Couples sauntered by, hand in hand, or pushing strollers. Teenagers usually waited until dusk before they pulled up in cutoffs and jean jackets, carrying brown paper bags of alcohol under their arms, rock music playing loudly from their car stereos. They sat on the hoods of their cars, passing the bottles until a cop cruiser crept up.

He'd found work with a company that repaired heating and cooling units in corporate buildings in the Loop. His parents hadn't heard from him and he planned to keep it that way. He convinced himself that it was a relief. He'd done as his brother had: one day you're just gone. He marveled at how easy it was to disappear, and he wondered how many others like him and Joe had done it, when he read the newspaper every morning, perusing the classified ads for missing persons:

Michelle Boyd, age 22, white female, 5'4", 110 lbs. May have dyed hair brown. Last seen on May 3, 1978.
Bradley Wade, age 31, white male, 6'1", 145 lbs. Tattoo on right bicep. Last seen on October 27, 1976.

Today, one way or another, he'd finally disappear for good.

Through the frost-covered windows at the end of the corridor, he watched students escaping into the parking lot, their bodies hunched over, moving close to the ground. He heard someone on a loudspeaker giving the girls instructions to raise their arms in the air as they evacuated. Could their parents easily distinguish their child among the trembling green-uniformed bodies, heads swathed in white?

He turned toward the loading dock; his work was done. According to his observations, at least twenty bodies had fallen. He could search out more students and teachers, but it hadn't been about quantity. He'd seen their terror-stricken eyes, heard their bloodcurdling screams.

He lowered his rifle and started to walk back from where he'd entered the school building. Then he heard a muffled voice and turned around. It seemed to be coming from inside the paneled wall. He listened closely. A woman's voice, speaking in a quick, hushed tone.

He raised his rifle again and touched the wooden lattice with his free hand. It reminded him of the confessional at his mother's church. Then he remembered. This building had belonged to nuns nearly a century ago. Now these people had taken it over. More than two decades ago, he'd sat at the Tempest village hall meetings, seething at the prospect of a Muslim school in his own neighborhood.

He'd stood side by side with the other protesters at the back of the room, holding up signs reading *Vote NO to Terror School* and *Keep Tempest Safe*. In the end, the board had failed to keep them out. And now they had no one but themselves to blame.

You can't act different and expect to be treated different, he'd told Eileen when incidents of vandalism made the front page of the *Daily Southtown*. When construction finally began on the school, he'd lobbed a wrench from his toolbox at a newly erected window on the first floor as he was passing late one night in his truck. He'd laughed with others at a local bar over stories they'd heard of people breaking in and taking shits on the fresh-tiled floors. It got so bad, two night guards were hired to keep vigil until construction was complete. This only further incensed him—it was at the village's expense to protect the school. His tax dollars, his hard work.

This room must be an old confessional. The wooden lattice was smooth against his fingertips.

The loudspeakers continued to drone with orders outside. He could hear young girls crying and calling to each other. A sheet of frozen ice cracked on the window across from the confessional. He remembered how quiet the early morning had been when he'd taken Jeni for a walk, snow blanketing their path.

He pressed his ear against the lattice of the confessional, then stepped back. With the full force of his boot, he kicked the door open, rifle poised.

1993

1

IT'S LIKE a stranger staring back at her. At first a disembodied face floating in the mirror, until it morphs into her own face: Her eyes, brown and thick-lashed, stamps of early crow's-feet appearing when she smiles. Her nose, its full bulb—matured into Baba's—is the same, and her lips, bare and pale, twitch at the corners, unsure of the reflection in the mirror.

Afaf touches the fabric along the top of her head and the folds gathered softly at her throat. Beneath the hijab, it's still her. And yet a great part of Afaf is gone, hidden, never to be revealed again in public, and then only in the presence of women. A pang of something tragically permanent goes through her gut. She's spent years hating her hair—its wiry and untamed waves, dreading all the hours she's spent blow-drying it straight. Now it's pulled into a bun at the base of her neck like a spool of thread. A wide inner elastic band keeps it in place and the forest-green shayla—a gift—wraps her head.

It's not like she's never worn a headscarf in public. Since joining the Center, Afaf's slipped it on for Eid parties and wakes, for prayers at the mosque. And yet how quickly she slipped it off as soon as she climbed into her car, shaking out her heavy hair, checking the rearview mirror, and patting down strands that were static-laced because of the synthetic fabric.

She touches the back of her head, feeling for her hair. Is this concealment a high price to pay for her submission to God? She'll no longer feel the Illinois winter rushing through her hair, tingling her ears as she leaves the apartment. Or the sun beating down on her head when she goes for walks with Baba along the lakefront, her scalp warm and moist with sweat.

Afaf will miss her hair, the way it completes her face, one she hasn't always loved.

"Are you ready?" Kowkab asks her through the door.

"Almost." It's been a long time she's been standing here in her friend's bathroom.

Afaf slips a finger inside the hem of the scarf and traces her hair-line all the way to her ear. Something else has been bothering her: One day, will Nada recognize her in this thing? She has always felt like her sister is waiting to be found.

Last month, she walked past Nada in an aisle at the supermar-ket. Afaf turned around, followed her, pushing her own cart full of groceries from the list Mama gives her every week, a task she's taken over from Baba. Nada's wavy hair had grown longer and her body had plumped with age. When her sister turned the corner, Afaf caught her profile. Her heart sank. It wasn't Nada.

It's never Nada. Over the years, Afaf has pushed her cart behind strangers, all the way to the checkout line, sometimes to the parking lot. She spots Nada in public places—at Navy Pier or in the bleach-ers at a White Sox game. Every time, her heart lodges in her throat and her stomach heaves with sick excitement at the prospect that she's finally found her sister. As soon as Nada turns around, it's a stranger's face smiling at Afaf in curiosity: *Can I help you?*

And now, will she, too, become a stranger, should Nada hap-pen to pass her by? Will her sister do a double-take at the young woman wearing a headscarf? Could she express to her sister how much Islam and the Tempest Prayer Center have meant to her? It had started with a sense of community; the first time, really, she'd felt she truly belonged anywhere. Wasn't that what Nada, too, had been craving? Perhaps it's much easier to understand. Um Zuraib, Kowkab and her family, the rest of the circle of women—they'd accepted Afaf, discarded her past, pardoned her flaws. Before she discovered God, she'd found family at the Center. And through their grace and her own devotion to Islam, she found Allah. She gave extra du'aa for Nada: inshallah one day they'll meet again. And if not in this world, in the next one she'll be waiting for her sister.

And though this gives her hope, Afaf still searches for Nada in the aisles at the grocery store.

In the mirror, Afaf adjusts her shayla for the last time and wipes away tears. She unlocks the door.

"Mashallah!" Kowkab throws her arms around Afaf, her friend's swollen belly preventing a full embrace. "You look beautiful!"

Afaf laughs at her friend's compliment, the kind you give to a woman standing in her wedding dress.

Kowkab claps her hands. "I knew green was your color! The color of the Prophet! Allah dayman yihdeeki, ya Afaf!"

She silently hopes, too, that God may bestow upon her His every blessing, every gift. She feels as though she's on the cusp of something greater and it's this force that will carry her outside, in public, her hair—like a pair of naked breasts—now a private part of her body.

Her hijab celebration is hosted by Suha Bakri, the previous woman to commit from the circle of women from the Center. A tradition has started among them: once you've donned the hijab for life, you honor the next woman to do so, in your home with trays of baklawa and fatayir. Since the late 1980s, some of the muslimat had started covering up in subtle ways: berets pulled down below their ears along with turtlenecks, or headscarves loosely wrapped like those fashionable women driving convertibles in the 1950s, tufts of bangs peeking out. Suha Bakri was the latest in an increasing number of women to completely pledge the hijab.

"How do I *really* look?" Afaf asks Kowkab, fussing with a tiny pin on the side of her head.

Her friend beams at her like she did that first time they prayed side by side on the run-down floor of the Center. Now they are twenty-seven years old. Kowkab is married, her first child on the way. At first Afaf had been suspicious of her fiancé Yazen, convinced no man could ever be worthy of her dear friend. He'd shown up at Kowkab's house with a small entourage of brothers, cousins, and uncles to ask for her hand, and Kowkab had officially accepted. Over their courtship, Afaf watched them together, a quiet affection between them, their love never on display. But now Afaf catches a squeeze of the hand when they pass each other at fund-raisers for Palestine, sees the lingering gazes they share across a table full of guests at Ramadan dinners.

Real, enduring love seems possible when she's around her friend and her husband. At their ceremony, the imam had recited: *Allah has created for you spouses from amongst yourselves so that you might take comfort in them and He has placed between you love and mercy.*

Afaf had listened, long jaded by her parents' marriage eroding like a fossil of something once living and thriving, obliterated by a natural disaster. Baba's devotion to Islam, and her own, have split her family: quiet alliances have sprung up between Afaf and Baba on one side, and Mama and Majeed on the other. Her brother rejects any "organized religion," as he calls it, and repeats that message when he checks in from college. But Afaf knows it's a rejection of Baba and what he's put Mama through since they were children. In Majeed's eyes, their mother is blameless, a woman uprooted from her family, then her daughter stolen from her. Baba only made things worse for them.

Mama's contempt for religion is less ideological than Majeed's, but just as personal. She barely speaks to Afaf, always cooking and cleaning, the TV veiling the silence between them. Afaf can feel her mother's eyes on her from the hallway when she prays in the family room on the same rug Baba brought home from the masjid all those years ago. She also watches her husband: is she yearning for something to anchor her? Is Mama's open disgust merely secret envy?

Fasting's good for the body and soul, Afaf told Mama last Ramadan, inviting her mother to join her and Baba for a month of spiritual renewal. She posted the iftar calendar on fridge, counting down the days to Eid with a highlighter. She'd catch Mama studying it, tracing her fingers along the timetable of prayer and fast-breaking.

Don't you worry about my soul, Mama had retorted. *I've got scores to settle.*

The corners of Baba's eyes crinkle with yearning for Mama. At supper, he shares the Center's latest news as he spoons turmeric-dyed rice onto his plate, while Mama puffs away on her cigarette, her back leaning against the kitchen sink. His lips twitch in anticipation. Afaf eats Mama's lima bean stew and nods at her father's incessant rambling. She feels as though she must compensate for Mama's indifference. Shouldn't this be a time of growing closer, their aging bodies bracing each other as they carry the grief and misfortune life has dealt them? Mama's rejection pushes him closer to his faith and he clings to it.

Two human beings living in such misery together have colored Afaf's belief in marriage. It seems far worse than deliberately being alone.

Kowkab reaches for Afaf's hand, her other rubbing her belly. "You're glowing."

Afaf takes her friend's and they head out the door.

The cardamom-spiced coffee wafts through the foyer of Suha Bakri's luxurious house. She lives in a well-manicured neighborhood in Tempest, part of a population of well-to-do Arabs who've migrated miles south of Chicago, along with thousands of white people, discarding their urban existence. The hypocrisy of her husband's liquor store is politely ignored—*Allah will judge each on his and her own merits*, the imam lectures them each Friday. Suha's husband recently donated to the youth field house to be installed in the spring.

A massive chandelier glitters above Afaf's head and gilded frames with Quranic verses hang on sponge-painted walls.

"Ahlan! Ahlan!" Suha gushes. "Welcome and congratulations, habibti!" She's wearing her hijab though she's inside her own house, and Afaf can tell she's still brimming with the excitement of her own commitment last month. One glimpse of Suha Bakri's house—a spiral staircase, cathedral ceilings, marble floors, and a Range Rover in the driveway—and Afaf can see how easy a transition it is for someone like Suha to devote herself to Islam. How else can one account for such wealth and comfort, for the blessings of healthy children? Afaf smiles to herself as she and Kowkab are ushered into a large family. It's a small sacrifice, a woman like Suha concealing her mass of thick, highlighted curls beneath a taut fuchsia fabric with tiny rhinestones.

The women are waiting in a circle to embrace Afaf. It's a flurry of lips and eyes and headscarves. She's moving so quickly through the line she can't recall whom she's just greeted. When she can finally stand back, she's happy to see her favorite women are present. Kowkab's mother and sisters, all sharing that same crooked smile, beam at Afaf. Rita Parker and her daughter Ashanti wave at her from the living room. They wear emerald turbans, their faces a shimmering deep bronze.

Afaf remembers the first time she met Benjamin Parker. Mama had recoiled at the presence of the heavyset black man Baba had invited into her small kitchen. With a stiff back, she served them coffee. Either completely oblivious, or magnanimously polite as Afaf has come to know him, Mr. Parker never stopped smiling and thanking Mama for her hospitality. He and his family are the first black members of the mosque. They live one town over from Tempest.

Baba was instantly taken by Mr. Parker's fervent beliefs. They spent hours at the Lower Delta Restaurant on Eighty-Seventh Street and Kedzie Avenue, arguing about muslimeen who profit at the expense of poor black folks.

There should be a rec center or day care on every corner—not a liquor store, brother, Mr. Parker protested, rubbing stubble on his chin.

Allah see the evil they do, Baba conceded. *He see everything.*

Um Zuraib waits for Afaf in the living room. Last year, her mentor had fallen outside her home, breaking her hip. Her once-robust body, its girth taking up a love seat, is now whittled down to a slack frame, her welcoming bosom deflated. She sits on a leather recliner, the other women fretting over her.

She reaches out her hands. "I'm so proud, ya Afaf," Um Zuraib tells her as Afaf bends over her. "You've come a long way, habibti."

Afaf kneels on the floor beside her, nodding, remembering that rainy day she and Majeed, timid and unsure teenagers, followed Baba inside that dilapidated building on Sixty-Third and Kedzie. The women accepting Afaf without question, without judgment. How she'd gazed across the lines of worshippers on the Persian rugs, their faith palpable. They made her believe she was worthy of something grander than Hoover High School, its white girls and their boyfriends, made her believe she could soar above a broken family with a disappeared sister and a vacant mother. This circle of women and their daughters propel her to do good, to love Allah, and learn that His love reflects back once you open your heart. Before she could fathom His great bounty, she had loved these women first, could touch and gather their kindness in her hands, could wrap herself in their grace until she could start to love herself again.

Now Um Zuraib squeezes Afaf's hands, then presses her palm against Afaf's partially covered forehead. "Inshallah your mother is not too far away."

A chorus of *Inshallah* rises from the women, like a geyser, gushing hope.

2

THE FESTIVE excitement surges and falls in Suha's house. Afaf escapes into a guest bathroom, gathering a few quiet moments for herself. She gazes at her reflection in the vanity mirror above the sink and thinks of Bilal. His face reaches from the corners of her mind, seeping into every recess. His irises are like two drops of honey, under heavy eyebrows. He'll be proud of her hijab. Though he's not the reason she's finally decided to wear it, she's glad it will please him.

Bilal Hamzić. *Ibn al ajnabeeyah*, as Baba calls him: *Son of the foreign woman.*

He showed up one weekend to take the English-language class Afaf taught to new refugees at the Center. He was always the first one to arrive and his eyes seemed to follow her every gesture, as he listened intently to each word she slowly enunciated while pointing to a chalkboard behind her. She could see it was more than ambition driving Bilal. There was a kind of muted desperation in his face, an urgent need to do well, to make something of himself. She'd heard his story told around the mosque, how he'd escaped eastern Bosnia. His father and uncles were executed.

The Center sponsored Bilal's immigration. In America, he was reunited with his mother and sister, who'd also fled. Afaf could see the debt Bilal carried for surviving the killings, a terrible weight on his shoulders under which he struggled. Now he would make the most of his spared life.

One day, he stayed after class. *You are very patient teacher.* His precise though broken words had startled her. He was usually quiet during the lesson.

You are a good student, Afaf told him, turning around to erase the board, avoiding his gaze. He was a handsome man, his skin the color of lightly steeped tea.

Are you a teacher of school?

Yes. I teach in Chicago. Third and fourth grades.

He nodded. *You are natural teacher.*

Afaf's cheeks flushed and she accepted his invitation for coffee. She'd received marriage proposals from other muslimeen, the brothers and cousins of women she worshipped alongside at the masjid. She smiled politely at the frequent string of accolades she was forced to listen to as she splashed water on her face during wudu in the communal washroom, or when she slipped her shoes back on after prayer:

Hatim is a second-year resident at Rush Hospital, ya Afaf. You'd be perfect for each other.

Mashallah, my brother Feras is opening a second jewelry location in the mall. Do you want to see a picture of him?

They're respectable men, but Afaf wasn't interested. There's something missing in them—or perhaps missing in her. After she joined the Center, being alone didn't feel like a plague. It wasn't the same as loneliness, the kind she'd felt for so many years without a sister, without supportive parents. When Bilal entered her life, he quickly filled up a space, like rainwater gathering in a watering can. It felt unexpected, though very natural.

They spent the summer outside the Adler Planetarium, sitting on the lakefront, watching sailboats like she did when she was a little girl. They ate falafel sandwiches and drank bottled iced tea. He told her about his time at the University of Tuzla and she shared anecdotes about her young pupils. They held back the stories of the things that had broken them.

One early October weekend they visited an arboretum outside the city, walking between great cedars and black maple trees. Afaf had stopped to pick up a fallen leaf and it crumbled at her touch. Bilal had grabbed her hand and pulled her close. Their lips met for the first time.

He guided her to a bench that faced a large pond bordered by blue spruces on the far side. Ducks waded in contentment, dipping their yellow beaks in the water. He and Afaf sat in silence for a long time before Bilal spoke in a low voice.

I come home from university. My village—it was burned to ground. My father, my uncles, my cousins, my friends. Dead. My mother and sister were already gone. His eyes crinkled as he looked at the rippling pond. *I keep moving. I stay hidden in the forest for two weeks. No food. Only tomatoes I steal from nearby farm. I drink water from creek.* He kept hold of Afaf's hand. *My mother. She still cries at night. She does not know that I hear.*

He turned to Afaf and tucked a strand of her loose hair behind her ear, held her chin in his hand. *I want my life to begin again.* It was his quiet proposal.

Afaf understands what it means to start over, to be given another chance. For Bilal, it's leaving behind the dead parts—his father and relatives, his ravaged country. And now he's looking ahead at a future, one that includes Afaf. They've been on the same journey, their paths happily converging. *Naseeb* is what her aunt Nesreen calls it—fate.

Had not Allah had a hand in it, too? Islam led her here. Would she have found Bilal otherwise if not for her newfound faith? Look at her now: a devoted muslimah, a public school teacher. And she owed so much of it to the circle of women from the Center. *Elhamdulillah*, as Baba says.

Bilal squeezed her hand, his amber eyes warm and expectant. *I will always take care of you.*

For the first time in her life, Afaf discovers that to be desired by another human being—to be needed—is an exaltation, one she hadn't anticipated. She's already loved by others: Baba, Majeed, Kowkab, Um Zuraib. But what Bilal offers her is different than their kind of unconditional love. With him, the memories of white boys fumbling with her bra straps, pressing their chapped lips against hers, have wilted like the fallen leaf crumbling in her hand that day.

They plan to announce their engagement next spring. Bilal has accepted an entry-level job with an accounting firm in Chicago while working on his college transfer credits. His dream is to develop a system of halal banking practices for muslimeen, to appropriate the interest a personal account earns toward charity.

If Afaf teaches summer school, they'll have saved up enough for a small wedding.

Back in Suha Bakri's spacious kitchen, Afaf waves to Bilal's mother Ilhana, who's helping herself to a small plate of desserts from trays of knaffa and baklawa arranged on a granite counter. She is a slight woman with small shoulders, ice-blue eyes. Esma, Bilal's sister, approaches Afaf, hugs her close, her headscarf the color of saffron.

"Mabrook," she says, her Arabic, like her English, stilted but sweet. She's inherited her mother's white skin and blue eyes.

Esma pulls an envelope from the pocket of her thigh-length tunic and presses it in Afaf's hand. She winks at Afaf before joining her mother.

Inside the envelope is a bookmark from Bilal. One side is embossed in Arabic calligraphy. Afaf traces the golden loops and dips with her fingertip. The artist's caption reads, "*Love* by Osman Özçay." Such is Bilal's affection. Quiet and solid, like oak wood—no hollow spaces, no echoes.

3

ON HER way home from the party, Afaf stops for gas to save her extra time in the morning. The late fall temperatures have not risen above fifty degrees. The sky is overcast and a soft drizzle mists her windshield as she pulls up to the pump.

"Twenty on number two, please," she tells the cashier, smiling and trying to pull the young woman's attention away from her headscarf.

The cashier doesn't say anything, slides Afaf's paper bill into her drawer, and presses a few buttons.

"Raghead."

Afaf turns around, her heart thumping. *Who said it?*

A group of teenagers snicker near the Slurpee machine. A man in a suit fastens his eyes on the newspaper he's purchasing, refuses to look Afaf's way. The cashier gives her a wicked grin.

Afaf heads to the exit, her cheeks flushed. The deep contentment she'd felt just a short time ago in Suha Bakri's home is gone, like she'd been blithely walking a tightrope, the safety net suddenly snatched from beneath her. Is this a prelude to what life will be like from now on?

Afaf's eyes remain fixed on the entrance to the store as she pumps gas. Patrons go in and out, and some cast looks at her, while others are oblivious to this woman with the wrapped head. Is she strong enough to bear the taunts?

Afaf thinks of Kowkab and Um Zuraib: *Allah will see us through anything.* That's what they tell each other, the circle of women, when things get hard. Like Bahiya Adwan and her father's agonizing surrender to dementia. Or like Randa Abdul Aziz, still reeling from an ugly divorce. When they lose children to disease and the unknown, they're told to recite Surah Al-Baqara:

> *O you who have believed, seek help through patience and prayer. Indeed, Allah is with the patient.*

Afaf climbs into her car and flips the mirror open on the visor. Only her eyes and nose are visible, bordered by green fabric. She shifts position, trying to capture her full head, but it's impossible.

She flips back the visor. *I can do this—it's such a small thing,* she tells herself. *A small thing.*

When Afaf gets home, Mama's at the kitchen table sipping a cup of coffee. On the same old portable television, she watches *Good Morning America* and *Phil Donahue*. She stays in the kitchen all day, cleaning and cooking and watching game shows, wiping down the counter though it's spotless. At night, she closes her bedroom door and watches more TV on another set Baba bought her. No matter which room she's in, the sound of the television obliterates the quiet, as though her mother can't stand to be alone with her thoughts.

"Alf mabrook," Mama says, green eyes gleaming with sarcasm. "Congratulations on the final step of your conversion. May the Lord redeem your soul." It's the same contemptuous tone she heard at the gas station: *raghead.* Mama grabs her mug and rinses it at the sink. The hem of her black abaya sweeps the floor, her long sleeves wide and flowing. The bodice is stitched in silver and gold and the open collar contains loops of tiny embroidered flowers. It's one of a dozen that Khalti Nesreen has brought back for Mama from the bilad.

The latest grievance—the most offensive, Afaf realizes—is Baba's journey to hajj last year. With contributions from the Center, her father had gathered several thousands of dollars and flew to Mecca to fulfill one of the most sacred pillars of Islam. It would have cost less to purchase a ticket for Mama to fly to Palestine, with a few hundred dollars put aside for gifts for her family.

"How can you deny what Allah has pressed upon us, ya Muntaha?" Baba says to Mama. But Afaf understands it's not really about religious obligation or even money. She recognizes the same vague fear in Baba's eyes—if he lets Mama go, she'll never return.

Mama's father passed away shortly after she married. Her mother died last year from pneumonia. It had been over twenty years since Mama had last seen her. A framed picture of her sits on Mama's dresser. In it Afaf's grandmother wears a tailored dress suit with broad shoulders and carries an infant in her arms—Khalti Nesreen, the last of her children. A little girl—Mama—timidly stares at the camera, clutching the hem of her mother's jacket. Afaf wonders what that little girl in the photograph was thinking—had Mama already predicted her life as a woman? Was that what made her expression so glum?

As customary, Khalti Nesreen hosted an evening of mourning in her house in Kenosha and she and Mama received friends and distant relatives bearing their condolences and offering aluminum foil-wrapped dishes full of rice and vegetables. The masjid sent a carton of fresh palm dates and a small donation. Afaf helped Khalti Nesreen serve the bitter, unsweetened coffee in tiny demitasse cups while Majeed and Baba sat with the men in the living room, Baba thumbing his musbaha, an onyx set of beads he'd brought home from hajj. Her brother stared at his feet. Ammo Yahya was showing a colleague an ancient map of Jerusalem that he'd found at a street art fair in Milwaukee.

In the kitchen where the women gathered, Mama wrung tissue paper in her hands, moaning about not seeing her mother before she died, complaining how it should have been her duty to host the azza as the oldest daughter—but how could she, when her apartment was so tiny it could barely hold the immediate family? Khalti Nesreen's girlfriends stole glances at each other, eyebrows cocked in disapproval.

"Khalas, sister!" Khalti Nesreen snapped at Mama. She arranged a platter of the fresh dates and handed it to Afaf. "Inshallah God has mercy on our mother's soul."

Since her mother's passing, Mama has become more unhinged. She'll go days without showering, and Baba or Afaf have to gently remind her, steering her toward the bathroom, turning the faucet on, and helping her undress. She stares listlessly until Afaf pulls back the plastic shower curtain and invites her in.

"Do you think I'm an imbecile? I can take care of myself," she snaps, alert again and disdainful.

On a bad day, Mama spends an hour scouring the stovetop with an S.O.S. pad; she's already scrubbed off most of the laminate on the burner trays. Then she stands at the sink and plucks out the tiny wires from her fingertips, her slender hands scalded red from running them under hot water.

Today Afaf's worried. Mama tends to wear the black abaya when she's in a particularly foul mood. Afaf must be cautious: any gesture, any word, could set Mama off. Her mother's like a caged tiger, gorgeous and deadly.

On the portable TV, a woman on a game show squeals in delight. She's won ten thousand dollars and has a decision to make: walk away with it or triple the amount in a final round. The host, a short, shiny-faced man, places his hand on her shoulder as the giddy contestant ponders her choice. The camera zooms in on the woman's face, then cuts to her family in the audience. They give her a thumbs-up.

"Dummy," Mama says. "Take the money and go home." She sets her coffee mug on the counter and leans against it. Her gray hair trails down one side in a loose braid; only a few strands of black remain. She's still quite beautiful—a phenomenon that makes it difficult for Afaf to hate her.

Afaf pours the dregs of the coffeepot into a mug. "The women asked about you," she tells her mother, taking a seat at the table.

Mama snorts. "They still think they can save me. Idiots."

Afaf has come to understand an unshakable truth about her mother, something she finds difficult to share with Um Zuraib and the other women: It isn't that Mama doesn't believe in God. She's simply denied His power, extinguished any flicker of faith that she might use to transcend her misery. The loss of her daughter, a troubled marriage, a lonely existence in a country where she never felt at home—she has no intention of relinquishing such injustices to prayer and fasting. Mama's pain is supreme and hers alone; no higher being can ever claim that.

The TV clamors with applause as the contestant poses herself in front of the camera, the lights dimming behind her. In the corner of the screen, the timer counts down as she spouts single-word answers to questions the host fires at her.

Mama stands at the sink as Afaf sips black coffee, her mother's eyes boring into her. The headscarf suddenly feels like a clamp on her head. Mama's scrutiny turns it into a joke that someone could never play on her. Afaf and the rest of them are fools in her mother's eyes, giving themselves up without question, without a tangible return on their pain.

Afaf touches the hem of her scarf, wondering if she's made a mistake, and a sense of perverse disappointment comes over her: she still wants Mama's approval. And for a moment her mother's power over her outweighs the Lord's. Afaf closes her eyes and silently prays: *Allah, keep me on the path of righteousness.*

In the absence of Mama's approval, Afaf turns to Baba—has done so for years—clinging to her father's esteem as if it were a branch on a cliff. Together they pray and fast, attend meetings at the Center, help organize fund-raisers. They carefully move around Mama like a stream split by a rock. Afaf wonders what Majeed will say when he sees her. His final semester is under way, then he'll go to law school. She doubts he'll ever come home to live again. His room has remained the same, his tidy bed in the corner, his old *Muscle & Fitness* magazines on his nightstand, free weights in a plastic tub. She remembers how awkward he was, his body taking up more space, puberty stretching his limbs and broadening his shoulders. The boy Majeed was who always surpassed Afaf when they were kids—the overachiever, the star athlete, the good son—would always be preserved in his room like the trophies still irreverently piled on his dresser. The man that he's becoming is elusive, someone Afaf doesn't know well, someone she suspects sleeps with girls at school and guzzles beer with his friends at bars off campus.

On the phone, he rails about the Oslo Accords and the desolate failure of the Palestinian Authority. When she tries to speak with him about Islam, he changes the subject. Afaf has prepared herself for a stern inquisition about her decision to wear hijab.

At first he was quiet on the line. *That's a big step, Afaf. Are you sure?*

Of course. I've been thinking about it for months.

Then I'm happy for you. As long as you're doing it for yourself.

In other words, *not for Baba.*

Though Majeed is devoted to the Palestinian struggle—he's the head of his university's chapter of Students for Justice in Palestine—he refuses to join Baba at Friday prayer. He'll meet him afterward at the Lower Delta Restaurant, where she pictures Baba recapitulating the imam's sermon on premarital sex, her brother squirming as he silently sips his tea.

The timer buzzes on the TV and the audience moans in displeasure. Just like that, the woman has lost it all.

"Dummy," Mama says again, shaking her head.

"The party was fun," Afaf offers. "Um Zuraib sends her regards." Since the group of women had adopted her, Afaf secretly hoped it might generate some jealousy from Mama, some fear that she might be replaced. Her mother is undaunted. Afaf's devotion to Islam has made her an enemy—just like Baba, both of them coerced into a war they hadn't started with Mama.

Mama snorts again as she lights a cigarette. For a moment, Afaf imagines the billowing sleeve of her abaya catching fire, then her hair, her mother's mouth opening in an awful scream though no sound comes from it. And Afaf just stands back and watches how brilliantly Mama burns before turning into a pile of ash.

In her bedroom, Afaf unpins her shayla and slips it off her head. She drapes it over one side of her dresser and the fabric licks the top of the old record player she keeps on a small table. She pulls a record from an old box beneath it. Nina Simone begins to croon. Her voice, deep and overcast, drowns out the noise of the game show and commercials in the kitchen. It was one of the very last records—*Here Comes the Sun*—Afaf purchased from a store in Chicago that sold vintage comic books and music. She's searched for Farid al-Atrash and Um Kalthum, hoping to surprise Baba. She'd kept all of the early albums Baba had brought home that day from a garage sale, their sleeves now worn and fringed at the edges.

Afaf gathers her lesson plan book from her messenger bag. Next week her third-graders will be honing their multiplication skills (five and six times tables) and practicing adverbs in their autobiographies, bound by construction paper they assembled themselves.

Had she ever pictured a life in teaching before Um Zuraib? She's forever indebted to this woman, a surrogate mother to Afaf, who, alongside her dear friend Kowkab, encouraged her through the tough coursework. *You have so many gifts to share with the world, ya Afaf.* It took her five years to complete her degree—she'd had to work, to help Baba with the bills—and still she'd graduated cum laude in elementary education.

She finds children are amazing creatures: eager to learn, quick to forget injury, open to change. At least until high school, when your world suddenly becomes smaller and you move awkwardly through your days, exposed like a raw nerve. At ten years old, all Afaf wanted was to be seen and accepted, to not have teachers look over her head as though she were invisible.

Her teaching career had started with volunteering at the day-care program run for low-income families by the Nur Society of Sisters, a committee of muslimat devoted to charitable causes. Afaf read the children all the books she'd loved at their age, the stories that offered a temporary reprieve from the old apartment on Fairfield Avenue where clouds of grief and anger hung over her family. Her favorite was still *The Phantom Tollbooth*, tears filling her eyes at the part that had meant the most when she'd felt so utterly out of place:

> *"It was impossible," said the king, looking at the Mathemagician.*
>
> *"Completely impossible," said the Mathemagician, looking at the king.*
>
> *"Do you mean—" stammered the bug, who suddenly felt a bit faint.*
>
> *"Yes, indeed," they repeated together; "but if we'd told you then, you might not have gone—and, as you've discovered, so many things are possible just as long as you don't know they're impossible."*

Something had shifted in her small chest all those years ago as she sat on her bedroom floor. She read those words twice, then three times. She'd walked to the library on her own the day she chose that book. Nada had shown her the way enough times and she visited at least twice a week, reading as many books as she could carry home.

The words echoed in her heart, a combination of nostalgia and plaintiveness: *So many things are possible just as long as you don't know they're impossible.*

She'd wanted to make every child feel they weren't alone, to fan their potential into roaring flames of hope and promises to be fulfilled one day. Teaching gives her a sense of purpose and, unexpectedly, intoxicating independence. No matter what, she knows she'll survive.

She looks over at the green shayla, thinks of the other headscarves folded neatly in her drawer—shades of melon, sage, and French rose.

That ugly word suddenly hisses again in her ear, bristling the hair on her neck: *raghead*. She's tried to put the incident out of her mind, but it's no use.

She opens her lesson plan book, wondering what tomorrow will bring at school.

4

ON MONDAY morning, Afaf walks into the teacher's lounge and her colleagues appear perplexed. She smiles and stows her lunch, pretending nothing's changed, ignoring the knot of anticipation in her stomach. She won't say anything first; if they have questions, they can ask. But they merely nod at her, weak smiles and raised eyebrows. Their silence communicates the questions she imagines they'll ask once she's left the room: *Can she wear that thing in a public school? Doesn't that cross a line of church and state? Is she some sort of radical?*

After a beat, they return to their morning gossip, several laughing over a student's spelling error that turned *liberate* into *lubricate*, and others rehashing the Bears' final score last night. Afaf grabs her coffee and walks down the hallway to her classroom.

Afaf's third-graders look at her with astonishment. There's no disguising their emotions. It's as if a stranger has taken over their classroom. She quickly reassures them it's still her and explains why she's covered her hair.

"So you don't sleep in it?" Jeremy Mann asks, always the first hand to shoot up with a question. He'd once asked why bees had to die once they stung people. It seemed utterly unfair to him.

Afaf shakes her head, stifling a laugh.

"Do you take a bath with it?" This from Mikaela Cummings, her strawberry-blond hair pulled into two high ponytails.

"Oh, no, Mikaela! I hope you don't take baths with your clothes on!"

The children giggle, hands over their mouths, vigorously shaking their heads. She can see they're relieved. They can move on to nouns and adjectives.

Afaf's aide, Mrs. Walsh, also appears relieved. "You look lovely, dear," she whispers, squeezing Afaf's hand. Her husband is a retired lieutenant colonel who served in the Persian Gulf War. He gripes about President Clinton and the demise of the country. Mrs. Walsh couldn't stand to be home with him every day.

"You'll pardon my saying so, but I might have pulled his shotgun on myself if I hadn't taken this job," she'd joked the first day of school, holding one side of the bulletin board trim as Afaf, a nervous new teacher, stapled down the corners.

During the Pledge of Allegiance, Afaf touches her headscarf, checking the fastening pins, slipping a finger inside the edges, as if her hair might vanish. Mrs. Walsh catches her and smiles.

As the morning continues, Afaf forgets about her hijab, consumed by the routines she's developed for her students. She walks down the aisles of small desks, guiding the exercises, waiting for a chorus of answers. Layla Hamad, olive-skinned and petite, concentrates hard as Afaf passes her. She's one of two Arab girls in her class. Afaf stops at her desk.

There's a star-shaped bruise on Layla's left cheek. Afaf taps her shoulder and signals to the little girl to follow Afaf into the hall. The rest of the class continues their drill, unbroken by this quiet disruption—their disciplined compliance pleases Afaf. She nods at Mrs. Walsh, who swiftly picks up where she left off.

"You're not in trouble, Layla," Afaf immediately tells her outside the classroom door. The fear in the little girl's honey-colored eyes begins to melt away, not completely disappearing. "I noticed that bruise on your cheek. Can you tell me what happened?"

Layla's hair is thick and wavy, reminding Afaf of all those childhood days Mama wrestled her hair into lumpy braids. Layla wears a sparkly headband, her tiny gold earrings dangling from delicate lobes. Most of the girls in Afaf's class aren't yet permitted by their parents to have pierced ears—Jumana Odeh, the other Arab student, wears cubic zirconia studs. Afaf feels a special bond to these girls: she remembers what it was like to be a poppy in a field of lilies.

Layla's lips move with the choral repetition of the math drill floating out to them in the hallway. Afaf glances inside the classroom. Mrs. Walsh walks down a row, moving her hands like a conductor.

"Don't be afraid, Layla." Afaf smiles and lays her hand on the little girl's shoulder. Layla flinches, eyes wide. "Did someone hurt you?"

She quickly shakes her head, confirming Afaf's suspicion. "Layla, please listen carefully to me." Her tone is gentle, though Layla is now fully alert, her small lips perfectly still. Math drills become white noise in the background.

"I fell down yesterday. I fell down at my house," Layla spills out. Her eyes flit everywhere but on Afaf. "It doesn't hurt."

"I'm glad it doesn't hurt, Layla, but I'm worried about how it happened." Afaf places her other hand on the little girl's shoulder, forcing her to look up. "Did someone hit you at home?"

Afaf can see all of the excuses Layla has rehearsed drifting across her face like leaves, settling in her eyes. The little girl bites her upper lip. Afaf knows too well how children quickly discover the truth can only make matters worse.

It's not the first time. Last week Layla's nostrils were crusted with dried blood. She told Afaf she'd fallen off her bike and her forehead had hit the sidewalk. Afaf had let it go. Today she persists. "If you can't tell me, Layla, I'll need to walk you down to Principal Walker's office and we'll have to get to the bottom of this."

"Please, Miss Rahman, don't tell on me," the little girl pleads, as though she's done something wrong.

"Did your baba hit your face?"

A little boy runs past them in the hallway, his lunch box clanking. Layla is temporarily distracted.

Afaf squeezes the girl's shoulders. "Layla, did your baba hit your face?"

She sniffles, then nods. Though she had expected it, Afaf's stomach sinks.

"Did he punch your nose last week?"

Another nod.

"Does he hit your mom?"

Afaf remembers Mrs. Hamad attending open house alone, a short woman with a pear-shaped body and curly brown hair pulled back with a studded headband, similar to the ones Layla wore every day. She seemed skittish, like a cat set off by every sound. She'd listened and nodded eagerly at Afaf's presentation on educational goals and yearly benchmarks. On clipboards Afaf had set on a long table, Mrs. Hamad signed up for every holiday party and school activity, though she hadn't shown up for any, not for the Halloween parade or the field trip to the Museum of Science and Industry.

Tears stream down Layla's face. "Please don't tell on us." Again she begs Layla, as though she and her mother are culpable in a terrible crime.

Afaf's throat constricts with pity. "Listen, Layla. I want you to take a deep breath. Look at me, Layla. Breathe. Like this." Afaf inhales through her nose. The little girl follows Afaf's diaphragm as it rises and falls. Soon she's calm. "Go to the washroom and splash some water on your face. Get a drink from the fountain and come right back to class. We'll talk about this later, but you don't have anything to worry about now. Okay?" Afaf's instructions are precise and clear. Layla obeys without question.

At lunch, Mrs. Walsh gives Afaf a stern look. "You have to report it, dear." She takes loud sips of herbal tea from her thermos cup and thumbs through her *Good Housekeeping* magazine.

Afaf remembers the awkward lecture on state-mandated reporters when she was in college, the professor laser-pointing at a screen. There was a long list of occasions and circumstances determining when you were supposed to notify the Illinois Department of Children and Family Services. Her chest had tightened with fear during class that morning. She'd discovered there were worse things than living with a mother who made you feel invisible. The professor rattled off case after case of neglect and abuse—cigarette burns on a child's neck, no food in the fridge for days, a drunken boyfriend cornering a little girl every time her mother was away. Afaf had hoped she'd never be in such a position to make that phone call.

Afaf nods at Mrs. Walsh, silently watching her pour another cup of tea and slurp it down. Afaf folds her sandwich back into its crinkled plastic wrap. She's lost her appetite.

Her professor's words echo back to her: *While it's important to use discretion, it's always better to be safe than sorry.*

Stephanie Roman comes to mind, a girl Afaf knew in seventh grade. She stopped coming to school for two weeks after she was taken from her parents' custody. A vengeful relative had reported that Stephanie and her brother were being sexually abused by their father. In the end, it was baseless, but Stephanie wasn't the same, growing sullen and detached from the other kids. She eventually transferred schools after her parents moved the family away.

But the evidence is not invisible here, hiding under Layla's skin. It's staring at Afaf in the shape of a star on her cheek. It wasn't like Mama's depression or Baba's alcoholism—things she'd been able to hide forever as long as it didn't show up in cuts and bruises.

And yet something keeps Afaf from walking to the office and making that call. It feels like a betrayal of some kind, as though she shares a silent code with Layla, arabiya like her. Their community is very small—almost stiflingly so. Through the Center, Afaf has learned how easily each family can be traced back to Palestinian clans.

"I'll make the call," Afaf announces, though Mrs. Walsh has already left to wash her hands before the children return to class running and laughing to their desks.

5

AFAF CAN'T remember driving home. She'd started the day imagining the spectacle of her hijab, though that had turned out to be the least of her worries. She replays the conversation in the hallway with Layla over and over in her head. She finds herself pulled up to the curb, the wind whipping at the hedges outside the apartment, surprised at how quickly she arrived home.

"Some woman called three times for you," Mama tells her before she can utter hello.

"Who is it?" Afaf unpins her shayla and removes the headband.

Mama watches what will become a ritual for Afaf each day she comes home. She snuffs out her cigarette and pierces cauliflower frying in a deep pan of oil. "I don't know. Her name is Sabrine. So pushy." Mama hands her the number she's scribbled down on a Chinese take-out menu.

"Thank you." Afaf takes the paper. "Why don't you change out of that abaya? I can wash it for you. Get it fresh again."

It's mostly easy to do things for Mama, helping her stay clean, keeping the apartment in order. Easier than hugging Mama or taking her hand, pressing it against her own cheek. Their relationship is practical, functioning. But today she wants to tell Mama what happened at school. And though Afaf knows precisely what she needs to do, it would still feel good to hear Mama say, *Khair inshallah. It will turn out all right.* She still desperately aches for that confidence—no matter how much Um Zuraib or any of the other women shower her with attention, it will never be the same as coming from her own mother.

Mama mutters low and goes to her bedroom. She returns in a sleeveless pink housedress. She holds out her abaya and dirty underwear like a child.

Afaf drops them in a small stackable washer beside the bathroom and dials the cordless phone. "Salaam, this is Afaf Rahman." She measures a cup of detergent and starts a cycle, balancing the phone between her ear and shoulder.

"Afaf! Salaam, habibti! It's Sabrine Khalil."

She scans her memory. "I'm sorry, Ms. Khalil, have we met at the masjid?"

There are children shouting and playing in the background. "Loolad! Quiet! Go outside!" The woman clears her throat. "I'm sorry, Afaf. We haven't really spoken before. I'm secretary for the Nur Society of Sisters."

It hits Afaf: Sabrine Khalil, a slender woman with horn-rimmed glasses. A cousin of Um Zuraib. "Oh, yes! Salaam, Sabrine! Are my registration fees due?"

Sabrine Khalil handles membership for the Nur Society, mails postcards for upcoming events. Afaf hasn't spoken much to her before.

"No, no, elhamdulillah, you're fine." The woman pauses, clears her throat again. "I'm calling about something rather sensitive, habibti."

Afaf carries the cordless phone into her room. Mama has settled in front of the television, and another game show theme song drones in the kitchen. "What is it, Sabrine?"

"You have my niece in class. Layla Hamad. She's my brother's daughter."

Afaf's stomach sinks, as it had earlier that day when Layla confessed to her. She waits for the woman to say more.

"Afaf, my brother and his wife have been going through a very hard time. He just lost his job, and with five kids . . . you know, habibti?"

I don't know, Afaf wants to tell the woman. She'd grown up with a father who nearly drank himself to death by ramming into a streetlight, but he'd never laid a hand on her or Majeed. She didn't know anything about a father hitting his child so hard a star had formed on her cheek.

So why hadn't Afaf made the call to DCFS today? She'd lied to her aide.

She feels hot, like her pores are closing in shame. She unbuttons her sweater, slips it off with one hand, the other still gripping the phone. The woman's words puncture her ears.

"Um Zuraib said I should call you and explain the situation. That you'd understand."

Um Zuraib? Of course. It was Um Zuraib who'd given her Afaf's number—how else would this woman know anything about her?

Afaf feels cornered, her back up against the wall. These women aren't asking for her empathy: they're demanding her silence. But Afaf can't give it to them.

"It's out of my hands, Sabrine. I'm sorry." Afaf hangs up, cutting off the woman's protests. The phone rings a few times and she ignores it, laying it down on her bed.

Mama appears in her doorway, the smoke from her cigarette swirling into Afaf's room.

"Who keeps calling? Is it that woman?"

Afaf stares at the gray snake of smoke that coils and disappears.

"Answer me, Afaf!"

"It's nothing, Mama. I took care of it." But she hasn't really. She'd cowered under some foolish sense of honor. "I have to pray al-asar."

Later that evening, Afaf sniffles on the phone to Bilal.

"You are doing the right thing, Afaf," he consoles her. "Children must always come first."

Afaf sees a flash of the forest where Bilal's sister and mother had hidden for weeks. How many children had crouched behind those trees alongside them? Where do Layla and her mother hide from her father?

There's a soft knock on her door. "Khair inshallah," Baba says, poking his head in. "Your mother says a woman's been bothering you on the telephone." He enters her room and lowers himself into the chair at her desk, his bones creaking with age. His speckled hair is shaved under the skullcap he wears nowadays.

Afaf sniffles back tears. "I took care of it, Baba."

"Tell me. What's happened?"

"A little girl I teach. Layla. She's been coming to school with bruises."

He thumbs his onyx musbaha, looped over his palm, each shiny black bead revolving through his fingers. "May God keep away evil."

"Her father's been beating her and her mother."

"Lah, lah, lah." Baba shakes his head, beads circling uninterrupted.

"I have to report it, Baba. I'm bound by the law." She stands up as though she must affirm this fact to her father.

"Even if you were not, you are responsible for this child." He points at Afaf and says in English, "You are her voice."

Afaf sits back down on her bed. "Um Zuraib has gotten involved.

Layla's aunt works at the masjid. She's the one who's been calling me all day."

Baba listens, and she can see how her predicament becomes clear to him. "A child is in harm's way, habibti." He stands up and crosses to her. "You have only one choice. To help her." He kisses her forehead and closes the door behind him.

~

It's Thursday and Layla Hamad is gone.

Afaf made the phone call to DCFS on Tuesday morning in the school's social worker's office. Then she waited, miserable and worried, watching Layla closely over the next few days as she colored meticulously inside the lines on her worksheet, listened as she echoed the correct answer along with her classmates. The star on her cheek had faded some. Afaf wondered if the little girl knew how much her life was about to change.

Today Layla's desk is empty.

Mrs. Walsh pats Afaf's shoulder as they sort completed worksheets. On some Afaf has attached bright-colored stickers, a few she's stamped with *Needs Improvement*. They slide them into cubbyholes on one wall of the classroom. The students are in art class, bending colorful pipe cleaners into animal shapes and flowers.

"She'll be in a safer place, dear," Mrs. Walsh tells her.

The school social worker told Afaf yesterday, *The consequences seem harsh on a family in these cases, but in retrospect, they're necessary.* Then she dropped her voice. *I know there's a code of silence among certain ethnic groups. You did the right thing, A-faf.* Her eyes lingered on Afaf's hijab.

Ethnic groups. Code of silence. Such terms instantly evoking images of honor killings and child brides. Is that what the social worker and other staff members think of when they see her? Do they think Layla Hamad is any different than the hundreds of other children in the custody of the state of Illinois?

And what of her hijab? Do they imagine Afaf's father or brother, swarthy and dangerous men, had forced it on her? Behind her back do they whisper, *Poor A-faf, another oppressed Arabian woman?*

In the end, she is glad she'd been the one to make the call, and not Mrs. Walsh or another staff member. She's ashamed that she'd nearly confirmed their ignorant assumptions.

But Afaf still has to face the circle of women.

6

SHE CONSIDERS skipping the women's hadith lecture at the Center tonight. No one else has called since she'd hung up on Sabrine Khalil. The silence feels dangerous. Not a word from Um Zuraib, either. Does she resent Afaf's involvement, or do they consider it meddling?

Afaf decides to go and confront the inevitable. Hiding suggests she's done something wrong. Her call to DCFS was mandated by law. She'd made a choice, hadn't left it to another staff member to intervene.

Afaf pulls into the parking lot as the last strokes of orange and pink brush the horizon. November has begun to rob the day of hours. The black alder trees that line the sidewalk around the mosque have grown to their adult size since its construction. Their leaves are now brown.

The Tempest Prayer Center still takes her breath away. It was built in the image of the Dome of the Rock in Jerusalem: the golden dome flashes in the daytime and its arched windows glow at night. Like the one in the painting of the old man carrying the holy city. It's like an ancient relic plopped down in the middle of white suburbia. It faces a main road, brick houses with tidy landscapes behind it.

Afaf remembers how proud Baba was at the ribbon-cutting ceremony years ago, standing beside the imam and the other men who'd brought him back to life. It had taken much time and patience to overcome the racist bureaucracy of Tempest, where they'd found an affordable plot of land. It was originally zoned for both residential and institutional—a church or recreational center. The attorney hired on behalf of the Center had strenuously pointed out that fact to the town board members who'd protested a "religious center," despite the presence of a Lutheran church only three blocks away.

There are two archway entrances: one leads to an enormous prayer room for men; the women go through the other, which takes them down a spiral staircase to the lower level. Slabs of white marble cover the floor. The first level contains a large office where the imam performs al keetab for couples before their wedding, or he ministers to feuding families haggling over ancestral land overseas. Blue geometric flowers pattern the walls and large mosaic windows filter soft light indoors. A recreational building has been added since the original construction, including an indoor basketball court and meeting rooms.

And more progress followed: a few miles away Nurrideen School, once an old convent, opened its doors with the sponsorship of Ali Abu Nimir, offering families a way to maintain their faith while educating their children.

But there were also a few steps backward, like the refusal to integrate the sexes at popular community events, or forbidding any discussion of contraception. And now Layla. Silencing her to protect the little girl's father feels like another antiquated practice that she'd ultimately defied. Afaf hopes the consequences aren't too harsh.

In the lower level, she slips off her shoes and places them on a large shelf against one wall. The lecture begins after salat al-maghrib—the sunset prayer. She performs wudu in the communal washroom, greeting other muslimat who crouch beside her on the tiled floor, holding plastic containers, water streaming beneath them to a large drain. A young girl stands with bleached-white towels, smiling with missing teeth.

Afaf finds a spot next to Kowkab. Her friend tugs at the elastic waistband on the bottom half of her prayer clothes. She looks like a large, unsteady barrel. Most of the women wear prayer clothes that completely conceal their forms, while others attend in long-sleeved abayas with glittering designs.

"What's wrong?" her friend whispers.

Afaf hasn't told Kowkab what's happened, though her friend immediately senses something's wrong. Afaf shakes her head and she squeezes her friend's hand, attempting a smile.

Um Zuraib is at the front as usual, seated on a chair because she's unable to stand for long or get into a prostrate position. There's a special row designated for her and the elderly women: Um Sajee, the oldest woman in their circle, who'd fled the Israeli forces in 1948 and lived in a refugee camp in Lebanon for thirty years; Um Wahab, whose two sons fled the States after committing coupon fraud at their grocery store; and Um Mohammad, whose husband had given the highest undisclosed sum to the construction of the mosque.

Afaf wishes Um Zuraib would turn around and see her, give her a reassuring nod. The old woman stares straight ahead, her wrapped head poised in the direction of the loudspeaker from which the imam's voice will bellow, leading the congregation in prayer.

Afaf scans the room again, two dozen women readying themselves for worship, their hands folded over their stomachs, right over left. There's no sign of Sabrine Khalil. Relief washes over Afaf and she tries to relax and focus as the imam recites the opening: *Subhanakal-lahumma.*

For a few minutes, Afaf is comforted by the bodies that surround her, their faith emanating each time they raise their hands and kneel on the floor. A sense of clarity floods her brain and tingles all the way to her fingers and toes. By the second rak'a, Afaf breathes deeply, a calm settling deep in her bones. She can momentarily forget her frustrations, let go of the uneasiness she was carrying before she began her salat.

The first time Afaf prayed within these walls, she could smell the fresh coat of paint. She'd stood between Kowkab and her mother and sisters, Um Zuraib taking her place permanently at the front line. By that time, Afaf had learned to pray on her own and had fasted every day of Ramadan except for a week during her period. Now, as her forehead touches the blue carpet, she's overcome by that first sense of optimism that had been ignited in her years ago.

When Afaf approaches Um Zuraib after prayer, her optimism completely dissolves. She searches for understanding in the old woman's eyes, cataracts clouding the corners. But she finds none.

"He had planned to meet with the imam," Um Zuraib informs her.

"Because he was caught?" Afaf's cheeks flush hot.

Um Zuraib ignores her pointed question. "It's out of our hands now. Layla and her brothers and sisters are in foster care. With amarkan."

Not with their own people, is what she means. That they'd been yanked out of their familiar surroundings, as unstable as they were, out of their mother's arms, precariously dropped into the homes of people who don't understand them. What if the women are right? What if she'd sent Layla and her siblings to a worse fate?

It's difficult to look into Um Zuraib's eyes. She doesn't blink, the kindness gone from her eyes like stars dimming in a night sky. "He was beating them," Afaf whispers. "I had to call."

Um Zuraib kisses her on both cheeks. "You did what you believed was best. Only Allah will judge." She limps away, a few women greedily vying for her attention, guiding her to a chair for the lecture.

Afaf sinks to the floor and wraps her arms around her knees. Um Musa begins the lecture with an excerpt from the Holy Prophet's hadith:

Whoever keeps secret a shameful deed done by a Muslim, God will grant him His cover on the Day of Judgment.

7

MAJEED COMES home for the weekend. He must have sensed Afaf's misery over the phone on Friday.

She's back from morning errands and finds him at the kitchen table with Mama, holding her hand as she smokes her cigarette. This closeness still makes Afaf jealous. She can see how, if only for a short time, Majeed can sweep away the cobwebs of depression hanging so delicately over Mama, which she and Baba have not disturbed. Her own husband and daughter have been an awful disappointment, but her son can still make her smile.

Majeed hugs Afaf. His hair is cut short and neat. His face is lean, his hazel eyes more mischievous. She tries to picture him with a family one day, a beautiful muslimah at his side, but the image doesn't fully materialize. His rejection of Islam is mostly quiet and respectful: he lets Baba talk at length about redemption and the blessing of marriage to a woman who will raise his children to be good muslimeen. Majeed only nods, though sometimes Afaf catches him scowling when Baba mentions the sin of alcohol.

He's *lecturing* me? he tells Afaf in private.

It's not lecturing, Maj. He knows firsthand how it can destroy you.

Her brother snickers. *A few beers with friends? I don't buy it, Afaf. Men do far worse than that in the name of religion.*

She's found she can still be close to Majeed as long as they don't discuss religion. Afaf recites extra du'aa for her brother at the end of each prayer, hoping he'll see the path Allah has lit for him. Couldn't he see how it had transformed his own sister? Was her brother's memory so short?

Now Majeed pulls her into his arms, touches a fold in her head-scarf. "Look at you, sis! I didn't think you could do it."

She hugs him tightly and he lets her hang on. "Could or would do it?"

He laughs. "Would, I guess. How does it feel?"

Afaf pulls back, self-conscious all of a sudden. She can read it on her brother's face: Majeed think she's been brainwashed, too, like all the women he believes have been duped into submission to worth-less men.

Mama goes to the stove, sprinkles cumin into a simmering saucepan, though she meant to use allspice. "Ya rubbi!" she snaps. She slams cabinets and clanks dirty dishes in the sink.

Afaf ignores her noise. "It feels fine. I mean—it was a little weird in the beginning, but I'm getting used to it." She doesn't tell him about the sneers and heckles at the gas station, or the uncomfort-able, foreboding looks from her colleagues.

Mama throws down a spoon. It clatters against a plate. "You're a fool, Afaf. A stupid, stupid girl." She throws her head back and laughs, trying to light another cigarette with sopping-wet fingers.

"Mama, come on. Have a seat." Majeed placates her with a new cigarette, guiding her to a chair. He places it in her mouth and lights it.

How long has she been like this? he mouths to Afaf.

She shakes her head. Afaf tries not to resent her brother. Majeed's been spared the daily challenges of life with Mama—her eruptive anger, sudden and consuming, or her vacuous stare when she doesn't speak for a whole day. He'd earned his scholarship, had worked hard every day of his education, but none of it changes life at home. Her brother escaped, leaving Afaf behind. Still her mother pines for the ones who are gone—Nada, Majeed—denying her and Baba, the ones who've stayed.

Mama catches their silent exchange. "What are you whispering about me?" She throws her cigarette in the sink. "Do you think I'm stupid? That I don't see what's going on? I know more than you'll ever know!"

"What do you know?" Afaf counters. Rarely does she engage her mother's outbursts. She wants to shout that Mama doesn't have a monopoly on suffering, but Majeed grips her arm.

Mama stands close to Afaf, her breath stinking of cigarettes and coffee, her body musty. "You think you're so special now, wearing that thing? Ha! If I wear one on my head will Allah bring Nada back? Will this misery finally end?"

Afaf is stunned by the mention of her sister and she turns toward Majeed, who looks like he's been slapped in the face. An invisible presence suddenly fills the kitchen, pressing against Afaf.

Before either of them can respond, Mama lunges at Afaf, clawing at her headscarf. A pin she'd securely fastened on one side stabs her scalp.

Majeed pulls Mama off of her and Afaf stumbles backward against the stove, knocking the long handle of the saucepan. Boiling liquid sears her arm.

"Afaf! Cold water!" her brother commands. He guides her to the kitchen sink and gently rolls up her sleeve. Fortunately, the fabric has absorbed most of the scalding soup, but her arm turns pink.

Afaf winces, but she refuses to cry as their mother watches, wild-eyed. Majeed firmly holds her elbow under the running water. "Don't move."

Her eyes are trained on Mama, afraid her mother will attack her again. Mama stares vacantly at the mess on the floor, the tomato liquid dripping down the front of the stove. She takes a step toward Afaf and Afaf flinches, alerting Majeed, and he looks up.

"Mama?" her brother says. It sounds like a question, like she's someone he no longer recognizes.

Their mother mumbles something before turning and disappearing into her bedroom. The television goes on, volume raised. Majeed won't look at Afaf. He's concentrating hard on her arm, though she can feel his indignation.

As soon as Mama closes her door, Afaf sobs. The cold water temporarily soothes her burned pores. Her skin still throbs—a patch of blisters has cropped up—but she's suddenly relieved by this physical attack, like she'd been holding her breath for the last twenty years. Mama has finally struck out at her. Afaf has nothing more to fear.

Baba comes home with fatayir, special treats for Majeed's visit. He's shocked by the scene in the kitchen, Afaf's brother mopping up the mess on the floor, her arm wrapped in a sheet of paper towels. Only an hour before, Baba had left them in good spirits.

"Lah, lah, lah." Baba carefully examines Afaf's arm and insists they go to the ER. His musbaha dangles from his jacket pocket and she wants to pull it out, to hold on to something to keep her from trembling.

"It's fine, Baba. I—elhamdulillah," Afaf stammers. "Majeed put some ointment on it."

"Forgive your mother. She's not well, habibti." He places both hands on her shoulders. *"Be merciful to others and you will receive mercy. Forgive others and Allah will forgive you."*

She wants to tell her father to stop preaching to her—that Mama's the one at fault, the one who's ruined their lives. Is there a verse in the Quran that speaks about such losses? Has Baba memorized that one, too?

Afaf drops her head, looks away from Baba's watering eyes. Despite her anger, she gives silent du'aa on behalf of Mama. She's doing everything she can to be a good person, and at every turn Mama tries to derail her. Does the loss of a child negate the existence of another? Is Afaf's life not worthy, too?

~

A noise wakes her. It's like a gurgle, like water down a drain. Afaf turns over in bed, forgetting about her burned arm, immediately wincing in pain. She sits up and smoothes down the edges of the bandage. Her digital alarm clock blinks: four-thirty a.m.

A sound again. She checks the hallway, holding her arm like a broken wing. It's dark except for a thin slice of light beneath the bathroom door. She knocks, expecting Baba to answer, though it's still too early for fajr wudu and prayer. "Hello?"

That strange gurgle comes through the door. Afaf turns the knob. Mama's lying in the tub, which is half full with water. She's completely naked.

"Mama!" Afaf screams.

One slender arm dangles out of the tub. There's an empty bottle of Drāno on the floor. Chunks of vomit float on the surface of the water, along her mother's splayed legs.

"Khair inshallah!" Baba pushes Afaf out of the way. "Muntaha! Muntaha! What have you done to yourself?"

Majeed appears in the doorway. "What the fuck is happening?"

"Call 911!" Afaf shouts over her shoulder. "Hurry! Baba, help me pull her out!"

Baba and Afaf hoist Mama out of the tub, and she forgets about the pain in her arm. Though she's no more than a hundred and twenty pounds, Mama's body feels bloated and heavy, like a bag of soaked rice. Water streams from her deflated breasts, down her still-flat stomach. Her pubic hair, still dark and full against her pale skin, looks like a bird's delicate nest. Baba carefully sets her head on the tiled floor and strokes her loose hair. Her arms flop at her sides like a rag doll. He shouts, "Muntaha! Wake up! Wake up, my love!"

"Mama, open your eyes. Yalla, Mama!" Afaf slaps her mother's cheeks. A flutter of movement beneath her lids. "Come on, Mama! Wake up! Wake up!"

Majeed hands her a towel and Afaf covers her up. "They're on their way," he says.

"Yalla, Mama! You need to open your eyes."

"Will she be okay?" Majeed's eyes are wide with the same terror Afaf recognizes from when they were kids that night they heard the detective telling their parents about "a body found" at the old stockyard. Or at the hospital when the police officer suggested that Baba could have died in the crash.

Afaf listens to Mama's chest; her heart beats softly but steadily.

A siren wails in the distance, then a thunder of footsteps up the staircase to their floor. Before they have a chance to knock, Majeed lets the paramedics in.

"Miss, give us some room," a female paramedic orders.

Afaf gently places her mother's head on the floor.

"You all need to stay in the hallway so we can help your mother." She places a stethoscope in her ears and leans over Mama's chest. She looks up at Baba. "Sir, is this your wife? Sir?"

Baba's face is ashen. Afaf grips his arm and he gives a weak nod, as if in acknowledging it he'll be blamed for her near-death.

"Any idea how long ago she drank the liquid?"

Baba shakes his head again.

Afaf's pajama top is soaked through and she touches her bare head, realizing the male paramedic has seen her without her hijab. But he's not paying attention to Afaf. He's busy covering Mama's nose and mouth with a respirator while his partner checks her blood pressure. They lift her onto a stretcher and strap her in.

Afaf clutches the wet towel to her chest. She can still feel Mama's heartbeat against her ear like a faint drum.

8

BABA PARKS in an underground garage and they climb out of the car, the cacophony of slamming doors eerily amplified inside the cement structure. They enter a different wing than the last time they were here, after Baba's crash. How terrified Afaf and Majeed had been that night in the ER.

Baba holds the elevator and the three of them enter. Afaf searches the directory of floors on the laminated placard:

LEVEL 3: PSYCHIATRIC HEALTH & CARE

A week later, Mama's transferred from the poison unit. Afaf wonders if this is the floor where Mama had stayed when she'd had a nervous breakdown. Is that the natural sequence of events, she wonders. You lose a child, have a nervous breakdown, attempt suicide. And how do you go back to your life when you've failed at ending it? Do you simply wait for the misery to swallow you up one day?

Afaf had heard about arabiyyat drinking Drāno or Mr. Clean, trying to teach their cheating or abusive husbands a lesson. She'd once overheard Khalti Nesreen telling Mama about a woman she knew from Milwaukee who'd succeeded. Her own children came home from school and found her lifeless poisoned body curled on the floor.

A white couple enters the elevator behind them. They stare at her and she instinctively touches the hem of her hijab, a habit she's developed. She's growing accustomed to it, even forgetting she's wearing it at times, until others remind her with their furrowed brows and pursed lips. They stare at Baba, too, with his skullcap, his musbaha looped across his hand. She can sense Majeed's body tightening, readying himself for a fight. Afaf hooks her pinkie finger on his and gently tugs it, restraining him.

They exit into a hospital wing decorated in pastel blue and green. Framed prints of Monet's haystacks cover the walls. At one station, two nurses wearing bright-patterned scrubs smile at them as they approach the desk. Afaf expects a muted mood, to match the hollowness she feels inside.

They walk down a corridor past patients' rooms with curtains drawn around the beds; a few doors are closed. A doctor speaks with two women—a mother and daughter, Afaf guesses—outside one of the closed rooms. Tears stream down the young girl's face.

Mama's room is open, the curtain pulled back from her bed. Her eyes sink in dark circles, her cheeks are gaunt. She looks like an aging sorceress, once beautiful and bright. Her gray hair fans out like silk against the white pillows. An IV drip hangs beside the bed. Mama's hands are in restraints, black cuffs enclosing her thin wrists.

"Salaam," Baba softly greets her. He sets a small Quran on her bedside.

Mama tilts her head in the direction of his voice, pulling her gaze away from the window. Majeed immediately moves to her side, gently lifts her hand. He chokes up at Mama's bound wrists. "Are these really necessary?" he asks, sniffling.

Afaf is quiet and remains frozen at the door, fingering the edge of a fresh bandage Majeed gently wrapped around her arm.

Mama looks feverish and her pupils are dilated. "I want to go home," she croaks.

Baba holds her other hand, the restraint grazing his fingers. "Inshallah you'll be discharged soon, and—"

"No. I want to go home." She tries to lift her arms, but the cuffs only permit them to move a few inches above her body. "Home," she repeats, with all the emphasis she can muster for a single word.

Afaf glances at Majeed and they watch Baba's face drain of blood, the same as when they found her in the tub only a week before. They understand what Mama is asking for.

All this time, Mama's been a ghost, wandering the present, searching for a portal to the past where she'd once been a young girl, carefree. Nobody's mother, nobody's wife. Only Muntaha, free from grief, treading lightly as a child who hasn't known pain beyond a scuffed knee or a sprained ankle, hasn't had a part of herself stolen from her.

Afaf had never imagined Mama had any other aspirations beyond motherhood—and she'd sorely failed that in Afaf's eyes. Had Mama suppressed other dreams of being someone else, not the mother of a lost child? Not the wife of a broken man? Something washes over Afaf as she studies her mother, in restraints, denied any control. For the first time, Afaf sees Mama as a shattered woman.

Baba nods at Mama's request, choked up. "Whatever you desire, habibti."

Mama turns back to the window and her fingers slip from their hands, letting them go.

Nurrideen School
for Girls

SHE WAS a slim woman. Her long-sleeved garment was loose-fitting, revealing a slight swelling of her bosom. Layers of fabric confined her limbs, a black headscarf tight around her head, the folds rippling at her neck. It was unsettling: her face and the skin of her hands were the only parts of her he could see. Her eyes were brown as hazelnuts, boring into him, her terror reflecting in each like pools of water. Tears streamed down her face and she continuously wiped them away with her sleeve. She fought to keep her composure, though she didn't make a sound—not a whimper.

"What are you doing in here?" he asked the Muslim woman. It seemed unlikely to him that she'd chosen this place to hide. The first-floor exit was only a few feet away; she could have easily pushed through the doors as soon as she heard the gunfire, joining the others who were safely outside. She must have been occupying this space before he entered the building. Perhaps he'd just missed her when he rounded the corner.

"I— Nothing," she stammered. He could see her working out her answer, gauging his reaction. She glanced at a small green rug on the floor, a pair of leather mules stacked neatly beside it. "I was praying."

With his rifle, he gestured for her to sit down on the solitary chair. She hesitated for a moment, glancing again at her shoes. When she settled onto the cushion she gripped the armrests, her torso straight and rigid. The lower half of her body trembled, and her chin quivered. She was completely attentive.

He studied the space. A table with a gold-embossed book. No other furniture. On the ceiling he followed a metal track running from one side to the other, splitting the room in half. He imagined a curtain had once hung down, separating the priest from the confessor.

He'd hated going to confession when he was a kid. His mother dragged him and his brother Joe every Thursday evening while their father waited in his pickup truck outside of St. Matthew's. He and his brother sat stiffly on a wooden bench across from the confessional, their mother inside. He'd wondered what she could possibly be confessing. She worked hard to make them a home, and what did she get in return? A man who seemed to despise the world. Why wasn't his father in there confessing his sins?

His own transgressions were relatively minor: cursing at Joe, drinking an extra bottle of rationed milk. He'd never confess to immoral thoughts of harming his father, or masturbating in the shower. While they waited their turn, he and Joe made funny faces at each other, each challenging the other to laugh first and break the somber quiet of the church. Behind them in the lonely pews, old women wearing short lace veils murmured prayers on their knees, rosaries tucked between their folded hands.

He couldn't tell anything about this Muslim woman behind her watery eyes and quivering chin. Her folded olive-skinned hands trembled in her lap, and he studied a solid gold wedding band that she rubbed with her forefinger.

He and Eileen never talked about marriage, easing into a life of cohabitation that resembled something like love—a close and simple companionship. The first time they had sex, he traced a finger over a thin and long scar on her thigh, like a stroke from a fine-tipped brush.

Lover's quarrel, she'd snorted. She lay flat on her back, her arm across his chest, and told him about her abusive ex-boyfriend who'd beaten her so badly she was in the hospital for a week. She'd lost her job as a secretary and for a long while waitressed until she could find something better.

"You got kids?" he asked the woman.

"Yes. Two boys and a girl." She hadn't taken her eyes off the rifle—had she looked at him closely? If in a miracle she'd make it out alive, could she identify him? He'd been invisible his whole life. Today that would change forever.

He leaned against the door, his rifle still trained on her. He was suddenly exhausted, but remained alert.

"My daughter attends here." She paused. "She's a senior. Her name's Az—"

"Shut up. You think I'll feel sorry for you if you tell me their names? You're ruining this country. Your people, your evil religion."

He remembered that day. He was at home in the morning; he'd been assigned second-shift at his heating-and-cooling job. All alone, he watched raw video of two planes colliding into two hundred thousand tons of steel. It was surreal, like a sci-fi invasion—unlike anything that could plausibly happen in his country, the most powerful nation in the world. Newscasters cut into the footage to report what they knew so far. President Bush had been reading to a bunch of second-graders in Florida when the first plane hit.

Eileen called him from the restaurant. *Holy Christ*, she whispered into the phone. He could hear her coworkers sobbing in the background.

It was all anyone talked about in his online chat groups: the 9/11 terrorists. Members declared positions that were as sound as an overhaul of pilot licensing, and as extreme as corralling all the Muslims until the government could get to the bottom of the attack:

Quit looking for 1 mastermind . . . Every Muslim is an enemy of the state.
Now will you take away my right to bear arms? Fuck dems and liberals and Political Correctness!
A holy war has begun . . .

He'd had no direct interactions with Muslims, though he'd suddenly seemed surrounded by them in Tempest when he moved from Chicago. They'd be in line in front of him at the Walmart, their kids pulling candy bars off the checkout shelf despite their mother's admonishment, or they'd be stopped at a traffic light beside him, women in headscarves perched behind the steering wheels of their luxury SUVs.

He'd started carrying a gun outside of the range, as times were increasingly dangerous according to the men at his shooting clubs and from what he'd been reading online. He'd started stowing a small handgun in the glove compartment of his car, keenly aware of it when he walked across a parking lot in a shopping mall and passed black teenagers hooting and hollering at each other.

The more he delved into the internet, the more alarmist the sites became, gripping him to his desk chair in the front room while Eileen knitted and watched *Wheel of Fortune*. Every blog transmitted information like an oracle proffering omens of a soon-to-be-destroyed society if his race did not rise up against every visible adversary. There was little sense of hope, only a resounding call to battle.

Afterward, he'd be in a terrible mood, Eileen wondering what had overcome him when she'd come home from her shift at the IHOP.

The hell's gotten into you? she'd say as he slammed kitchen cabinets. *It's that crap you're reading on the computer, isn't it?*

Never mind, he'd tell her, grabbing Jeni's leash for a brisk walk to shake off his anger. He'd cut through the park across from the Willow Wood Apartments, children gleefully shrieking as they barreled down slides and bounced on seesaws.

Now, over a decade since 9/11 and the cataclysmic failure of the Obama administration, the most popular topic was still Islam—"*Will You Submit to Sharia Law?*"—and thousands of users left comments detailing incidents where they'd clashed with "Mussies" and "Hajjis." One member had reported almost strangling a woman with her own headscarf. "*Makes it easier to lynch these koran-thumping whores—they supply the noose.*"

When the body of a little boy washed up on a Mediterranean shore, he'd felt numb. Eileen had covered her mouth in horror as she watched the news report. He'd already seen it on his Facebook feed:

Wish they'd all drown.
Like the Red Sea purging the Egyptians . . .

He studied the woman in front of him. He remembered the village hall meetings he'd attended, smoldering in his chair as a brown-skinned lawyer argued before the board to reopen the convent, make it a school for Muslim boys. He'd volunteered to pass out flyers at local grocery stores and the public library protesting the project.

The woman looked back, shifting her gaze from his rifle to his face. "I'm sorry for your pain," she said quietly. "We can talk about it."

The sirens wailed. How much time had passed since he'd entered the building? The only shard of natural light came from beneath the door. The light bulb cast a shadow of the woman's head—the shape of a cave in a distant mountain.

"What do you know about it?" he sneered. "You don't care a goddamn bit about me or this country. You don't belong here."

"I was born in this country—just like you," she said, leaning forward, her hands fluttering like birds in her lap.

"Yeah? You sure don't fucking act like it." He shook his head vehemently. "Naw, lady, you don't belong here at all."

And he believed it now. It was a message that suddenly resounded louder than all the times he'd heard it or read it online over the years: *They don't belong here.*

Like most true citizens, he'd perceived them as mere outsiders, a nuisance. But everything changed on 9/11. Now they were killing innocent citizens with their suicide missions, believing their Allah would gift them with virgins in paradise. On that fatal morning, he clocked in at work and headed toward the break room to store his lunch when the planes crashed into the World Trade Center.

"I'm not your enemy," the woman suddenly blurted. She shifted in her chair and he instinctively raised his rifle chest-height again.

"Yes, you are," he responded. She happened to be one kind of enemy he'd encountered up close.

2002

1

"WE SHOULD cancel hajj," Afaf says, pouring almond slivers into a saucepan sizzling with butter.

Bilal sighs as he sets the kitchen table. "I will not allow monsters masquerading as muslimeen to control our lives. The trip is paid for. We are going."

Her husband's English—no contractions, no slang—is as meticulous as his place setting: he folds the paper napkins precisely, like hospital corners on sheets.

Bilal pretends he hasn't lost three more clients this week, one who'd told him she was taking her business elsewhere, to "real Americans." Another client apologized profusely when he closed his account with Bilal, confessing his fear of the feds. Bilal continues to reassure Afaf that his financial consulting firm will survive the country's backlash. *After all*, he'd said, *most of my clients are muslimeen.*

Ayman ambles into the kitchen on small crutches. "I'm hungry."

"Soon." Bilal helps their seven-year-old son onto a kitchen chair. Ayman sprained his ankle sledding with neighborhood kids. He props his bandaged leg on another chair, his little body parallel with the table. He's grown nimble at maneuvering around the house on one leg. It amazes Afaf how resilient children are. His first scrape, his first lost tooth sent Afaf into hysteria, yet how quickly her son overcomes any physical setback, how quickly he adapts to new conditions.

"I'm worried about my father," she insists, stirring the almonds, careful not to burn them as they turn golden in the bubbling butter. The kitchen is pungent with the aroma of yogurt and lamb. "How can he travel in this terrible climate?"

"It is his choice, draga moja," Bilal says. "You can try to persuade him, but you will be wasting your time." He eyes their son. "No games at the table, Ayman."

Their son grudgingly powers off the Game Boy and stows the console in his sweatshirt pocket.

Afaf turns off the flame under the almonds and stirs a pot of rice. "And what about you? They might not let you leave the country."

Bilal sighs again. "They cannot prevent me from traveling, Afaf. No matter how much they try to intimidate me."

It doesn't help that Bilal's the head of a halal consulting firm that helps muslimeen properly disperse their interest into charitable organizations to avoid riba. It is perhaps what's most interesting to the intelligence agencies. Bilal's dream of starting a financial business that observes halal practices had come true, only to fall under federal suspicion.

Would they be prevented from going to hajj, to a country that was the cradle of Islam and home to fifteen of the nineteen hijackers? Bilal is much more optimistic than Afaf. She's ready to postpone their pilgrimage for another year or two. Since September, she's heard too many stories of men and women—some of them teenagers—detained without cause, barred from legal representation. From the circle of women, Lamise Abu Nasser's brother-in-law has not been heard from in three months since his detainment in Connecticut. In Brooklyn, a group of underage boys from a mosque were taken into custody, their parents unable to see them until they appeared before a circuit judge. A college student from Fairfax, Virginia, was interrogated for eighteen hours after she posted comments about illegal arrests on her Muslim blog. Dozens of stories emerge every week, terrifying Afaf.

Her son Ayman shifts in his chair, listening, his brows furrowing as he tries to comprehend their conversation. The day after the planes collided, a classmate called him a terrorist, a word he'd never heard before, as insidious to Afaf as *rapist* or *pedophile*. Words that make adults cringe, yet too awful for a child to hear, let alone be called.

When Afaf became a mother, she'd stopped sleeping soundly, her ears perking at the slightest cough or whimper. She lay on her back, rubbing the scar on her arm from the boiling soup her mother had spilled so many years ago. She tries to avoid the news, though the faces of the terrorists—nineteen men who were once sons, brothers, husbands—haunt her everywhere she goes. The mushrooming clouds invade her prayers. How could so many lives be taken in the name of God? It's not her God or Baba's, the one who'd saved them both.

Sometimes Bilal stirs awake and they make sudden love, clinging to each other in that early morning darkness before he drifts off again. It's more frequent these days, like new lovers discovering each other all over again. She listens to Bilal's soft snoring, her body pressed against him, his broad back like a reservoir wall, holding her in.

Then the alarm clock sounds and she prepares for a new day to teach at Nurrideen School, where three hundred young muslimat in defiant hijab arrive. Before joining the Islamic girls' school, Afaf taught in Chicago, combatting unemployment and poverty, gangs and daily violence. Skin color determined how much funding their school would have, what her students' neighborhoods looked like. Now it's a child's religious upbringing—their faith—that incites hateful vandalism on their family's garage, or being spit at in the parking lot of the Walmart.

They'd gone from *towel-heads* to *terrorists*.

Afaf's unwilling to take off her hijab, though it sometimes feels heavy. A week after the towers fell, she considered it: *Just for a little while, until things settle down,* her brother Majeed had urged her. But it felt more like a humiliating surrender than protection. How many people had died rather than denounce their own beliefs? It seems they've always engaged in this strange dance with their Christian brothers and sisters.

It's not the same God, a white teacher at her last school had declared. She and Afaf had been debating the commonalities of Christianity and Islam. Her coworker balked at the notion that they were worshipping the same biblical Lord. Afaf had brought her literature the Center had produced in an effort to forge interfaith relations among their communities. Afaf saw the pamphlet lying on top of a heap of discarded foam coffee cups in the staff break room.

A few muslimat from the Nur Society have taken off their hijabs—Suha Bakri, and one of Kowkab's sisters—their husbands worry about their safety. Just last week Afaf heard about a woman who was shoved and kicked by a white couple at a supermarket while she was unloading her groceries. Others hadn't been so lucky to escape with mere injuries. Afaf grimly recalls the images on the news of women donning blond wigs to deter Son of Sam, the same year Nada disappeared.

Last month Afaf had gone into a Victoria's Secret at the mall to purchase a bridal shower gift for one of the younger women. A middle-aged white woman and her friend had sneered at her as she carried a lacy negligee to the salesclerk: *Isn't it a sin for them to shop here?* As if muslimat were incapable of being sensuous beings. Or did not wear underwear. But she hadn't turned around to argue these things with those white women. She'd simply purchased her gift and left, eyes straight ahead to the exit.

Haven't women always been most vulnerable in difficult times? Sister Nabeeha reminds them at the women's hadith lecture about the special burden they carry. *We experience the pain of menstruation, of first intercourse, then hours of labor and years of rearing our children.*

They nod, the younger girls blushing at the mention of sex.

But those burdens are no less gifts. We will be exalted in His kingdom. Did not the Prophet, peace be upon Him, declare, 'Heaven lies under the feet of your mother'? Nabeeha charges them, *Sisters, do not abandon your hijab. We can withstand more than men.*

Still, several women have resorted to hats with low brims instead of colorful headscarves.

Akram scampers into the kitchen and tugs at Afaf's shirt. "Mama! Can I feed the fish?" Her five-year-old hops from one foot to the other. Akram favors his father, thick brown hair with a natural side part, penetrating amber eyes.

"No, habibi. You fed them this morning." She tickles his stomach. Akram giggles and squirms.

"Come, baby, wash your hands for dinner." Bilal swoops Akram off the floor, their son's shrill laughter echoing down the hallway.

There's a ring at the front door, then Baba's shuffling feet, his cane clacking against ceramic tile in the foyer.

"Salaam, habibti. Your favorite." Baba hands Afaf a brown paper sack with grease stains on the bottom. He holds her face with both hands and kisses each cheek. He steps back and she sees how much her father has aged. Perhaps it's this trip to hajj, or perhaps it's how the world has just turned topsy-turvy—Baba looks like an old man, no longer virile and straight-backed. He leans against his cane, shoulders stooped. His body seems to shrink with every passing year.

"Thank you, Baba." Tangy sumac spices and chopped onions permeate from the bag: spinach pies. Afaf finishes spooning steaming rice onto a platter and sprinkles the golden almonds on top.

"Smells good," Baba says. He loves Afaf's mensaf, though she predicts he'll only have a few bites before putting down his fork. His appetite has diminished over the last few months. He refuses to talk about anything regarding his health. It's a battle seeing to his blood pressure medication and daily supplements. Since Mama moved to Palestine, Afaf and Bilal have asked him repeatedly to move in with them so that she can better monitor his condition, but he refuses. Baba still lives in the old apartment in Chicago. Nearly every white person has left her old neighborhood; now it's mostly young immigrant families from Mexico with whom Baba exchanges greetings in English. Afaf and Bilal purchased a home in Tempest to be closer to the Center.

When Afaf frets over a missed dosage of his latest prescription, he tells her, "It's in Allah's hands, habibti."

This has been Baba's way: this unquestionable surrender of his health to God despite his doctor's recommendations. And it's the same for everything else in his life—financial matters, the plight of the Palestinians.

Everything except when it comes to Mama. Afaf doubts there's any verse in the holy book that has eased Baba's loneliness. It's been nearly eight years and he still misses her. She's returned to her parents' home, residing with her younger brother's family. Mama will never come back to the States. Baba's pride keeps him from traveling to Palestine without her invitation, though she and Majeed have the means to send him. When Afaf dutifully calls her long-distance, Mama refuses to speak to Baba, only politely asking Afaf and Majeed about him as though he's a distant relative.

Still, Baba wires her money every month like he's paying off some exorbitant debt he owes Mama. Afaf and Majeed, too. For Eid, she sends Mama pajamas and house slippers, and kitchenware for Mama's sister-in-law Huda.

Your mother is too quiet, habibti, Huda chirps on a long-distance call. *She's in her own world. And all that walking she does! No wonder she still has her girlish figure.* Her aunt's tone is a tad more than envious.

Mama never went on walks, barely left the apartment, in Chicago. Afaf tries to picture the villagers watching Mama with awe as she strolls down their dusty roads like a prodigal daughter returned from a failed life. To them, she's a cautionary tale that America isn't a land of dreams, but one of nightmares, a place that snatches your child and ruins your marriage.

"Have a seat, Baba." Afaf pulls out a kitchen chair for him. He waddles over to Ayman, pats his grandson's hair.

"Keefak, habibi?"

"Salaam, Siddo Mahmood." Ayman kisses the back of Baba's hand as Bilal has taught their sons to do. "I don't want to go back to school tomorrow."

"You're going," Afaf says.

Baba slowly lowers himself in the chair. "Where's my other boy?"

"Here he is," Bilal says, Akram bobbing at his heels.

"Ahlan! Ahlan!" Baba kisses Akram's head and holds it for a moment longer, his lips moving in du'aa. He pulls out his musbaha and with his other hand he tugs at his short beard. "I was at the hospital with Benjamin. Maskeen. It's very bad."

Mr. Parker, Baba's longtime friend, is dying. She remembers, so many years ago, a bear of a man sitting in her mother's kitchen, arguing about systemic racism. "May Allah give him strength. How are his wife and Ashanti? I haven't seen them at the masjid."

"They spend every moment with Benjamin at the hospital. They would be pleased to see you, habibti."

"Inshallah next week."

Baba turns to Bilal. "How's your mother?"

"Elhamdulillah, Uncle. She started dialysis." Something pitches in Bilal's voice, imperceptible unless you're listening closely. He escorts his mother to every treatment and stays with her for four hours, three times a week. They speak in their native tongue, remembering what it was like before the war. He taps away at his laptop, evaluating financial portfolios while his mother's blood flushes through tubes, a steady humming in the small room at the dialysis center. A nurse sits across from an imposing machine, monitoring the procedure.

His mother still sings to Akram at naptime a folk song from the country she'd fled forever with her own two children:

> *Maghrib has come, the sun went down,*
> *The shine is left on your face.*
> *Maghrib has come, your face*
> *Shines more beautiful because of the sun.*

I would like to warm myself
In the beauty of your face.

Baba turns back to Afaf. "Have you heard from Majeed?"

"Yes. He's fine. Still working on that settlement for that food service." Afaf speaks to her brother once a week, suspecting he might
not call her if she didn't initiate their conversations.

The real question twinkles in Baba's eyes. "Have you spoken to your mother?" He thumbs his musbaha, pretending to be
nonchalant.

"Yesterday." Afaf pours him a glass of pomegranate juice. "There
was a muzzahara after the Friday prayer. Two shot dead."

"Lah, lah, lah. Allah yarhamhum. May the Lord grant them
patience and peace." Baba looks at her, eager for some personal message, a sentiment from Mama that she misses him, too.

"Mama sends her regards," Afaf tells him, refusing to delude him
with false messages. Perhaps it's cruel, denying an old man some
slice of joy. But Afaf believes she's no crueler than Mama, who'd left
her wedding band behind on her dresser. Afaf had hid it before Baba
discovered her mother had discarded it.

He looks down at his musbaha, but not before she catches his
eyes clouding over, his shoulders sinking at Mama's indifference.
Mama remains as distant as ever, by an ocean and her own poisoned
mind. She might never know Afaf's sons, that each has one dimpled
cheek, or that Ayman always sleeps on his back, how Akram stutters
when he's excited. And she'll never know that Afaf learned to prepare meals from cookbooks and from recipes the women from the
Center swap after hadith lectures. Afaf has made a good life without
her mother's guidance, and yet Mama's absence looms like someone

erased from a photograph, leaving an empty space to which your eyes are perpetually drawn in the frame.

Afaf changes the subject. "Baba, we've been talking about going to hajj. I think we should postpone it until next year."

Baba gestures with his musbaha. "Why delay it? Are you worried about the boys?"

Afaf is the youngest muslimah to travel to hajj this year from the circle of women, some of them surprised that she'd leave behind her two young sons. She and Bilal have had long conversations about it, had decided a summer ago. They want to fulfill this important pillar while they're relatively young and fit.

Who knows what next year might bring? Bilal says. Her husband keenly understands how, in a precarious whim, life can force you to flee from your country, after your father has been brutally executed. He's taught Afaf to never plan too far ahead, to appreciate every waking moment, no matter the hardship that accompanies it. Together they watched two planes hurtle through the World Trade Center, instantaneous flames revealing how dangerously short life can be.

Afaf sits across from Baba at the table and serves him first. "It's you I'm concerned about, Baba. Are you sure you want to do this again?"

The first time her father planned to fulfill hajj, Baba had thrown himself into prayer, spending hours reading the Quran and performing du'aa, Mama glaring at him from the kitchen sink. His musbaha had become a new appendage of his hand, the beads in a perpetual cycle through his thumb and fingers. The prospect of a second pilgrimage seemed to offer some solace; the old light in his eyes flicked on from time to time.

Baba holds his hand up, halting another heaping scoop of rice. "I must go. When a Muslim cannot make the journey himself, another can go in his place." He's going for Mama, though she's not asked him to.

When Baba returned from hajj the first time, Mama had stood in the corner of her bedroom as he unpacked his suitcase, pulling out tiny bottles of Zamzam water and mosaic jewelry boxes inlaid with mother-of-pearl. He handed each gift to Afaf, who gathered them in her arms. Mama had sneered with contempt.

He'd also come home with a urinary tract infection. How much can his battered body stand anymore?

"I know you can go in someone's place, Baba." She wants to say, *But Mama doesn't want you to do this on her behalf—doesn't want you—can't you see that?* Instead she argues, "But Allah overlooks such things when he knows what's in your heart—your neeya. You've already made the journey."

"And I plan to do it again with you and my son." He pats Bilal's arm and her husband looks at Afaf with an expression of, *I told you so.*

"It's the timing, Baba. I think it's not a good year—" She instantly winces at her choice of words. But it's too late.

" 'A good year'? When is it *not* a good year if one's body can carry him to that holy place?"

"That's not what I meant, Baba. I—"

He holds up his musbaha. "Nothing can stand in our path towards God. We cannot give in to fear, habibti. Muslimeen have endured worse in the history of man. We cannot lose faith."

Ayman and Akram are oblivious to the adults' conversation, making goofy faces at each other, tapping their bowls with their spoons until Bilal hushes them.

Baba is obstinately ignorant of how much the world has changed. He thinks he can still talk to strangers about Allah and the Prophet and amarkan will be amused by this old man who speaks with an accent, recounting verses from a mysterious text. The Islam they've seen on TV is a dangerous religion that plunges through buildings with planes, regardless of life. She'd wondered, too, how these men had come upon this path of destruction. The liberal news outlets debated the failure of U.S. policy, that somehow this heinous act could be at least understood. It is still beyond Afaf's own understanding. She reads the same scripture, prostrates in the same direction toward the Ka'aba, utters verses in the same language. And still there is no reconciling their Islam with hers.

Afaf leans back in her chair. Bilal takes over serving the food, the boys eagerly holding out their bowls. She can see she's getting nowhere with Baba. A part of her is afraid that the pilgrimage will take an irreversible toll on his frail body; another part is happy the three of them will be together in that holiest of places.

Afaf only wishes Majeed could be with them. He seems to move farther and farther away from her and Baba. First to law school in St. Paul, then to a firm in Indianapolis. Now he's accepted an offer from a firm in Sacramento, will move again across the country, a single man, no wife and children.

Her brother hasn't been quite the same after the night they'd discovered Mama in the bathtub, her body bobbing naked in the vomit-filled water. He blames Baba, Afaf knows it, and perhaps he's resented Afaf, too, all these years.

Religion doesn't make reality go away, he'd said bitterly to Afaf in one of many arguments they've had.

*But it shields us from the ugliness sometimes. We need that, Maj.
Even if it's not permanent. Isn't this what civilizations have been doing
since the dawn of time? Since the Mayans and Greeks? It isn't mass
delusion, as you call it. It's the most primitive human instinct. Religion
eases suffering, Maj.*

It was the first time she'd shut him up. But not for long.

It couldn't help Mama, he'd challenged. And now the attack by
so-called Muslims. Majeed had sounded bitterly vindicated.

Afaf shreds some lamb for Akram and watches her boys vying
for their grandfather's attention, not permitting him to get a word
in edgewise. Baba smiles and nods, slowly chewing, making a show
of eating. After dinner, each boy takes her father's hand and he lets
them guide him to the family room, where he'll strum his oud. It's
too cumbersome to carry back and forth from his apartment; Baba
is content to leave it at her house, playing only for her children nowadays. It's one of two artifacts from her childhood: the record player
sits on a console in the family room, a stack of old records untouched
beneath it. Sometimes Afaf will play *Hair* while she's mopping the
kitchen floor or folding laundry, amused by the erotic lyrics to which
she and Majeed had been blithely ignorant as children.

Bilal stacks the dishes on the counter and wipes down the table.
He touches the small of her back as she stands at the sink rinsing
dishes. She lifts her face toward him and he kisses her, his lips soft
like the bristles of a paintbrush.

A song about a tiny bird floats into the kitchen:

*A tear fell on its cheek. Its wings tucked underneath it,
It landed on the ground and said, "I want to walk, but I can't."*

It's the same one Baba sang to her and Majeed, their favorite Marcel Khalife song. Baba plucks the strings with his pick, Ayman and Akram listen intently and smile up at their grandfather from the floor. The music drifts to her, each note lingering a beat longer in her ears, the melody slower, more melancholic. The song is a sad one, but she hadn't paid close attention until she heard him first sing it to Ayman. Now it sounds like a brand-new song though it has always been so familiar. Afaf hadn't been listening closely.

2

THEY FINALIZE their will and fax it to Majeed. In case Afaf and Bilal don't return, Esma will take custody of her boys, and all of Afaf's material possessions will be liquidated into their trust fund, which Bilal carefully prepared. Her gold dowry from Bilal—among them a beautiful pair of bangles, and a heart-shaped pendant and earrings set—will be equally divided between her sons, her clothes given to the Nur Society of Sisters, her books to a local library. The old beloved record player will be shared—six months with Ayman, six months with Akram. Her brother Majeed had long relinquished his rights to it, another relic discarded from his past. Instead, she offers him Mama's wedding band and pair of gold earrings in the shape of almonds that she rarely wore. Bilal has his great-grandfather's gold pocket watch, curlicues carved onto its protective case. It's the only thing he'd managed to hold on to when his family fled the Balkans.

This part had been easier than Afaf imagined: counting up what they owned, declaring its value, and dividing it up. But what about the things that really mattered? How do you stipulate them? There's no space in a will for how to raise her sons to be dignified and strong, or the number of times to hug them in a single day until they're finally able to pull away, or how to watch for the slightest trace of heartbreak or fear—no matter how much they'll try to disguise it—or how to treat all whom they love with respect and constant affection.

At the Center, Sister Nabeeha pans the room of women, preparing them for hajj. Her eyes are sharp and alert, like a schoolteacher's. *What's left to do once you've taken care of your will and debts? Forgiveness. You must seek forgiveness from anyone you've wronged.*

She's asked for Baba's forgiveness, though he'd brushed her off, gently grabbing Afaf's face, kissing her forehead. *You are my best daughter.*

She hadn't been good enough for Mama, could never ascend to the heights of pleasing her mother—even after Nada has been gone all these years.

And what of forgiving others? she wants to ask Sister Nabeeha. Had the time come for her to forgive Mama? Did it even matter anymore? Her mother excised herself from them like a machete that slices off a finger, the stub bleeding for a long time before new skin grafts the wound and scar tissue appears—the only evidence she'd been there in the first place.

Afaf calls her the day before her flight and Mama tells her two neighbors are also making the pilgrimage.

"Allah protect them," Afaf says.

"Yes. They are fairly young women, though Um Sameer already has six grandchildren." She doesn't sneer about it and Afaf wonders if being back home has softened her mother's view about religion. Perhaps when you hear the muezzin's call to prayer five times a day you finally relent to your hijab-covered neighbors who nag you over for tea. You begin to see things in a new way. Or perhaps your losses have finally blunted to a bearable throb.

"Forgive me, Mama." The words dart out of Afaf's mouth. For what is she asking her mother's forgiveness? Never being able to replace her sister? Twenty-six years later, Nada's face appears less frequently to Afaf, sometimes emerging from the corner of a long day like a shadow elongated across the floor. She no longer sees her sister in public places and she wonders if it's because she's stopped looking for her. But Mama could never let Nada go.

Her mother clears her throat on the line. "May you safely return to your children, habibti."

Afaf hangs up and opens a tiny notebook of du'aa from the circle of women, a ledger of all the prayers they want her to say on their behalf—for their parents to recover quickly from surgery, for their brothers with legal problems, for their children's safekeeping during this ominous time. She'll be praying in a place believed to be closest to the ear of the Lord.

Afaf also will pray earnestly for her mother. That's all there's left to do.

~

Before Afaf, Bilal, and Baba head to O'Hare International Airport, they say goodbye to the boys at Esma's house. Her sister-in-law's children quickly steal her sons' attention, and they squirm out of her arms to go play. The only tears shed are Afaf's.

Esma hugs her tightly. "Say prayers for my mother, draga moja. My brother will take care of you and Abu Majeed. Do not worry."

Afaf nods, dabbing at her eyes with the sleeve of her overcoat. Esma and Bilal exchange three kisses on alternating cheeks, a tender gesture they share with their mother. He pulls his sister close for a long embrace.

"Allah be with you," Esma says, waving from the driveway.

Snow crunches under the taxi's tires as they pull away, leaving behind naked maple trees and gray sky. In twenty hours, they'll be in a desert where the Prophet once traveled to deliver his final sermon. An ancient place Afaf has only seen in books and on TV.

The international terminal at O'Hare is a mix of citizens and foreigners: brown-skinned and blue-eyed; women in colorful saris under winter coats; men in patterned dashikis and hats. It's a blend of ethnic and Western fashions.

There's a flock of muslimeen bidding tearful goodbyes to their adult children. Her heart lifts at the sight. She's been dreading the airport. It's comforting to see fellow pilgrims. As she passes them, Afaf catches white strangers staring at this display. Can they detect the notes of love ringing in the wishes and blessings these families exchange for a safe journey to hajj? Or do they only see potential terrorists standing before them?

They approach the security queue and a female officer waves Afaf over. "You'll need to remove that"—she points at Afaf's head-scarf—"and your coat." Afaf touches the zipper of her abaya, royal-blue, tiny pearl beads on the hem and sleeves.

Bilal steps forward. "Miss, this is ridiculous."

"It's TSA policy. If you refuse to remove these articles of clothing, we'll need to search you in private, ma'am."

"Do you think she is concealing something under her scarf?" Bilal says in a loud voice. People around them are suddenly more alert and skittish: *Will this man attack us?* Afaf can see the question furrowing in their brows.

She squeezes Bilal's hand, placating him, wanting to end the quiet spectacle around them. "It's fine. I'll see you on other side, okay? Take care of my father."

"Don't worry, habibti," Baba tells her. "We'll be waiting for you."

Afaf is led to a small area siphoned off by tall partitions. She hears the regular traffic of people on the other side of the partition, the loading of small bags and electronic devices on the conveyer belts, metal detector wands beeping.

"Please undress to your undergarments."

Afaf strips down to her long slip. A beautiful woman stands across from her, her white cotton bra and half-slip gleaming against her black skin. She looks over at Afaf, her eyes impassive. Afaf closes her eyes as another female officer waves a metal detector over her body. Her face flushes hot with humiliation, perspiration gathering between her breasts. This isn't like a visit to the doctor's office for her annual pap smear, or crouching among the muslimat at the communal washroom to perform wudu. She's suddenly seized with the terror of being exposed: *What if the partitions topple over?* A hundred strangers gawking and pointing at her partial nakedness.

"I'm going to be sick," Afaf tells the officer. The vomit heaves from her throat and she retches into a wastebasket someone quickly hands her.

"No reason to be nervous, ma'am. Unless you've got something to hide," the officer says with a sneer. Afaf squeezes her eyes shut again as her stomach churns.

When she can finally dress again and is permitted to fasten her hijab, Afaf is physically drained, and a trickle of bile is tickling her throat. The officer leads her out of the makeshift room and she immediately spots Bilal and Baba. They wave and she catches more steely stares as Bilal hugs her. She bites her lip, refusing to cry.

"Are you all right?"

She nods, forces a smile. "I need to use the restroom."

She walks around a custodian mopping the floor and splashes cool water on her face. She catches a woman next to her staring at

Afaf's reflection in the mirror, unsmiling. Afaf stares right back, defiant. The woman drops her eyes, lathering her hands noisily. When she passes behind Afaf, the woman flicks water at her headscarf.

"Shame on you," Afaf snaps back. "What have I done to you?" What has she done to any of them? Is she not a citizen of this country like them? How naïve to believe she's ever really belonged—with and without her hijab. Before and after a terrorist attack.

"You're all evil, bitch." The woman's awful words trail behind her like streaks from the custodian's dirty mop across the tiled floor.

The other women quickly rinse their hands, herd their young children out, roll their luggage past Afaf, not looking her way. One snickers before closing her stall door.

Afaf leans against the mirror, pressing her forehead against the cool glass. She wants to ask these strangers how she—one woman, a mother and wife, a teacher, if they'd only ask—can be a menace to them. How can she make them unafraid?

She lets the tears roll.

"Are you all right, miss?" An old white woman pats Afaf's shoulder.

"I'm fine."

The woman turns on the faucet next to her. "Human beings can be awful." She smiles kindly at Afaf in the mirror.

"Will this be life from now on?" Afaf asks her.

The woman is silent, gives Afaf a weak shrug, and dries her hands.

3

THE FIRST time Afaf felt Ayman in her belly it was like a delicate flutter of wings. A tiny human being was growing inside her, absorbing her nutrients, quietly thriving. The pain of his birth was so extraordinary, then instantly—miraculously—it halted as soon as he slipped out, and she'd been light-headed with euphoria.

But in this place. No earthly experience has prepared Afaf for the holy city of Mecca, a marvelous clash between antiquity and modernity. Lavish hotels break up the desert sky, cars speed along busy highways driven by men with women clad in black niqab, only their eyes staring back at Afaf. A gigantic clock tower, its ticking mechanism designed to last a hundred years, stands outside of the Masjid al-Haram, where Abraham almost sacrificed his son Isaac before an angel of God intervened.

The holy mosque teems with thousands upon thousands of men and women from every walk of life, every corner of the planet, moving in one direction, counterclockwise, bodies huddled close to each other in a wave of white like clouds across the sky. The opulence of the outside world is temporarily discarded.

At their hotel, they bathe and dress in a pure state of ihram before they enter the site of the Ka'aba at the mosque. Baba and Bilal wear white garments draped over one shoulder. Afaf wears a white cotton hijab and abaya, her notebook of du'aa inside a small purse fastened closely to her hip. She and Bilal are careful not to touch, sparking any sensual contact, though they'll be absorbed by the bodies of strangers.

All together they recite talbiyah:

Here I am in Your service, O Allah, here I am. Here I am . . .

Bilal smiles at her, tears in his eyes, and she's blinded by her own as their bodies fuse into the massive crowd circling the Ka'aba. All the distress of the airport—the hatred, the undeserved animosity she'd absorbed from passengers over a dozen hours before—seeps out of her consciousness. For the first time in her life, she belongs. Here among the pilgrims who chant a palpable humming, lifting Afaf's spirit, she's found her place.

Baba loops his arm through Bilal's, his cane keeping him steady and upright. Afaf moves behind them, imagining Abraham and his son building this magnificent black house of God. For over two decades, she's faced it from the west each time she prayed, from eleven thousand miles at home in Tempest, Illinois. Her stomach flutters with humility and the tingle goes through her entire body. They aren't near enough to touch and kiss the Ka'aba, so they raise their hands in acknowledgment:

"Allahu Akbar! Allahu Akbar!"

For a moment, Afaf is arrested by fear: What if she faints, her body trampled by the other pilgrims? Hundreds of muslimeen have died during the journey, stampedes breaking out, fires burning through makeshift tents. She squeezes her eyes shut and breathes deeply, wiping morbid thoughts clean from her brain. She is in His grace now. She focuses hard on prayer: *Bismillahi allahu akbar wa lillah hil hamd . . . Bismillahi allahu akbar wa lillah hil hamd.* Then she opens her eyes, lifts her hands to the bright sky, and gives du'aa for her sons, for Majeed and Esma and her mother-in-law, for Mama and Nada, tears streaming down her face.

Ahead of her, a young man has tied a rope around his body and corrals a group of elderly women with it—each one has a loop around her waist—leading them forward. It's a spectacle Majeed would have scoffed at, though the pilgrims are oblivious, consumed by their worship.

By the third circuit, she can tell Baba has grown tired. His bare head glistens with sweat. His collarbone juts out of his white garment. She has four more circuits to go, then they're off to Mina, where they can rest and meditate until sunrise. Bilal is patient and kind, wrapping an arm around her father's shoulders, letting Baba lean against him, and Bilal absorbs his weight.

Afaf completes the seventh circuit and rests for a while. The hours begin to morph and stretch, the passage of the sun the only evidence of time passing. They follow seven times the path that Abraham's wife Hagar took in search of water for her infant son. The spring of Zamzam appeared before her and they drank until their thirst was no more. She remembers the small vials of water Baba had brought home from his first hajj.

Hours later, an air-conditioned bus takes them to Mina, a veritable tent city where men and women segregate for prayer and meditation. Afaf is nauseous as the bus ambles along a heavily congested road and takes sips of water from her plastic canteen. She checks on Baba, sitting next to Bilal. His face appears sallow.

"Baba, stay hydrated," she instructs him, handing him one of the fresh bottles of water the bus driver offers the passengers. "We'll be there soon and you can rest."

"Allah yird'aa layki," Baba prays. "May God bestow all blessings upon you." He smiles weakly before laying his head back on the high-cushioned seat and closing his eyes. Even that appears to take effort.

Afaf gives Bilal a worried look. He nods and his lips move in du'aa.

Outside the window of the bus, she watches pilgrims walking along the road. In the distance, the muezzin's call—a human voice so bottomless it is as disquieting as it is uplifting. Afaf is awestruck by its reverberation in the desert air. It reminds Afaf of the melancholic melodies Baba plays on his oud, and she's already decided it will be what she misses most about this resounding place.

They pass mountains, and the sun hangs over them midway in the sky. It's asr prayer, when the day begins its decline.

~

The vicinity of Mina is covered with air-conditioned tents. Generators drone twenty-four hours a day during this special season. After the devastating fire of 1997, the Saudi government replaced the cotton tents with ones made of fiberglass and Teflon, color-coding camps and paving pathways between them. Bilal escorts Baba to the men's camp, and Afaf joins a company of fifty women, complete strangers who've become her companions for the night.

Inside their tent, everyone feels generous and relaxed, though the quarters are tight, with floor mattresses crammed side by side and little space to move around. They perform salat al-isha'a, the last prayer of the day, and silently meditate.

Has it been merely two days since she'd hugged Ayman and Akram? Has it been only five months since the planes crashed in New York? In this region, the horizon seems to expand beyond human measure. There's no talk of money or politics, of war or famine. A veil of spirituality hangs over the pilgrims, shielding them from the world's suffering.

Afaf lies down on a soft mattress next to a woman from Melbourne by way of Sudan, her skin the color of soos—the licorice drink vendors were selling in the bazaar outside of Afaf's hotel when they'd arrived. She speaks perfect Arabic. "Inshallah you are granted good pilgrimage."

"Inshallah you as well." Afaf smiles.

Tomorrow they must reach Mount Arafat for their journey to be validated by the Lord. Afaf says extra du'aa for Baba and his health, that Allah will see him through this experience which so many are granted only once in their lifetime. Will Mama ever appreciate the sacrifice her husband's made for her?

That night she sleeps soundly in the tent—her first sound sleep in many years—under a blanket of stars, the same ones that twinkle above Ayman and Akram though they are two worlds apart.

At daybreak, she prays with her tentmates and the pilgrims begin their journey to Mount Arafat. She rejoins Bilal and Baba and finds they've acquired a wheelchair for her father. Afaf worries even more: he must be feeling very badly if he's consented to a wheelchair. Bilal pushes her father and she keeps pace, making sure Baba takes regular sips of water from his plastic canteen.

"Stop fretting, habibti," Baba scolds. His face looks jaundiced, his eyelids drooping as he gazes up at her.

Pilgrims flock the path, hundreds of black umbrellas poking out of the masses, shielding them from the sun.

They reach the great boulders of Mount Arafat, a magnificent pinnacle swarmed by pilgrims like ants on an anthill. The younger and healthier climb its peak with ease, the elderly and disabled repent at its base.

She prays and begs for forgiveness, forgetting her exhaustion. Fear tugs at her spirit—how will she ever be able to make amends for every wrong she's committed? Could she have been a better sister to Majeed? Might she have been of greater comfort to her parents, especially Mama? Had she done enough for every child she's taught? What unseen injury had she inflicted upon others, consumed by bouts of vanity?

The peak of the mountain is blurred by the sun and she can only see undefined forms—*are they angels?*—coating its slopes. She prays that the Lord will give her the strength and fortitude to be a good Muslim. She clings to a new sense of transcendence, this knowledge that she's more than merely encased in a physical body.

Afaf looks over at Bilal, his eyes closed, hands raised to the sky, lips moving silently. She remembers the story of Adam and Eve and is grateful for Bilal. They are two broken people whose losses somehow made them whole.

They move on to Muzdalifah. The traffic of bodies is overwhelming. The three of them are relieved to have fulfilled the greatest obligation on their route. They head toward an open area where they'll collect stones to cast at three pillars representing the devil that thrice tempted Abraham.

Bilal signals that Baba needs to rest and they make their way to the side of the road, which is still dense with bodies. Water basins and portable toilets are erected along the path.

She wipes the sweat from her forehead, gulps water from her

plastic canteen, then gargles and spits it in a direction away from the throng.

Bilal is on one knee, facing her father. "What is it, Uncle?" Afaf hurries to Baba's side.

Her father's face is ashen, his eyes rolling back in his lids. Baba clutches his chest with one hand. "I can't breathe," he wheezes. "I can't breathe."

She falls to her knees and grabs his other hand. "Hold on, Baba! Let's get you out of the sun."

Time suddenly speeds up as Baba releases a gasp and his hands go limp.

"Baba, no. Please, hold on, Baba!" Afaf cries. She waves her arms for help. The pilgrims keep moving, eyes straight ahead or toward the sky. From a distance, she must look like she's praying, too, as she wildly throws her arms up. "Please help us!" she shouts in Arabic. "In the name of God, help us!"

Bilal checks Baba's pulse. He presses two fingers on Baba's neck, then spreads his hand over her father's head and says a prayer.

She clutches Baba's hands—hands that held her face, prayed over her sons, balanced his oud. They are lifeless. "No! Please! No!" she screams, but no one hears her above the pelting of stones, thousands of pilgrims striking the devil from their paths.

4

BABA IS buried in Jannat al-Baqi, where the close relatives and companions of Prophet Muhammad are buried in the city of Medina. It is a desolate place, plundered and rebuilt over the centuries. Rocks designate the graves in the sand, so that it looks like a weatherworn beach.

The dead are laid to rest quickly—no ostentation or pageantry, no bouquets of flowers or wreaths. Afaf is asked if she'd like to repatriate the body, to carry it home to the States. But she declines. She knows Baba would want to be buried in this holy place. And she knows she'll never return to read Al-Fatiha over Baba's grave. She'll have to pray for him a continent away.

According to the Saudi imam who performed the funeral rites, they've fulfilled hajj, exempted from the last duties if they pay for a sacrificial slaughter at Eid. Baba had held on until Mount Arafat. His final gesture of love.

Her eyes are raw and sore from crying, her muscles atrophy in misery. It's difficult to sit up and hard to sleep for long periods. She's staggered by how fierce this grief is, how it levels her body. Nausea comes in waves and she retches bitter bile in the toilet. How can one accomplish any ceremonious task—preparing the body, praying over it, burying it—when one can barely stand?

Bilal tries to feed her at the hotel, but Afaf can't keep anything down. He brings her a tangy addas soup, tearing bits of bread for her to chew between spoonfuls. She remembers when Khalti Nesreen prepared the same soup for Mama when Nada disappeared. Had it also tasted like death?

A woman in a black hijab comes to the room. She doesn't appear to be Arab, her eyes disarmingly wide and black as onyx, her skin a yellowish copper. When she speaks, she confirms she's a migrant hotel worker.

"Salaam." She holds up clean sheets.

Afaf nods. "Salaam," she croaks, surprised at the sound of her voice. She realizes she hasn't said much in the last twenty-four hours. Or has it been longer? Once again, time warps. She can't tell if it's day or night until the housekeeper draws the blinds and sunlight pours into the room. Afaf vaguely recalls Bilal leaving for a while, assuring her that he would return with more food. When had she eaten the soup?

Afaf struggles out of the bed, making way for the housekeeper. Her head feels light and hollow, like a doll's, then becomes heavy with fatigue. As soon as she stands, her legs give way beneath her and she crumples to the floor.

"Miss, are you all right?" The housekeeper is at her side, crouched down beside Afaf, holding her arm.

"I'll be fine." She tries to lift herself up, but it's no use. Baba's gone. Nothing's going to change that, even in this miraculous place. Afaf simply has no energy to move on.

"My father died," she tells the housekeeper in English.

The housekeeper seems to comprehend—or perhaps she's familiar with this kind of anguish. She guides Afaf's head to her chest and steadies Afaf's trembling body. Afaf presses against her small breasts as the woman hums a tune.

Afaf folds herself into this stranger who smells of dried sage leaves and lemons, wishing she were Mama.

~

It is Majeed's face she sees—the only face among the crowd at O'Hare International Airport. Families flock around their loved ones, welcoming them home with bouquets of flowers and new babies that pass from one pair of outstretched arms to another. Afaf is only aware of her brother waiting at the end of the gate, every other sound a far-off echo of happiness. Bilal pushes the luggage carrier ahead of her, glancing over his shoulder as though she might disappear.

The path seems interminable ahead of her and passengers whisk past, eager to reach the end. At last, she is in Majeed's arms.

"Afaf, I'm sorry. I—" His body heaves against her and she holds him close, muffling his sobs.

"He loved you so much, Maj. He was so proud of you."

They stand clinging to each other a long time until Bilal urges them on.

5

THE CENTER holds a special azza for Baba. The men and women gather in separate quarters of the mosque to mourn, the imam's voice coming through loudspeakers from the corner of the low ceiling. He's a young man from Yemen, has taken the place of the retired Abu Nabeel. His beard, red like rust, and his short height offer a disarming countenance without diminishing his authority among the congregation.

"Hold your tears," the imam implores, a twang in his Arabic accent. "For they only torment the soul of the deceased, keep him from a peaceful eternal rest."

The women bob their heads, draped in black, assenting as they dab their eyes and blow their noses into their tissues.

If Baba had passed away in Illinois, his body would lay in repose at Hammond Funeral Home, owned and operated by a nondenominational family. For years, they've permitted muslimeen to prepare the body of their beloved themselves, to pray over their souls and shroud them in white. No embalming, no delay. Who might have performed these duties for Baba here? Majeed? Even now her brother looks lost among the men, sitting beside her husband in a close-fitting black suit and dark blue tie. Bilal guides him through the rituals, instructs him what to say when mourners offer their condolences. Majeed even joined the funeral prayer, following Bilal's movements. Afaf feels an incredible tenderness for her brother. The dilapidated second floor of the Islamic Center of Greater Chicago flashes back to her, a teenage Majeed wedged between Baba and a stranger as they prayed, she standing beside Kowkab, both out of place. Perhaps Majeed might have found some solace in washing their father's body, tracing the scars from Baba's crash, pressing the calluses of Baba's fingertips from strumming his oud all those years.

Could Majeed finally forgive Baba? Had she done the same for Mama? Their mother's been calling, and Majeed fields the calls. Afaf can't speak to her—not yet. To communicate Baba's death—to try to articulate her grief—over a telephone feels sacrilegious. A part of her hoped Mama would fly back to the States to mourn with her children. To offer her physical body to Afaf. She didn't need words, just the hollow space between her mother's neck and shoulder, where Afaf could lay her head. It is an unfamiliar place—one she desperately needs. Had Majeed craved the same from Baba? Her heart swells with sadness.

In the women's quarters, Kowkab hovers over Afaf during the times when she and Esma are not seeing to trays of unsweetened coffee and pressed dates. That morning her friend gave her a Valium to calm her trembling hands, to still her perpetual tears.

"You're surrounded by love here," Kowkab whispers in her ear before jetting away to greet a small group of women. Folding chairs have been positioned in a horseshoe shape, Afaf seated at the top of the arch.

Mrs. Parker and Ashanti hug her at the same time, their tangerine scents comforting her. She whispers to them, "My father loved Mr. Parker."

They nod, sniffling and wiping their tears. They hug her again and hand her a basket wrapped full of organic tea and biscuits.

Khalti Nesreen and Ammo Yahya have arrived from Kenosha. Her aunt's shoulders are slightly stooped, her slender frame, like Mama's, carries a thin ribbon of fat around her waist. Her hair is cut neatly into a graying bob. Afaf wonders when her aunt had aged so much.

"Wallahi I loved your father, habibti," Khalti Nesreen tells her, gripping both of Afaf's hands as if she's trying to convince her. "He had his flaws, but he had a big heart. Allah yarhamo." She sniffles into a crumpled tissue. Still, Baba would always be the man who had failed her sister.

Someone wheels over Um Zuraib, her body shrunken like a snail forced out of its shell. Afaf remembers meeting her for the first time when Um Zuraib pressed Afaf into her enormous bosom and she'd felt safe there. Afaf leans down to embrace her. Her sunken cheeks feel like paper, her wrinkled hands cold and small. As with Khalti Nesreen, Afaf startles at the old woman before her, her face swallowed up by a black headscarf. Has she, too, been aging so quickly?

"Your father did you the greatest deed by turning you to Islam," Um Zuraib says.

Afaf nods, tears welling up again. "Yislim deenak wa emanak. Thank you, Um Zuraib." Things never quite returned to normal after their falling-out those years ago. Afaf had heard through the circle of women that Layla Hamad, the little girl with the star-shaped bruise, was eventually reunited with her mother, who'd stayed married to her abusive husband. They moved away. Layla would be sixteen years old now. Had that been the worst she'd been through in her life to this point? Or did Layla now feel as worthless as Afaf did at that age? Did she rely on the irreverent hands of white boys to remind her she was alive?

Kowkab is by her side again. "How're you holding up, habibti?" She places a Styrofoam cup of coffee in her hand, making sure Afaf has grabbed hold of it before Kowkab peels her fingers away.

"Fine, fine." Afaf blows her nose and settles back into her folding chair. She's cold, but feels strangely calm. The Valium slowly stems the sadness. At least for a little while.

One by one, the women approach her with their condolences. She's too tired to stand and receive them; instead, she lets each one lean down to offer a kiss on each cheek. Some who knew Baba well relate times he'd been generous to them; others offer polite sentiments about someone they'd only seen around the masjid and to whom they'd never spoken. The same words: *Your father was such a decent man.*

The line is never-ending. Kowkab winks at Afaf to be patient. She wants to go home, gather her sons in her arms, slip under the covers. Her body craves sleep, though it hasn't come since they returned home.

A woman steps up and lingers for a moment as though uncertain whether to greet her or move on without saying a word. The other mourners wait behind her. Her headscarf is ill-fitting, and she tugs at the loose fabric on her forehead, trying to capture a few curly strands of auburn hair that have escaped. She's wearing a puffy short coat, conspicuously out of place among the weeping mourners.

Afaf holds out her hand, prompting the stranger to speak.

"I'm—I'm so sorry for your loss," she finally blurts.

There's something strangely familiar about this woman. Afaf looks more closely. "Who are you?"

The woman shakes her head, glancing behind her. The line extends to a dozen women. "It's me, Afaf." She says her name, and it echoes from the past like the strings of Baba's oud, like a song she hasn't heard for a long time.

"Nada."

Her sister nods, tears streaming down her cheeks. "I'm sorry. To come like this."

Afaf doesn't say any more. She stands and they fall against each other like they're bracing against strong winds. A hundred questions spring to Afaf's lips.

"How did you—where have you—?"

Nada nods, holds both of her hands. "We have so much to talk about," her sister tells her.

New tears surge, and Kowkab hurries over. "My sister . . . she . . ." Afaf cannot summon words. Kowkab's face breaks with understanding and her friend embraces Nada.

"My address," Afaf manages to say to Kowkab, who nods and recites Afaf's home address as Nada quickly jots it down on a folded envelope she's pulled from her purse. "Come to the house tonight," she tells her sister. Behind Nada, the line of women has doubled. Afaf must fulfill her obligation, receive each and every muslimah who wishes her father eternal salvation.

Nada nods, squeezes Afaf's hand before another woman quickly takes her sister's place, hugging Afaf close, telling her how much Baba was like a father to her.

6

AFAF PACES back and forth in the kitchen, glancing at the clock on the wall.

It's like a dream.

Nada is back.

Nada is *alive*.

Afaf trembles with this extraordinary truth. She's filled with something she can't quite name—is it relief, anger? It presses against her being.

Majeed emerges from the basement. He's changed from his suit to an old college sweatshirt. He's been sleeping in the spare room. Bilal insisted her brother stay with them, though he'd already made reservations at a Holiday Inn a few miles outside of Tempest. In the past Majeed wouldn't have relented, fiercely clasping to his privacy on short business trips to Chicago. It hadn't taken much convincing this time; she and Majeed are all they have now.

And Nada.

"What if she changes her mind?" Majeed's face is strained, but Afaf catches a flicker of hope at the prospect of Nada disappearing again. It would be easier if Nada were dead—he won't admit it, but Afaf knows her brother, how difficult it has been for him to grasp the complexities of life. For him, Baba was a drunk and a cheater; Mama an isolated, grief-stricken mother. Nada's reappearance forces them to contend with an unwieldy past and their uncertain future.

"She's comes this far, Maj. She'll be here." In each other's presence, neither one has been able to utter their sister's name, as though it might unleash a curse, breaking the spell of avoidance that had long been spun over their family.

"Seems a little late," Majeed mutters. He runs his fingers through his thick hair. Each time Afaf sees him, more gray tinges his temples, runs through his crown.

She understands his anger; her own threatens to break the surface. But beneath that is a deep well of longing. After all these years she still wants her sister back.

Bilal enters the kitchen, lightly touches Afaf's shoulder. "The boys are finally sleeping."

He can sense the tension between the siblings. "Have either of you eaten? Majeed?"

"Thanks. I'm fine." Her brother heads to the family room, sinks into a recliner.

Afaf prepares a tray of teacups, opens a tin of Pirouette wafers from the Parkers' basket. Years ago, Baba would bring them home from the arrabi grocer; she and Majeed loved to crunch down the rolled wafer straws to their fingertips when they were kids, racing to see who could finish first.

"What time will your sister be here?" Bilal asks.

Your sister. How do the three of them fit back into each other?

The digital clock on the microwave shows ten-thirty p.m. "Soon," Afaf says. She wonders where Nada is staying. Should she extend her an invitation to stay with them? How many times had she done the same for other guests? This is her own sister. She, Nada, and Majeed under the same roof again.

Bilal hugs her close. "And you?" he whispers in Afaf's ear. "How are you handling all of this?"

"Elhamdulillah," she automatically answers. How easy it is to revert to that word, despite the tumult lashing inside her heart. Since Baba's death, her faith feels fragmented, like the seams of a well-worn coat coming undone, no longer able to shield her from the bitter cold. She could always shroud herself in Islam, in the trust she has in Allah to see her through anything. But, with Baba gone, that sense of transcendence at hajj is gone. She dabs her wet eyes with the hem of her billowing sleeve, before tears fall onto her husband's shoulder. Perhaps this is Allah's plan, His strange magnificence snatching Baba from her and offering Nada.

Afaf pulls away from Bilal and walks to the foyer. She turns around, taking in the home she's made with Bilal. Thirty-five hundred square feet, three bedrooms, four bathrooms, a finished basement. They've done well for themselves. Their sons will never go without. What will Nada think of the life she's made? Does she remember where they began in the old apartment on Fairfield Avenue? Living paycheck to paycheck, Baba taking the bus to the factory, Mama serving leftovers until the pots were bare.

Afaf catches her reflection in the mirrored panel of a china cabinet. She's been avoiding looking at herself, apprehensive at the sight of a faded woman. A pale and drawn face peers back at her from the dining room, like someone who's been sick for a very long time.

She hears Majeed's cell phone buzz, and he speaks in a low voice. It's probably a girlfriend he doesn't want to introduce to his family. He's been secretive about his personal life and Afaf has stopped asking. She adjusts her peasant blouse, its linen fabric dyed a sage-green. She changed out of her black abaya, opting for a less morbid blouse, the one she'd found at her favorite thrift shop in Chicago. Does Nada shop resale? Is she frugal like Afaf, or is money of no matter to her?

Her stomach rises in a wave of anticipation. There's so much she wants to know about her sister, things that they would have naturally learned and already known had they grown up together: Her favorite food, her worst fear. Colors that look terrible on her, or the familiar scent of an ageless perfume that lingers long after she's left the room.

What about family? Is Nada married, with children?

Thoughts race across her brain, one question sparking another before she can answer the first.

The doorbell rings and Afaf catches her breath, the chime an eerie sound this late at night. She touches her bare head, her dark strands gathered in a long ponytail. Bilal and Majeed appear behind her in the foyer.

Nada stands in the doorway holding a bouquet of carnations strikingly pink against the backdrop of night. Her head is covered by a knit cap, her hair a mass of curls beneath it. It's a lighter shade than the auburn Afaf remembers, with a few nomadic grays near the crown. Nada is slightly shorter than her.

"I'm so sorry," her sister begins, handing her the bouquet.

"May God grant him mercy and salvation." Afaf's words feel stilted and rehearsed, the same she'd repeated to the women at the azza hours before. And yet there's no proper expression, no satisfying euphemism to salve that burn. And it stings even worse now that Nada is here, Baba departing without ever seeing his firstborn again. She clears her throat.

They don't shake hands or hug, the flowers replacing any awkward physical gestures for the time being.

"Maj?" Nada takes a step toward the men. "I can't believe it. You look exactly the same."

When Nada says *Maj*, broken shards of memories gather again in whole images. The three of them quietly eating their dinner while Mama banged pots and pans in the sink. Nada soothing Majeed when he fell off his bike, pressing an iodine-filled cotton ball against his knee. That walk to the library for Afaf's very own card. Nada had been a big sister for a little while. Does Majeed remember, too?

He only nods in response, doesn't speak. Nada appears uncertain—should she reach out and embrace their brother?

Afaf breaks the awkward moment. "This is my husband Bilal." She puts a hand on his arm.

Bilal steps forward, shakes Nada's hand. "Hello. I am so happy to meet you. Welcome." It seems easy for her husband, his indispensable hospitality unflinching. Nada is a stranger in his home like any other he's met for the first time.

Nada beams at him, relaxes a bit. Her cheerfulness is undampened by Afaf and Majeed's somber mood.

Afaf gestures with her flowers. "Come in, please."

"I will leave you now. Inshallah a good night." Bilal kisses the top of Afaf's head and squeezes Majeed's shoulder before going upstairs. Her brother heads to the kitchen.

Nada removes her boots and hat, unzips her puffy coat, revealing a gray wool sweater. A heart-shaped pendant hangs from her neck, a tiny ruby in its center. Nada touches it nervously as she studies the photographs mounted on the wall of the foyer. She points to one of Afaf and Bilal on their tulba when Baba officially gave her away in marriage.

Afaf watches Nada as she moves along, a small smile playing across her sister's lips, an expression of someone who's meeting people for the first time. There's one of Afaf and Majeed on Eid and the one of Baba with his arm around her brother's shoulders at Majeed's graduation from law school. In another Baba holds his grandson Ayman for the first time at the hospital. Nada had been absent from so many moments—occupying the empty spaces in the photographs discernible only to Afaf.

Nada points up at the school portraits of Ayman and Akram, toothy smiles across their faces. "Your sons?"

Afaf nods, and a pang of desire for them goes through her heart. She wants to seize them in their beds, touch and smell them. Wrap herself in their innocence, their simple beings.

"Does Maj have any?"

Afaf shakes her head. "Inshallah one day." It sounds silly to say, when so much of Majeed's life to her is like a shuttered house.

Nada pulls a few loose photographs from her purse. "I have one daughter. Hope." In one, a teenage girl smiles in a prom dress.

Afaf's stomach rises. A niece she's never known. Her fingers graze the photograph, one corner dog-eared. Hope could be mistaken for a white girl, with crystal-blue eyes and peachy skin, except her hair might give it away. She inherited Nada's curly strands.

"Mashallah. She's beautiful," Afaf tells her sister. Hope: Amal in Arabic.

Nada nods, continues browsing the photographs on the wall. She pauses in front of one with Mama in her green velvet dress the night Baba fell in love with her a lifetime ago when their fates were sealed. Nada touches the edge of the frame. "I remember this one," she says quietly, fingers returning to the pendant around her neck.

Afaf stands silently aside, giving Nada time to examine each photograph.

How strange it must be, to see them all like a whole other family she'd never belonged to, glimpses of their life stories captured in neatly posed pictures. How much did Nada remember? Could she still hear Mama crying, her fights with Baba? Or had she completely excised those sounds, along with every smell and taste from that old apartment on Fairfield Avenue? Can she imagine the life she'd left behind? Is she sorry?

In the kitchen, Afaf's brother and sister sit across from each other at the table. Majeed looks down at his hands. Afaf steals glances at Nada from the stove, where she prepares a pot of green tea. Like Afaf, Nada has Baba's face, her features softer versions of their father's: it's Baba's nose with a slenderer bulb; a disarming dimple in his pointed chin; his dark eyes framed by delicately feminine brows. Her body is thin and lithe. Like Mama's. Like Afaf's own body. The teapot whistles and Afaf pours them each a cup. Their silence veils each passing minute.

Nada speaks first. "I did a search online. Found Baba's name on the LISTSERV page for the Tempest Prayer Center." She lifts her teacup, puts it down before taking a sip. "That was probably four, five years ago."

A small stab in Afaf's heart. She glances at Majeed. He's listening, his face impassive. Why had Nada waited so long?

"I signed up for the newsletter, just to keep track. A few days ago, I received an email alert." She puts her hands in her lap. "It was about Baba's passing."

"Why didn't you come sooner?" Afaf says, knowing it's what Majeed is thinking, too, though she's sure he wishes Nada hadn't turned up at all.

"I tried. I didn't know how to reach out. I thought you hated me. One day I finally got up the nerve and skimmed the white pages. I couldn't find either of you." Nada looks at her. "I was sure you'd gotten married, Afaf. Changed your name."

Afaf nodded, though she hadn't changed her last name. People call her Mrs. Hamzić from time to time, or Um Ayman at weddings.

"Baba's listed in Chicago." Nada's tears begin to fall. "I really wanted to reach out sooner. I just—I'm sorry. I didn't know how." She drops her head, and her shoulders quake with sobs.

Afaf reaches across the table, covers her sister's hand.

"Why have you come back?" Majeed suddenly speaks up, unmoved by their sister's sorrow. "Baba's gone. Mama's overseas. Who have you come back for?" His words cut like a razor.

"For you and Afaf. I'm sorry—" Her wet eyes beseech them.

"Sorry for what exactly? Running away? Leaving us behind in a crazy house?"

Nada pulls a napkin from the center of the table and dabs at her eyes, blows her nose. "You were too young, Maj. I don't expect you to understand why I left."

"Why did you leave?" It's the real question Afaf has been waiting to ask.

Nada's eyes well up with fresh tears and she sniffles. She pulls another napkin from a wooden dispenser on the table and blows her nose. "I—I couldn't stand it anymore. I felt like an alien in that house. Like I didn't belong."

These words are startling to Afaf: Had she felt that way about their family, too? Mama had never allowed her to get close. They circled each other for years, never breaking their orbits.

"You both were so young. I convinced myself you'd be okay."

She paused. "I guess I was young, too." She vigorously shakes her head as though the past has suddenly seized her and she needs to wrestle away from it. "I couldn't—I had to leave."

Majeed is silent again. He looks down into his teacup. None of them have drunk their tea. Afaf can feel the slight vibration from the tapping of his foot under the table. He's trying to maintain control.

"Where did you go?" Afaf's voice is soft. She flashes to those pictures the detective had shown her parents. In her child's imagination, she'd attached Nada's head to the battered body, scaring herself to sleep for months after her sister had disappeared.

"I met someone at the roller rink. Remember Disco Wheels?" A small embarassed smile creeps across Nada's face.

Afaf remembers the place. Teenage girls in halter tops and boys with tight shirts and flared jeans, hands in each other's back pockets as they glided across the rink in laced-up skates. Nada would bring along Afaf and Majeed—her excuse to get out of the apartment—and give them a few bucks for a hot dog and a game of pinball. Majeed was afraid to skate, so he and Afaf hung over the railing, watching the older kids skid by. "Another One Bites the Dust" blared from the stereo speaker and the lights dimmed when a slow song came on. When Nada passed with her friends, Afaf and Majeed would wave wildly at her and she'd give them a nod of her chin, but never waved back. Afaf reaches back into memory, but the faces of the boys sidling up to Nada, some holding her waist from behind, their legs gliding in sync, are a blur now.

"His name's Robert. We fell in love." She blows her nose again. "We moved to Florida. He got a job and I finished high school. It was tough, making ends meet. Rob enlisted in the army. We got married before he went to boot camp. He's a CW4 now. Chief warrant officer.

Mostly oversees systems operations." She looks at Afaf and Majeed for some sign of compassion.

Afaf only nods, unsure how to absorb this information. She looks at Majeed. His face doesn't soften; his jawline tenses at this information. Her sister married amarkani, who served in an army bent on destroying Muslim countries. It feels like another betrayal. How outrageously disparate and contradictory the hand of fate! Naseeb had given her Islam; another destiny had been dealt to her sister. But hadn't Nada forged it on her own, the day she decided to leave them?

Nada sips her tea and continues, "We've lived in different places. In Germany for five years. Ten years in Bahrain."

Germany, Bahrain. What different lives they've had. Had Nada been happy all those years?

"We finally came home to Jacksonville after the first Gulf War."

A two-hour flight. Nada and Bilal had taken the boys to Disney World last year—how many hours is that from Jacksonville? It had taken Nada over thirty years to arrive.

"The only thing I've ever regretted is losing you and Majeed," Nada tells them.

Majeed clears his throat, but doesn't speak anymore.

Afaf says, "We were always here. You didn't lose us." She clutches her teacup, fights back tears. "You left us."

"You're right. I made that choice. But when you're seventeen and feel completely out of place—it's like the real you will never survive and you have to find somewhere you can be yourself." Nada's eyes dart between her and Majeed. "I found that with Rob. It hasn't been easy. I don't want you to think we headed off into the sunset without any trouble. People didn't always accept me. The chief warrant officer's *Arabian* wife."

It gives Afaf satisfaction knowing Nada hadn't been able to completely shed her skin married to a white man.

"How's Mama? You said she's overseas?"

"She's fine, elhamdulillah," Afaf automatically responds. "She's been living in Palestine for ten years." She rises from the table, pours a glass of water from the tap. With her back to Nada, she says, "It hasn't been easy for us, you know. When you left they were never the same."

Majeed snorts and leaves the kitchen. They hear a faucet running in the hallway washroom. Afaf returns to the table, watches Nada sniffle into her crumpled napkin. "Baba drank. Mama slowly lost her mind." She closes her mouth, presses her lips against the details of their mother's attempted suicide. She wants to punish Nada for her selfish abandonment, for leaving them behind with unhinged parents. She was their big sister, meant to protect them. Instead she'd run away. "We've been through so much, you know?" Afaf is tempted to list all that Nada was spared. But she holds back. Nada is here now. Allah has returned her sister. He's taken Baba and given back her sister. Her anger begins to lift. It will take time, especially for Majeed. But they're a family again—whatever that is, whatever it may be.

The clock in the foyer chimes. It's almost midnight. The heat cycle fans through the floor vents. Snow has begun to fall in big flakes. Through the skylight, Afaf peers up at the waxing moon.

Nada reaches across the table, covers Afaf's hand. "I never imagined it would ever get easy for any of you. I'm so sorry."

Tears well up and an old grief coats Afaf's chest again. Afaf pats Nada's hand over hers. She tries to imagine the journey her sister has taken without a mother and father, or siblings who look out for each other.

"You're here now," Afaf tells her sister. "That's all that matters." She remembers Baba's words from a long time ago: *Be merciful to others and you will receive mercy. Forgive others and Allah will forgive you.* Could she have mustered forgiveness without the benefit of Islam? Who would she be if Islam hadn't entered her heart? To whom might Nada have returned?

Her sister nods toward the washroom. "Maj hates me. I can't blame him." She dabs at her eyes with a napkin.

"Give him time. He'll come around." Afaf smiles, though she knows Maj too well. He can hold a grudge forever.

"What about Mama?"

"Would you like to talk to her?" Afaf imagines Mama's face when she hears Nada's voice. An old pinch of jealousy returns. She glances at the microwave. "It's morning there. We can call her if you're up for it."

She's been holding off any conversation with Mama, and here she is now about to call her with incredible news. She assumes Mama will be thrilled—hadn't Nada been the true love of her life?

She dials the cordless phone and listens to several long rings signifying the long-distance reception.

"Aywa."

"Mama?"

"Afaf! Yislim rassik. May he find eternal peace." During azza, mourners strung accolade after accolade around Afaf. Even those who had only briefly known Baba offered some small expression of praise. But Mama is still incapable of summoning anything more about Baba.

"Thank you," Afaf says.

"How's everyone there? Has Nesreen paid her respects?"

Afaf pictures her mother sitting on the barranda of her child-hood home, looking at a valley, a small glass of thick coffee in one hand, a cigarette dangling from the other. A world away from Afaf, as she had always been. "Yes, Khalti was here today."

"Good, good. And how are you?"

"Better." Afaf stands up, turns her back to Nada. "Listen, Mama. I have some news."

"Khair? What is it? Did something happen to Majeed?"

"No, no. Elhamdulillah he's fine." She turns back to her sister, who's worrying her pendant and looking up at her with anxious eyes. "It's Nada. She's here."

Silence on the other end.

"Mama? Are you there?"

"What are you talking about?" Mama hisses. "What's this crazy talk?"

"Mama. Listen to me. Nada's back. She came back to pay her—"

The line goes dead. Afaf looks at the screen of the cordless phone. *Call Ended.*

"She hung up. I guess I expected that," Afaf says. Fresh tears wet Nada's eyes. Afaf puts a hand on her shoulder. "It's amazing—your coming back. You can imagine what a shock it is for Mama."

The phone rings. It's her mother. "She's alive?" Mama's voice is brittle.

Still, after all of these years, Mama can't bear the thought that Nada had left of her own will. She probably feels the same as Majeed: that it would have been easier if she had stayed gone. Mama's life has been shaped by Nada's absence. Afaf feels she hasn't known her mother in any other way.

"I'm going to put her on." She hands the phone to Nada, who stares at it for a moment. She stands up and takes it.

"Hello. Yes, Mama. It's me." Nada sinks back down on her chair. She cups her forehead with her free hand. "I'm sorry, Mama," she sobs into the phone.

Afaf gathers her now-cold tea and heads into the family room, giving them some privacy. A mother and sister who were never quite there her entire life are like two ghosts meeting again.

~

Afaf wipes her mouth with the towel Bilal holds out for her, still clutching the side of the toilet bowl. After Nada left, she could barely sleep. Nausea pulled her from her bed.

"It could be viral. Something you caught from hajj," Bilal says, gently gathering her hair and twisting it away from her face as Afaf retches again. A trickle of bile, sharply bitter, burns her throat. She sits back on her haunches, breathless, trying to muster speech.

She shakes her head. "I'm pregnant." And as soon as Afaf says it, she knows it's true, like someone on your doorstep, someone you hadn't been expecting, but you know has been waiting there for some time before they finally ring the bell.

Nurrideen School
for Girls

THE MUSLIM woman folded and unfolded her hands and he could see her become afraid again as he pointed his rifle at her.

"How am I your enemy?" she implored him. "You don't know me. Or any of the girls—" She seemed to choke on this last part. He wondered how much she'd heard of the ambush in the music room while she'd been locked in here. He looked around the confessional, then at the ceiling, a dusty vent directly above her head.

"I know everything I need to, lady," he said, watching her tears fall into the folds of her headscarf. How could she stand that thing on her head? But he was all for modesty, was sick to his stomach seeing the way women dressed nowadays, calling attention to their bodies, then blaming men for having the wrong idea.

The woman said, "Tell me about your pain."

"What pain?" he said. He wouldn't share anything with her, make himself vulnerable, allow her to play mind games with him. There was no use in giving his pain a voice, permitting it a space outside of his body. He could bear its low, constant thrumming as long as it remained contained inside of him. He and Eileen managed without ever talking about the things that happened to them— things others were responsible for. If Eileen had nightmares about her ex-boyfriend, she never told him. And he'd never mentioned a thing from his past. They were like injured birds, no longer able to fly, sidling against each other in a nest.

The woman looked again at her shoes, snot dripping from her nose. "I know about losing people you love," she whispered.

The sirens were closer now, then an eerie silence engulfed the building like the moment before an explosion. The only sounds were coming from the woman's sniffles and the soft tapping of his boots. He was certain the SWAT team was poised to capture the building—the calm before the storm.

"I don't give a shit what you lost," he told her. He looked closely at her now. Her lips were pale as she chewed on the lower one. Her eyebrows were dark like brown felt. Was her hair the same color? Or a charcoal-black like the Indian woman in his apartment building?

The family had moved in at the start of summer: an Indian man and his wife, their twin boys, and a newborn. He'd been in their apartment twice, once to repair the lockset on the front door. It was damaged by the corner of a wooden dresser the movers were hauling in. The new tenant had stood over him, smiling and watching while he removed the metal plate and drilled a new one. His wife stood in the narrow hallway, her shiny black hair in a long ponytail. Against her shoulder, she soothed a swaddled baby, startled by the shrill noise. She patted its tiny back, and softly murmured in its ear.

The new tenant gave a nervous chuckle. "These things happen, I'm sure," he said, his accent thick. He glanced at his wife, who remained silent and unsmiling.

"This ain't Calcutta," he told the man, shaking his head as he drilled. "You gotta be careful around here."

The new tenant's smile disintegrated and he didn't say another word to him after that. The man turned toward his wife and spoke briskly to her in their language. She lingered for a few more seconds, then turned down the hallway and disappeared into a bedroom.

Two weeks ago, he'd been called to Unit 204. A windowsill was in need of caulking. During his layoffs, he serviced Willow Wood Apartments. The management figured him for a handyman—he was the guy from Unit 103 who drove a white utility van. He could make a little extra on the side while collecting unemployment.

That morning's email work order was brief: moisture seeping through a kitchen window. He checked his toolbox for some weather stripping and a tube of caulk and headed to Unit 204.

A severe winter storm had cloaked the branches of maple trees lining the western stairwell. Slowly melting snow dripped from the ledges of the walkway. The parking lot was empty except for a minivan that hadn't moved for weeks; it was caked in a pristine layer of snow. He'd made a mental note to call the building's association to find out whether someone had abandoned it.

He reached the second floor and stood for a moment at the landing, catching his breath. Black-capped chickadees lined the railing, then flew off to the electrical poles when he advanced on the walkway, his toolbox clanking. The units did not have a balcony; some tenants placed stools outside their doors to sit in the summertime on the walkway.

There was music playing inside Unit 204 and he heard muffled talking. He rang the bell once, then knocked on the door, but no one came. A minute passed. He turned the knob and the door opened.

"Hello," he called, craning his neck inside the unit. A worn leather sofa with rows of beaded pillows and an easy chair were arranged around an area rug. Beside the sofa, infant rattles and tiny stuffed animals spilled from a cane basket. He peered down the narrow hallway that led to the single bathroom, two bedrooms, and kitchen. He stepped into the unit, closing the door behind him. Heat instantly warmed him through his work jumpsuit.

The unit bore little resemblance to his and Eileen's place, though it was an identical layout. A flat-screen television faced an oversized sofa. The new tenants had installed shelves on the walls, holding varying sizes of framed photographs. Some looked recently taken: the man and his wife—visibly pregnant in one—their twin boys standing in front of them. They were dressed in suits and ties, with garlands of flowers around their necks. The woman wore a purple sari with silver embroidery, her black hair parted down the middle and pulled into a tight bun.

In a large black-and-white photograph, an old man and woman stood before an orchard, and in another, several young men knelt beside a wading water buffalo. On a separate shelf were school portraits of the twins. They smiled timidly with missing teeth. They were identical, though he could see one boy's eyes were set slightly wider, and the other boy had a tiny mole on his chin. Between the frames, single-stem dahlias—yellow, orange and pink—poked out of small brass urns.

The voices and music grew louder as he walked down the hallway. From the kitchen, a spicy-sweet smell emanated. He stopped at the master bedroom, its door open, and he could see a small television set mounted on the dresser that had gouged the door plate earlier, during the summer.

The Indian woman was sitting on the edge of the bed, her partially naked back to him. She was nursing her baby, one side of her linen peasant shirt pulled off her shoulder and the fabric draped in a soft pile around her waist.

He gripped the handle of his toolbox hard, not making a sound as he watched. The baby made garbled noises as it suckled. He stood listening and it felt like a long time before she turned her head and saw him. Her dark hair was in a braid, a few loose strands framing her face. She quickly stood, frightening the baby. It stopped suckling and gave an indignant shriek at the disruption.

In a flash, he saw the woman's breast.

"Out! Out!" she shouted at him. She shielded her baby against her chest, the empty sleeve of her shirt falling at her side as she slammed the bedroom door in his face.

He heard the lock turn and stood there a moment. When the woman's high-pitched voice rose again, shouting into a phone, he hurriedly left, the contents of his toolbox rattling inside its metal walls.

Back at his own unit, he carefully closed the door behind him and set his toolbox down on the carpeted floor. Jeni ran to him and he knelt down, burying his face in her fur, the dog's panting in rhythm with the quick thudding of his heart. He approached the bedroom and listened at the door where Eileen was sleeping after her night shift. She liked to sleep with the clock radio playing soft instrumental music. The strumming of a guitar mingled with her snores.

He locked himself in the bathroom and unzipped his jeans. He pulled down his underwear, lowered the lid of the toilet seat, and sat down. Against his closed eyelids, the Indian woman appeared, her small round nipple protruding from a prune-dark areola, her shining black hair falling out of its braid. Leaning back on the toilet seat, he breathed deeply and stroked himself. When he was finished, he balled up the soiled tissue paper and flushed it down the toilet.

At six o'clock that evening, his doorbell rang. He and Eileen were watching *Wheel of Fortune*. Her shift at the restaurant began at eight o'clock. She sat on a sofa opposite his leather recliner, already wearing her uniform. On her feet were a pair of fuzzy pink slippers. She knitted from a ball of pastel-green yarn as she guessed the word riddles.

The doorbell rang again and Jeni barked at the intruder.

"I'll get it," he said when Eileen shifted on the couch.

Through the peephole, he saw the Indian tenant, his hands on his hips, waiting.

"Who is it, hon?" Eileen asked, laying her needles across her lap.

He opened the door. He hadn't noticed the first time how much taller the Indian man was—two inches, perhaps three—and much thinner than him. He'd gained twenty pounds since he was let go from Excel.

The tenant dropped his hands to his sides. "Please do not enter my home without my permission," he said, the black pupils of his eyes shining like marbles. "And only when I am present, sir."

Jeni barked at the stranger.

"Quiet, Jeni!" Eileen commanded, pulling the dog aside by the collar. She stood behind him, listening and not saying a word.

He was silent, too, and the two men looked at each other, the Indian waiting for some kind of assurance, and when he got none, he walked away, shaking his head.

He closed the door, unable to look at Eileen.

"What the hell was that about?"

"Nothing."

"What'd you do?"

"They had a leaky window."

"Was his wife alone?"

"Yeah."

"And?"

"And, nothing. I didn't do nothing, Eileen. Relax."

"What did you do?"

"No one answered the bell. I walked in." It was hard looking at Eileen. "I had a work order." His eyes dropped to her fuzzy slippers, which were turning gray along the edges of the soles.

"For Christ's sake! What the hell is the matter with you? You don't go into someone's apartment without being invited in." She grabbed her needles and ball of yarn, slamming the bedroom door behind her. Jeni whimpered and scratched under the door for a few moments, then returned to the front room.

He sank into his recliner, tired all of a sudden. His muscles ached as though they'd been pumped taut with air and were slowly expanding under his skin.

He'd gotten away with a warning. As far as he could tell, no one else had been notified. He stared at the television screen for a long time; the images of contestants spinning a wheel and wildly clapping did not register in his brain. All he could see and hear was the Indian man, facing him, his thick words playing back: *Please do not enter my home . . .*

The tenant had called Unit 204 "home." He looked around his own unit, a place he and Eileen had inhabited for twelve years. There were no real tokens of a family within the space, nothing really to call it home.

He and Eileen had never discussed children—they were both in their late forties when they met. She spent her free time knitting baby booties and caps for her coworkers and her sister's grandkids, whose pictures she had tacked up on the refrigerator. He looked at a basket full of balls of yarn at the foot of the couch where Eileen had been sitting. The basket he'd seen in Unit 204 was brimming with toys. And on the wall were photographs of people in places he'd never see. They'd all had places they came from that they wanted to remember. He'd wanted to forget places. He'd left each place he lived, shaking each of them off his back. Still they clung to him.

He sat on the couch, Eileen sulking in their bedroom. Anger brewed, replacing his earlier fear of getting caught. He'd been humiliated by that filthy brown man. How dare the man show up at his doorstep? Who the hell was he? Why didn't they all just stay in their own damn country?

When Eileen left for work without a word to him, he unlocked his metal storage cabinet in the second bedroom and withdrew his Ruger semiautomatic pistol, the one he'd shoot at the range. He tucked it inside the front of his pants, pulled on his jacket, and left the apartment. He knocked loudly on 204 and the Indian man appeared, his eyebrows furrowed.

"Yes?"

"If you ever threaten me again, there will be trouble." He flicked his jacket back, revealing the butt of his pistol pressed between his belt and stomach. "This is my country. You don't belong here. Do you understand me?" The words spilled from his mouth and at first he wasn't sure he'd actually uttered them out loud. He'd heard them a dozen times inside his head, read them online week after week. Now the words hovered in the space between him and the Indian man, whose face slowly drained of blood. He felt a strange satisfaction, like a first drag on a cigarette, once you conquered the coughing and unpleasant taste.

One of the twin boys poked his head under his father's arm where he was holding the door slightly open. The Indian man swiftly commanded his son back inside. To him, the man loudly said, "How dare you . . ."

He zipped up his jacket and returned to his unit, walking slowly and deliberately, ignoring the neighbors on that floor who'd come out to hear the commotion.

The Tempest police showed up a half hour later at his door, their squad car lights rotating in the parking lot, casting a noiseless, cacophonous glare.

"Good evening, sir."

He could see them gauging the danger he posed, peering over his shoulder into the apartment. But they didn't ask him to come outside.

"A Mr. Ba—" The first officer deferred to his partner.

The second officer tapped his notepad with a pencil. "Bat-na-gar."

The first officer nodded. "Yes. Mr. Bat-na-gar stated that you brandished a gun, sir," the policeman said. "Do you have any weapons on the premises, sir?"

"Yes, I do. And they're all legal and licensed," he told them. "You can come in and check all my paperwork."

"Listen, sir," the second one said. "You might have rightful ownership, but you can't intimidate your neighbors with firearms."

"I didn't," he lied. "I went over there to talk. You gonna believe that piece of shit over me? I've lived in this building longer than him. I maintain every unit. I was born in this country, goddammit."

The policemen looked at each other. He remembered the guys in one chat room complaining: *Pussy police won't stand up for justice anymore. Too worried about being politically correct.*

"Sir, we're just trying to get to the bottom of this. Your neighbors said they saw you leaving Mr. B.'s place. Consider this a warning, sir. Keep your weapons safely locked up and call us if you're experiencing a problem. We wouldn't want a little argument to escalate, now, would we?"

He hadn't seen the Indian man or his wife since that day, only their twin boys, whom he'd watch from his first-floor unit as they climbed into the school bus like they did this morning.

A bell rang, jarring him back to the confessional. He aimed the rifle at the silently weeping Muslim woman. She was as foreign to him as the backdrops he'd seen in those photographs in the Indians' apartment, as distant as the faintly inked places on Mr. Hillocks's maps. But today he'd get closer to knowing.

"Take that thing off your head," he commanded. "I want to see your hair."

Here and Now

1

AS THE shots echo through the ceiling vent in the confessional, Afaf's first thought is Azmia.

Which period is her daughter in right now? Which classroom? What floor? But she can't focus. It happens so fast—one moment she's praying, and the next she hears gunfire, which she takes at first for firecrackers. Then screams echo through the ceiling vent. The blood drains from her legs, and she falls back against the wall. She calls Lou again, but he doesn't respond. She is alone. With trembling fingers, she presses 911 on her cell phone.

"Please state your emergency," a Tempest police dispatcher demands.

"Shooter in the building. Nurrideen School. Fifty-five West Chelsea Avenue." She is amazed at how precisely she provides the information; it is a mysterious force that allows her to construct a coherent sentence.

Her mind suddenly splinters from sheer terror as she tries to focus and remember. Remember what? What should she do next?

Run away as fast as you can. Bits and pieces come rushing back to Afaf from the police trainings she and her staff are required to complete each year.

The shots had come from Miss Camellia's music room. The first-floor exit is only a few feet away. She can be in the parking lot in less than a minute.

But she won't leave Azmia.

She calls Bilal.

"There's a shooter in the building."

"Where are you?" His voice is thick with fear.

"I'm safe."

"And Azmia?"

"I don't know—I can't remember which period she's in. She hasn't texted me."

"Calm down, draga moja," he soothes, and that term of endearment sends her body into wracking sobs. "Breathe, Afaf. Breathe deeply. Get ahold of yourself."

A siren cries in the distance.

Once the police arrive on the scene, our primary mission is to stabilize the danger. Medical assistance is secondary after enforcement agents clear the threat from the building.

She tries to resist images that come to her of her students, arms and legs splayed across the music room. Metal stands toppled over, ballad sheets fluttering to the floor, soaked in blood. How many are still breathing, perhaps playing dead, desperately praying the white man would turn and step out the door?

When she regains her speech again, she tells her husband, "I can't leave her."

"Get out now if you have a chance, Afaf. Do not be foolish!"

She isn't seeking his permission to abandon their daughter. She doesn't want to be blameless when they can look back on this event. She'd rather die.

But there is no time to negotiate. She hears a deliberate shuffling of feet—it isn't the sound of a young girl running away. The shooter is outside the confessional door.

If you're trapped, stay hidden. Silence your electronic devices.

"I love you." She ends the call as the door suddenly opens. The intruder will not blight their final communication.

The two-way radio. Her leather mules. Her cell phone. The Holy Quran. All in her possession. Afaf thinks about throwing them at the white man who kicked open the door. Throw whatever she can to foil him, like they'd trained her and her staff to do.

Throw anything you can at the shooter, the muscled police officer had instructed them. *Don't hesitate. Startle him and attempt to secure his weapon. But if you're far enough from him, run away as fast as you can.*

The white man stands with a rifle, an object she's never beheld outside television and movies. She's never even held a gun before in her life. The man before her doesn't look powerful—had the sound of his own gunfire scared him, too?

The crisis trainers had referred to the perpetrator as *he.* Had she imagined anyone else besides a man—a white man—in those scenarios? Did he look like this one, who was aiming a rifle at her now? The truth was Afaf had never imagined it at all. Not even in a nightmare.

How could she or anyone ever fathom such a thing? If she hadn't been paralyzed by fear, she would be admonishing herself for being so naïve. What unspeakable carelessness. All those bomb threats, those acts of vandalism, had been precursors to this moment, had they not? She was principal of Nurrideen School for Girls: she'd failed at her duty to protect her students and staff.

She follows the white man's slow movements, her eyes blurring with tears. She silently prays, *La howla wala koowa illa bi lah. There is no power or strength except in Allah.*

The shooter's rifle is an extension of his arm, gesturing to her to sit down. And she is glad to sit, before her body collapses on its own. She hopes it will be quick:

There is no power or strength except in Allah.

He surveys the confessional, glances at the ceiling. "What are you doing in here?" His voice sounds raspy, as if he has a sore throat. The butt of an old-fashioned-looking pistol pokes out from his holster. He slumps against the door, the mural of Gabriel and Mary partially obscured by his body.

"I—Nothing." Should she admit she was praying as she does every day at this time? Or would it further enrage him? Perhaps if she hadn't been trying to steal a few solitary moments out of her hectic day she might have seen him down the hallway and stopped him, requested to see his work order. Perhaps Lou had taken him for a repairman. He's wearing a work jumpsuit—it would be easy to mistake him. Or is Lou a part of this heinous plot? Her stomach turns. Has she ever wholly trusted Lou? His expression toward her and the student body has been one of indifference, though she can still see that flicker of disdain when she'd interviewed him. White people would never believe they are the same as them. And yet she had trusted him enough to hire him, inflating his sense of superiority, wielding it over her. So arrogant was Lou, he'd let a killer in without checking his identification and demanding to see a work order. Because the killer is white.

"I was praying," she finally says.

He nods vaguely. For a moment Afaf imagines him setting down his rifle. But he holds on to it, quashing her foolish hope. Then he asks her about her children. Hope flickers again in her chest.

"You got kids?"

She wants to tell him everything, all the stories of her two sons and daughter up until that point of time. How Ayman had been a fussy eater, and how Akram had stuttered until he turned twelve. And how both of her sons stared at their baby sister Azmia as she slept in her crib, marveling that they could have been so tiny at one time in their lives. These glimpses appear in a montage across her mind, a film reel of their lives speeding up and slowing down all at once.

Humanize yourself, your loved ones.

Where had she heard that? An old movie thriller she'd watched with Bilal one night after they'd put the boys down to sleep. The kidnapper was holding a blond-haired boy hostage and the boy's mother, her husband's arm wrapped around her shoulders, was speaking at a press conference, appealing to the kidnapper's compassion, his humanity.

She'll call Azmia by her name, but what of the other four hundred girls for whom she is responsible? She wants to recite each and every muslimah's name, to have the white man hear the life and potential surging through each syllable, foreign as they may sound to his ears.

"Yes. Two boys and a girl. My daughter attends here," she starts to tell him. "She's a senior. Her name is Az—"

He swiftly silences her. She wants to ask the white man if he has children, too. Whose father is he? What stories does he have of his son or daughter? How has he arrived at this point? Had he lost and found a sister? Afaf wants to know, though her terror chokes her, threatening to make her pass out. Perhaps that is best. Lose consciousness, cradled by oblivion. She may not feel the bullets then. But she fights to stay focused. If he is here in the old confessional with her, he's farther away from Azmia, from the other girls.

She wants to know. What has carried this man to this moment?

The school bell rings, jolting her, and she looks at the confessional door. It's an eerie sound: no thunder of footsteps follow, no chatter of young girls reaching a humming crescendo. Is it already fifth period? Azmia would be in AP psychology—there was a big test today. Azmia's note cards were scattered across her bed last night, words written in her daughter's characteristic block letters.

And now here Afaf is, trapped in a room with a menace she hadn't foreseen.

Or had she? She's always felt indefensible around white people. Inferiority had slowly fermented inside her, beginning when she was a young girl and teachers squelched her potential because they didn't believe she was smart enough. In her daily life, white women silently look down on her as though she is a threat to their existence. Men sneer at her, a noiseless storm of violence in their eyes when she passes them in airports, in parking lots.

The shooter shifts his weight on the floor, still pointing his rifle at her. She studies his face: gray, unflinching eyes, the wrinkles in his forehead, the broken capillaries blossoming from his nose. Had his father been an alcoholic like Baba? Perhaps his mother had also suffered some kind of mental illness they did not yet have a name for when he was a child.

The tip of his rifle scratches the floor. Every movement, every gesture is momentous as Afaf tries to decipher his thoughts, gauge his next action. Then his face clouds over, the memory of something suddenly catching hold. *What is it?* Afaf wonders. Is there a hand pressed on his shoulder, a voice whispering in his ear to go no further? But it passes and he jeers, "What do you know about me?

You don't care a goddamn bit about me or this country. You don't belong here."

She swallows a painful lump in her throat. How many times had she heard that? "I was born in this country—just like you." She leans forward, pleading.

"Yeah? You sure don't fucking act like it." The shooter's eyes flit over her body, rest on her hijab. "Naw, lady, you don't belong here at all."

"I'm not your enemy."

"Yes, you are."

"How am I your enemy? You don't know me. Or any of the girls—" She can't complete her sentence.

"I know everything I need to, lady."

Afaf wipes away her tears with her sleeves and they become damp, like the times they slipped back down her wrists as she performed wudu, the seams wet from the cool water she splashed on her face."I want to know about your pain," she whispers to the man.

"What did you say?"

"Your pain. Tell me."

She can see something shift in his composure, as if he's about to lean forward, ready himself for a conversation.

"What pain?" he sneers.

"I know about losing people you love," she whispers.

"I don't give a shit what you lost," he snaps back. "Take that thing off your head. I want to see your hair."

She instinctively touches her headscarf as she so often does under the scrutiny of strangers, their disdainful expressions deflating the start of a good day. Sometimes the women are worse, giving her a look of hatred and pity, a question twitching at their lips: *Does your husband make you wear that thing?*

The white man's face is impassive. Her stomach churns with horror and shame. So is this what it comes down to? A piece of fabric? And yet what power it had held from the first time she'd slipped it on at Kowkab's house, a stranger in the mirror staring back at her. And when Mama had tried to tear it off her head before attempting to take her own life with a bottle of Drāno. Her hijab had become a thing that attracted sheer hatred, fear. And yet where would she be without it?

She's devoted herself to being a good muslimah, fulfilling each pillar and raising her children to be devout and moral beings. Betrayal stabs her gut: *Is this how Allah would let it end?* She feels suddenly duped by her complacent submission, Mama's wicked grin searing her brain. What if she'd refused to follow Baba that day over twenty years ago, climbing the stairs of a decrepit building to a floor full of blithely waiting believers? She could've run off instead with the first boy to offer her an escape after graduation from Hoover High School. Like Nada. It would've been easy to toss a garbage bag full of her clothes into the backseat of a car and drive away without saying goodbye—not even to Majeed. Perhaps she would've crossed the state line into Wisconsin, or driven east toward Indiana, never looking back.

And today she might have been spared. Today would play out in someone else's nightmare.

Or has Allah decided this would be Afaf's fate—if not here, in some other place? A car crash on a congested highway. A fatal fall outside her residence. The end of an agonizing bout with cancer.

She clenches her eyes shut. *There is no power or strength except in*

Allah. She will not falter. Her faith is all that remains to her, something still palpable, though it has momentarily fumbled from her grasp. *It's in Allah hands*, her own words echo back to her from only a few days ago, when she'd reassured one of her teachers that life would go according to a greater will beyond their own. No matter how hard one tries to circumvent destiny or to run away.

When Afaf opens her eyes again, a peculiar calm settles in her bones. She looks at the shooter and demands, "Will taking it off save my life? Will it make me a human being?" These words numb her present fear like frostbite after hours of severe cold.

The white man is silent, still pointing the rifle at her head. "That rag makes you evil. You don't belong when you choose to wear it."

"I was born in this country," she tells him again. "Like you." Anger shoots through her veins. He hasn't killed her yet—she pushes on, challenging this white man, though these may be her final moments.

He shakes his head, a slight swaying that turns into vehement jabs back and forth. "No. We're not the same."

"Is this what separates us?" She tugs at the folds of fabric around her neck. "Does this stand in our way of understanding each other?"

"We're not the same," he repeats, though Afaf can hear something relinquishing in his voice. His rifle leans against his leg, his finger still on the trigger.

Throw anything you can at the shooter.

Before fear returns to her, Afaf flings herself at him, the mural behind him a blur.

His rifle drops to the floor. He punches her shoulders, the side of her head. She claws at his face, knees him in his groin.

There is no power or strength except in Allah.

He grabs her by the throat and thrashes her body. She kicks and slaps, but he grips her more tightly. He throws her against the chair, toppling the table. The holy book falls to the floor beside her. Time slows, and she feels as if she were underwater. She sees him pull the pistol from its holster, point it at her.

She raises her hands before the bullets tear through her skin like white-hot surges of electric voltage. Flecks of blood splatter against Gabriel's wings.

No power or strength.

She feels each bullet penetrate her stomach, the pain so severe she ceases feeling it, like she's being plunged in fire. Then, gratefully, numbness.

Except in Allah.

Bursts of light follow, each like a star exploding and releasing a dormant memory: The first time she sees her mother. Raising her tiny, infant fingers to Mama's lips.

More bursts of light, these revealing mysterious truths: Azmia is still alive.

She's certain now. It comes from some primordial place inside her, beneath layers of skin, tissue, organ, bone. More fundamental than her cells, their nuclei.

There's no image, no vision, only an indecipherable sense of peace and safety she's never experienced before, like deeply exhaling after holding your breath for a very long time.

She can let go now, and let the light enfold her.

2

A WHIRRING din. Like hundreds of tiny flapping wings. Then the sounds break apart: a siren squealing, metal wheels rolling against pavement, a young girl's voice.

Mama.

No pictures, only sounds. Some are hushed like whispers, others are piercing like shrieks in a still forest.

A heartbeat. Is it hers?

Mama.

There's light, but she can't see anything. Only sounds.

Mama.

I want to go home. Familiar words she'd heard a lifetime ago. And others drift toward her in the light:

You should take comfort in the fact that she's still out there.

See what happens when you give your daughter too much freedom. This country will snatch her up.

I want my life to begin again.

It's in Allah's hands, habibti.

We're not the same.

Explosions again. Pressure builds inside her skull. Heat sears through her abdomen. She's floating while air leaves her body.

Mama.

Afaf. Can you hear me?

Her lids are heavy, like sandbags. There are obstructions in her nose, her throat. How can they expect her to answer?

∼

IVs running through her wrists, Afaf moves through a new kind of consciousness, rediscovering the most familiar things: the sound of her own voice, the taste of chicken soup.

Her family hovers over her. She's never alone, it seems, between waking and sleeping. Ayman and Akram are like giants looking down at her, their eyes wary of all the tubes running through her body. Azmia removes the thick hospital socks, massages her legs and feet, keeps Afaf's chapped lips moist with balm. At first she watches them through narrow slits of her eyes, her limbs weighed down to the bed like they've been pumped full of lead.

Her sister Nada flies in from Florida, caring for Azmia and keeping her company, while Bilal sits beside her bed reading the Quran and caressing her bare arm.

She hears Majeed speaking to Mama overseas on his cell phone as he stands by the window. His voice breaks and recovers. Even now, he's the only one who could ever console their mother, reassure her that everything will be fine.

In the corner of her hospital room, a mounted flat-screen television is never turned on, silent like a black hole against the taupe-painted walls.

Bilal won't tell her anything. "In time. When you have found your strength again. You must focus on yourself, draga moja."

What they do tell her in precise terms, a band of surgical doctors and revolving nurses, is everything her body has endured.

Three bullets to her abdomen, one through her left hand, between the webbing of her thumb and forefinger. Hemorrhaging, two blood transfusions.

She slowly absorbs their terminology like the drip of an IV: *primary and secondary fragmentation*. She learns the latter is worse: it's very difficult to predict what complications might arise from damaged organs.

Only time will tell, one of the doctors tells her. *Fortunately, your liver and colon are fine.*

Elhamdulillah, Bilal breathes.

But what she wants to know they won't tell her.

Have they saved the others? Her girls? Those who had tried to escape in the music room as she listened to their screams above her—are their young lungs and hearts still whole and untainted, free of the vicious fragments of bullets? And Miss Camellia, the music teacher?

Kowkab, her dearest friend, visits her every day and Afaf finally whittles down the woman's resolve. Kowkab offers her small pieces of the aftermath, feeding her bitterness like bites from a sour plum. And still Afaf demands more.

"How many?"

"Fourteen girls and Miss Camellia, Allah yarhamhum." Kowkab sniffles into a tissue paper.

Afaf imagines the other girls crawling out from under the cafeteria tables, others bursting from washroom stalls and from behind gymnasium bleachers. They find their sobbing parents waiting anxiously on the curb. The parents sweep their daughters up in their arms and never let go.

And she sees the other parents, waiting and waiting, praying that God has spared their children, that they'd get to hold them again, and forever.

But their daughters never emerge from the building. Fathers and mothers cling to each other as the gurneys roll out of the exit doors one after another, carrying bodies wrapped in plastic bags.

And the shooter? Afaf wants to ask, but can't bring herself to say it. She'll find out later from the relentless news reports that the shooter tried to kill himself when the SWAT team closed in.

"It's Allah's will," Kowkab is saying, breaking Afaf's reverie. "May He have mercy on us all."

Afaf vaguely nods, her bandaged hand suddenly throbbing, in need of something to clench, of something to never let go of.

3

THE FEMALE guard pats Afaf's body, examines the folds of her hijab, fingers crunching the fabric around her neck. "All right. Go ahead."

A male guard gestures to her and she passes through a metal detector. They search the contents of her purse on a metal table. The guard holds up a packet of breath mints. "You can't take these in." He throws them away and they clink against the inside of a large metal trash bin.

Another guard motions to her. "Okay. Walk along that corridor line."

She reaches an area that reminds her of the DMV. There are mostly women here, young and middle-aged, standing in lines cordoned off by rope. Everyone looks tired, as though they've been waiting a long time. The queue moves slowly.

When it's her turn, Afaf offers her driver's license and a copy of her birth certificate. She fills out the prisoner's name and her own. The clerk scrolls on a computer screen, then looks up at her more intently now, recognizes her from the news.

"Wait over there," she tells Afaf.

What do you hope to gain from this?

That's what her therapist asked her. After weeks of sessions, Afaf revealed she wanted to visit the shooter.

Her therapist is much younger than Afaf, a white woman who

wears false eyelashes and sips Starbucks coffee with one hand and takes notes with the other on a legal pad propped across her lap. She suggests that Afaf keep a journal to chart her daily emotions. At their first session, she asked Afaf whether therapy was discouraged in her *religious culture*. Afaf hates the sessions, where she turns herself inside out, but she still goes. She can tell this stranger all the things she keeps from Bilal. Her nightmares, her constant fear that someone will lash out at her in public places.

And she confessed her desire to speak to the shooter.

But how will seeing him help your recovery, A-faf? You're making great progress here.

Progress is defined in small achievable goals. Taking a walk around her neighborhood once a day. Leaving the house at least three times a week to run an errand.

And eventually return to her job at Nurrideen School for Girls. But for the time being, it's unfathomable to Afaf.

She can't go back. Not without reasons, not without understanding.

The trial was held in June and was televised on a cable network. Afaf conscientiously watched from home with her sister Nada, who'd put her own life on hold to be with Afaf when Bilal finally went back to work. Her sister could finally be there for her in a way she'd never been. Afaf absorbed the footage of the exterior of the school on that day, young girls running into the street without their winter coats and book bags, their arms raised as local police ushered them away from the building. She couldn't make out who each individual girl was, their identical uniforms and hijabs blurring the bodies. The footage was taken by a witness on his cell phone and the edited clip was played in intermittent breaks from the testimonies. It was surreal sitting in her family room, watching what had happened outside the school building while Afaf had been trapped inside the confessional, a rifle pointed at her.

At the sentencing hearing, the parents of the dead girls took turns standing up in court to face the shooter. They told him whom he'd stolen from them, how wonderful and smart and beautiful their girls were. How they volunteered for good causes, and loved America and Allah. *Victim impact statements.* You tell the killer how he's forever turned your life upside down. Miss Camellia's brother tried to speak and broke down, her parents sobbing in the aisle behind him.

I need to know why, Afaf told her therapist.

I don't think we'll ever understand—

No. He has to tell me why.

The defense attorney fought down first-degree murder, painting a picture for the jury of a lonely, disgruntled middle-aged man who'd gotten caught in a cyber web of hatred. The prosecution strenuously enforced the term *hate crime*, though the defense categorically objected. In the end, the jury—made up of eight white men and women, three black women, and one Hispanic man—deliberated for twenty hours. Their verdict of second-degree murder and attempted second-degree murder fueled the ire of civil rights activists for days afterward.

Afaf has recovered from her wounds. Though her hand suffered the least damage, a ghost-pain twitches between her thumb and forefinger. Stitches have left a tiny row of scar tissue like broken train tracks; Afaf unconsciously rubs the scar when she watches the news. Her insides have silently healed. She doesn't feel any residual pain, takes pills only to ease her anxiety and depression, to slacken the rope lashed around her brain. Nothing helps her sleep at night. She refuses even a mild sedative, afraid her nightmares will bloom into something much worse, like the events of that day. In her nightmares she watches from a distance, screams and gunfire coming to her as muffled noise down a long corridor. Sometimes it's like a silent horror film as she passes from classroom to classroom, trying to open locked doors, pounding with her fists, hearing nothing in return. Sometimes she sees Lou the security guard and calls to him. He waves his radio at her, then slips down a hallway.

When the shooting began, the surveillance camera recorded Lou bolting out the front entrance of the building where he was stationed. His call to the Tempest police came from the parking lot, minutes after hers from the confessional. He testified that he hadn't asked to see any identification from the shooter.

He looked normal. Like he's there to do a job, you know? Lou had told the jury.

The public excoriated him, calling him a coward and an embarrassment to his years of police service. So far, he's refused any interviews.

The press won't stop hounding Afaf. She's the Muslim principal who sat face-to-face with the shooter. For a month after her release from the hospital, network television vans camped outside her home, lining the street down her entire block. Through a slit in the drapes, she watched from her bedroom window as neighbors elbowed their way through reporters, carrying aluminum trays and baskets of fruit. Her sister Nada hastily thanked them and closed the front door to a barrage of questions reporters shouted at her from the lawn.

What do you hope to gain from facing him again, A-faf? her therapist asked at the last session.

Whatever this thing is—hate, fear—she wants to look at it, hold it in her hands, pull it apart. How can she—how can any of them—move on without getting close to it? He must answer for those girls and Miss Camellia.

She wrote him one letter a week requesting he add her to his visitation list. Forty-three letters went unanswered until a few days ago. An envelope arrived with her name handwritten and the state penitentiary's return address. The shooter's name and his regulation number were also handwritten. Her husband intercepted it.

What is this? Bilal demanded, waving the letter at her. *Are you out of your mind?*

Her sons stood by their father. *Why, Mama? Why would you want to see him again?*

Her daughter Azmia has been more understanding though she, too, is shaken. Afaf has learned how youth demands truth, how it hungers for meaning. *Do you want me to go with you, Mama?* Afaf has managed to mostly shield her daughter from the press, though Azmia has insisted on speaking about the shooting on her own terms. Her account of her experience went viral on social media, #NurrideenGirls and #Azmia trending within hours of the shooting. Overnight Azmia became the poster child against anti-Islam bigotry in this country, a young woman whose own mother came face-to-face with extreme hatred. Between preparation for graduation and college, Azmia has been organizing vigils for the slain and weekly protests at the state capital. She boards a chartered school bus every Friday morning at six a.m. with a dozen other young people equipped with homemade signs: *Hate Kills. Gun Control Now. Seventeen* and *Teen Vogue* have run stories on her.

A guard leads Afaf to a room with two chairs. The space is divided like a polling station. She'll be seeing him through a window with tiny holes. Another female visitor is there seated with her back to Afaf. Afaf can't see who's on the other side.

Afaf sits down, sets her purse on the floor. A faint odor of bleach riles her stomach and she swallows down the bile.

When he enters the room on the other side of the window, he looks smaller than she remembers. His hands are cuffed in front of him and he holds up his arms like he's about to catch a ball. A guard guides him to a metal chair across from her, doesn't uncuff him. This time there's a barrier that separates them and there isn't a gun pointed at her. Still, Afaf clenches her hands in her lap, unable to quiet their trembling. He's grown a beard, speckled and bedraggled—she might not have recognized him if they passed each other on the street. Their fates are twisted like the mangled steel of a totaled car—neither can escape the wreckage of events.

"What do you want?"

The sound of his voice rushes back to her now from the confessional. Her legs lurch and tremble. The chair keeps her body from collapsing. She wonders if she's made a terrible mistake.

Maybe give it some more time—a year? her therapist advised her last week when Afaf showed her the visitation letter.

Time won't dull this piercing in her brain—she owes it to her girls, to Miss Camellia.

She cups her knees, straightens up. Breathes: *La howla wallah koowa illa bi lah.*

"Why did you do it?"

He shrugs. "I don't have to say a thing to you, lady."

"You agreed to see me. There's something you want to say."

She had begged him to see her as a person, a mother of two sons and a daughter whose life he had put in danger.

When the federal agents interviewed her in the hospital, she tried to summon the exact words spoken between her and the man. She began wondering whether he'd uttered a single word—had she imagined the entire exchange? The agents wanted to know if he was visibly distraught: *Did he cry? Did he mention a recent loss, or troubles with his family?* She shook her head and they didn't return for further questioning. The prosecution hadn't called her to testify, and she was grateful.

He avoids her eyes now, looking over her shoulder through the window.

Anger fills Afaf. Fear and uncertainty float away, freeing her. "Why did you write me back?" she demands.

The female visitor sitting adjacent to her shifts and Afaf lowers her voice. "You approved my visit."

He focuses on her again, his defiant eyes softening and his face tense. She can tell he's lonely—perhaps that's the reason he finally agreed to see her. She remembers an interview with his live-in girlfriend, a slender woman with dull, thin hair. *I had no idea what he was up to. I didn't realize how mad he was at the world.* Has she abandoned him now?

For weeks, Afaf lay awake trying to imagine his family: Were his parents alive? Did he have siblings? Besides his attorney, there hadn't seemed to be anyone present on his behalf in the courtroom. Looking at him now, it's hard to picture him outside of these walls, outside of the confessional. Is it the same for him? Can he see Miss Camellia outside of that music room? A brand-new, beloved teacher? Or those girls with parents who quibbled and doted over them, and sisters who wanted to be just like them, and devoted friends who held their every secret, defended every petty grudge? All the years of their lives snuffed out, obliterated in a matter of seconds.

For a long time, they sit in silence, both resting their arms on the ledge in front of them.

Then Afaf tells him, "I can't sleep anymore—can you?"

He shifts in his chair, drops his cuffed hands in his lap again.

"Please tell me how we got here." She braces herself for what he might spew at her like the vile emails she received immediately after the shooting:

He should have blown up the entire school. Killed all you ragheads.
He's an American hero.
Terror-islam must be wiped out.

Other strangers who reached out to her were kind and compassionate:

How can a thing like that happen in Tempest?
We are all God's children.

But their messages hadn't offered her a way to make sense of it all.

"Tell me why. I'm listening."

He'd already heard who each girl was, the families and the prosecution sketching his victims as vividly as they could, adding as many details as possible to make a canvas of those lives. Every flourish of accomplishment, every stroke of potential.

He clinks his handcuffs on the ledge, leans forward. He weeps, long and hard.

Afaf's body suddenly unwinds and she sits back in her chair. She waits for more and watches him, his face contorted in anguish. She'll wait as long as she can, as long as they'll allow her to sit here.

Epilogue

AUGUST IS hot and humid. On one side of the main entrance of the building, clusters of dahlias slouch from their long stems, red and purple heads heavy from the heat. On the other side a new wrought-iron bench has been bolted to the cement. Several of the more conservative board members and parents voted against any ostentatious display. They settled on a bronze plaque in the shape of a dove. And a simple inscription:

إِنَّا لِلَّهِ وَإِنَّا إِلَيْهِ رَاجِعون

We belong to Allah and to Him shall we return

Inside the car, Afaf hesitates for a moment, gripping the door handle.

"You do not have to go back. Not right away," Bilal tells her, squeezing her hand. He insisted on driving her this morning. "Let someone else run the school for a year."

Afaf rubs the graying whiskers of Bilal's beard. Her husband is not the same man she married. He looks unsettled, his eyes full of fright if she leaves the room for a moment. He's no longer the father who countered her every fear and worry with hope and optimism. It had taken weeks for him to finally let Azmia go to California.

I'll be home for Thanksgiving inshallah, Azmia told them, the last

of her boxes arranged on her side of the dormitory room. Her Suda-
nese American roommate had smiled reassuringly at them.

Bilal wept on the drive home. She remembers Sister Nabeeha's
words so long ago: *Women can withstand more than men.*

Afaf isn't the same woman, either. "Everyone's moving on," she
tells Bilal. She still carries fear, though it's tucked behind a wall of
invulnerability. It's not courage—but resignation. She survived the
worst thing imaginable; she could go on with her life.

Once a week, she calls Mama and detects an unfamiliar joy in
her mother's voice. Did not the Prophet say, *Heaven lies under the
feet of your mother*?

Afaf walks to the main entrance of the school and sees the lock
on the door has been replaced with a new security apparatus. She
presses a button and a young woman buzzes her in. Her assistant
Sabah isn't coming back for the new semester. Two teachers had
immediately resigned.

"Ahlan, Miss Afaf! Mashallah, you look well!" The woman
embraces Afaf. She wears an amber-colored abaya and tiny pearls
dot her beige headscarf. "I'm Yasmine. Your new assistant." She
holds out a plastic fob. "That's your temporary key. Until we get you
settled again." She gestures to Afaf. "Let's get you to your office."

How strange to be managed by someone so young, but Afaf follows Yasmine down the corridor as though it's her first time in this
building. A lifetime ago Afaf had entered the school a young, ideal-
istic teacher. Nurrideen had felt like home for the first time in her
career. Then she became its principal, crafting a new legacy of pro-
gressive education for young women. Would that be forever marred
by that fateful day last winter? The blood of fifteen muslimat had
been washed away, and walls had been painted over, window panes

replaced. But a tremor still pulsated beneath Afaf's feet as she walked down the corridor—did her new assistant feel it, too?

"Mr. Abbas has been using your office," Yasmine tells her. "He'll be here later to catch you up."

Afaf nods, listens. Her office appears unchanged except for a messy desk—the interim principal is not as tidy as she.

"Can I bring you some tea, Miss Afaf?" The young woman stands in the doorway, waiting.

Afaf shakes her head, smiles at her new assistant. "Thank you. I'm fine." She pulls out her leather chair and sits down.

"Let me know if you need anything." Yasmine closes the door behind her.

Her cell phone buzzes. *Everything is okay?*

She texts Bilal back: *Elhamdulillah . . . Don't worry abt me.*

She fights hard against the urge to call him to take her home. There's something she needs to do.

"I'll be right back," she tells Yasmine. Her assistant stands at her desk and looks like she'll follow Afaf. Instead the young woman only nods.

The corridor is quiet. Afaf turns at the end of it and walks past the cafeteria. A banner hangs from the ceiling, the printed names of the deceased and signatures of support punctuated with hearts and crescent moons. Afaf doesn't stop to read them, turns at the next corner.

She stops in front of the confessional and runs her fingertips along the wooden lattice. Her shoulders tremble as she turns the small doorknob and enters.

The lamp table and chair are gone. Her prayer rug, too. The space seems oddly smaller in its barrenness. The walls have been repainted a dull eggshell. Boxes of textbooks line one wall. She looks up at the vent in the ceiling, and tears fall into the hem of her hijab.

Afaf turns around, toward the back of the door. The mural has been painted over. She runs her fingers over this new coat of paint where Mary had once gazed into the face of an angel. It's smooth against her touch, and there are no traces of what had come before.

Acknowledgments

THIS NOVEL proves to me how a book can be written but it only enters the world through many valuable people. I am deeply indebted to my incredible agents, Katelyn Hales and Robin Straus, for supporting my vision in a time when this story might have otherwise been stifled, and for patiently guiding me through the publication process.

My boundless gratitude to my editor, Jill Bialosky, her assistant editor, Drew Elizabeth Weitman, and the rest of the meticulous and diligent team at W. W. Norton, who rigorously steered my book to its fullest potential.

Thanks also to the individuals and communities who contributed to this book and my writing in ways that are known or unexpected to them: Rebecca Makkai and Story Studio of Chicago, who provided me with a space for an exploratory draft and a lasting mentorship; my dearest friend, Nina Dellaria, still my first conscientious reader; my amazing writing and self-care sisters, Vimi Bajaj, Gulnaz Saiyed, and Marya Spont-Lemus; Leila Ben-Nasr for her faithful correspondence and uplifting friendship; Radius of Arab American Writers, who perpetually elevate our community; my Homewood-Flossmoor High School family, whose support for this second life of mine never wanes; Patricia McNair, still raising my stories; many brilliant authors whose books inspire and rattle me, and those who personally took time and care to read mine; and my online community, who boost my work and graciously remind me that we're on the same rewarding and challenging journey of creating art to combat this climate of hatred, fear, and despair. Our words, though sometimes slow and painful, are hope.

Finally, I want to thank all of my beautiful family, including my husband, Khalid, and daughters, Sabah and Sabrine; my mother, my sisters and brothers, my in-laws, and other lovely relatives and friends who are perpetually eager to read my work and show up for me. All my love, always. دائما إن شاء الله